BROKEN CIRCLE

J.L. POWERS
M.A. POWERS

This is a work of fiction. All names, characters, places, and incidents are the product of the authors' imaginations. Any resemblance to real events or persons, living or dead, is entirely coincidental.

Published by Akashic Books

ISBN: 978-1-61775-580-4
Library of Congress Control Number: 2017936100

First printing

Black Sheep/Akashic Books
Brooklyn, New York
Twitter: @AkashicBooks
Facebook: AkashicBooks
E-mail: info@akashicbooks.com
Website: www.akashicbooks.com

More books for young readers from Black Sheep

Changers Book One: Drew
by T Cooper & Allison Glock-Cooper

Changers Book Two: Oryon
by T Cooper & Allison Glock-Cooper

Changers Book Three: Kim
by T Cooper & Allison Glock-Cooper

Game World
by C.J. Farley

Pills and Starships
by Lydia Millet

The Shark Curtain
by Chris Scofield

To Annie, Nora, Grace, and Owen. Thank you for making life fun! You kids have to go to bed now. I'll read the book to you when you're a bit older. Don't forget to tell Aunt Jessica that she's awesome next time you see her!

—M.A. Powers

To Matt, because this book wouldn't exist without you. It's been fun . . . with more to come!

—J.L. Powers

The space between dreams and Limbo is the width of a frayed hair strand. Tread carefully in the land of sleep lest your soul lose its way and you fail to find the warmth of the bed in morning light.
—Marie-Balthioul Eshu (circa 1865)

To Live is to embrace Death as friend.
—Adrial Grim Reaper (circa 1488)

The Soul is eternal. Love of the Soul is a brush with the infinite.
—Antonio Mors (circa 1820)

PROLOGUE

It happens sometimes when I go to sleep, not every time but more and more frequently. My father is there. My father and the Monster and me. I know I shouldn't be here but here I am, and it's all so—it's all so *real.*

Dad's back is tall and very, very straight. He weaves in and out between gravestones, always marching forward, one foot in front of the other—the way he walks the streets of Brooklyn. It feels like I've been looking up at those same black coattails all my life.

He doesn't know I'm here. I'm not sure where here is. A cemetery of some kind. It feels like we're looking for my mother.

The sky is drizzling. Our shoes slurp through mud and my short legs struggle to keep up with his long strides.

We pass a series of moss-covered angels crying over a sarcophagus. Blackened gargoyles guard the tomb next to it, rusted bars covering its opening. Just looking at it makes the hairs on my arms stand on end.

The sun breaks through the clouds as we reach the heart of the cemetery. A marble monument flames orange and yellow in the setting sun's reflected light. A woman dressed in rags huddles at the foot of the grave. I catch a glimpse of fish-white flesh and the dark hole of Her mouth, the shocking blue-black of a starless night. Her fleshless fingers, skin dangling off dry bones. She smells like rotten vegetables.

She looks up . . .

Through my father She looks . . .

She

our eyes meet

She

and I know and our eyes meet and I know . . .

It takes only one second and then She's coiling toward us, snakelike. Pebbles skitter away from Her as She moves, covering ground faster than a twister.

"Dad!" I scream.

He whirls around and recoils when he sees me. "What are you doing here?" he shouts. "Run, Adam! Run! Get out of here!"

She melts right through him as She reaches for me.

I shrink back against a tombstone, its grip hard and cold.

She tries to gather me in Her arms. As if She wants to hold me. Or kill me.

"Stop!" Dad commands. His hand shakes as he lifts it to halt Her embrace, his voice gaining strength as he repeats himself: "Stop! Stop! Stop stop stop!"

A thin sliver of black smoke curls up from the crack of earth where the headstone is wedged. She and the smoke are one. She lunges at me, slips between skin and bone, and pierces me with sharp talons. We plunge into a pool of black liquid lapping the foot of the grave.

I open my mouth to scream and lukewarm oil rushes inside, warm and wet, and chokes me.

And now I'm falling through the dark.

I fall

and fall
and fall . . .
A woman screams—is it Her?—
a breathless scream that gets fainter as we fall . . .

Then after.

After, when I can no longer resist the darkness, I sense light. Not light I see but light I feel. It surrounds me. Protects me.

I know this light. It's my father and suddenly I realize I'm not alone.

CHAPTER 1

I shiver awake, sudden and cold. The apartment smells like old garbage and was I screaming? Maybe it doesn't matter because Dad's out of town but the family next door might have heard. Damn it, how could I fall asleep? And how long was I out?

The cell phone light illuminates the time—8 p.m., Friday night—and I've been stone-cold asleep for several hours. My whole body aches. Drops of blood seep through the sleeve of my shirt from gouges up and down my arms. Apparently, I beat myself to hell while I was sleeping.

I turn the lamp on next to the couch and text Sarah to meet me in the basement of a Presbyterian church near her apartment. One of the things I like about Alcoholics Anonymous is that there's almost always a meeting going on somewhere in Brooklyn. And those meetings always make me feel safer. Not safe—that's impossible. But at least, when I'm there, I'm not alone.

My name's Adam, I'm fifteen years old, and I'm not an alcoholic. But there is something my body craves that I want—no, *need*—to avoid.

I slouch in late, still rubbing sleep from my eyes, and scan the room for Sarah or her shadow, whichever I notice first. She hasn't arrived yet so I grab a cup of crappy coffee from the back table, shake some totally fake chemical creamer into my Styrofoam cup just to flavor it, and take the first available seat, smiling at the black guy sitting on the end of my row and the young mom type sitting just behind me. Puffy eyes betray her and her shadow is all jumpy, her hands *tap tap tap* against her thighs, and I want to tell her, *It's okay, everybody here is cool, you're going to be okay*. But of course I say nothing because she might not be okay. Everything might be on a downhill slide, that's why she's here. Still, when I smile at her, she smiles back, wobbly but genuine.

I find myself wishing I was her kid. I mean, obviously she's got problems—she's at an AA meeting—but then, nobody's perfect. When I think about my mom—which is every single day—I think she would have been like this lady. I imagine she had the same kind, wistful smile. I imagine she was always trying to do better than before, wanting what was best for her kid.

An ex-priest is sharing his story when this guy with a death wish skulks into the seat next to me. He's dressed all in black, heavy black eye makeup and ghost-white foundation smeared all over his face. I don't understand people like him, people who want to die. Every time The Dream wakes me, it feels like I've come back from the grave. Death doesn't seem peaceful or welcoming or something to desire—certainly not if it includes Her.

The death-wish guy stares at the speaker but his shadow leers at me. Covertly, I give it the finger. He shifts and glances in my direction, as if sensing it. I give him a chin nod when what I really want to do is scoot over cuz he smells horrible but that would be rude so I just sink low in my seat, sweatshirt covering my nose, eyes focused on the front.

Sometimes I play this game: if the zombie apocalypse begins now, do I need to worry? At the moment, I feel pretty safe. I can run faster than the death-wish dude, for sure.

Sarah touches my shoulder lightly from behind and whispers, "I'm here, Adam." She winks as she leans back in the folding chair.

I'm relieved that she came. In all the world, Sarah is my favorite. Her shadow? Also my favorite. It's light and bubbly, champagne, laughing and winking, like diamonds in the sunlight. She's the only person who knows I don't like to sleep. That maybe I'm afraid of it. I haven't explained why but she hasn't asked, she's *that* kind of friend.

Sarah: dark glossy hair, pretty brown eyes, skin freckled and browned a deep café au lait from the summer sun. She's drop-dead gorgeous.

I guess that's an unfortunate choice of words. Sarah's older sister died in June. I mean, she literally dropped dead. Of a heart attack. Came out of nowhere. Sarah's been beat up about it ever since. *Beat up.*

I wish I knew how to make her feel better. One time, she said, "I mean, you know what it's like to lose someone, right, Adam? You know how bad it is?" and I just said, "Yeah." I couldn't tell her I'm not even sure I really remember my mom. All I have are fuzzy outlines. But I do miss her. Is that possible, to miss somebody you don't really remember?

The ex-priest finishes and we wait to see if anybody else is going to get up and share something. Somebody coughs. The kid next to me clears his throat.

I've never stood up because what would I say? I imagine it now, rising to my feet. *Hi, I'm Adam Jones and I'm not an alcoholic. My problem? When I fall asleep, a demon woman from Hades tries to hug me to death. She drags me into the bottomless pit of hell. And no, I don't do drugs. Raise your hand if you also struggle with inappropriate demon abduction! Come on! Don't be shy.*

Of course I don't get up. Maybe I'm too frightened to ask for help. I mean, really ask. In a serious way. Where do you find courage when Fear is calling the shots?

Afterward, the young mom approaches me. "What are you doing here, a nice boy like you?" She sips from her coffee cup, then grimaces, squinting at its contents as though wondering if it's really coffee.

"What are you doing here, a nice mom like you?" I joke back.

Her shadow—a clown with a happy/sad face painted on it, big fat teardrops rolling down and smearing the makeup—is making friendly faces at mine.

"How do you know I'm a mom?" she says.

I pause before I answer. When I meet women like her—mothers, nice ones, young pretty ones with kind smiles—I suddenly feel like I haven't eaten in days. "How do you know I'm a nice boy?" I finally say.

"I just do." She glances around at the hall filled with people from all walks of life—the shifty homeless guy in the corner, the businessman in his nice suit, the ex-priest. "I'm real nervous about being here."

"First time to a meeting?" I ask, hopeful that that's the

cause of her anxiety. Because sometimes people get anxious just being around me.

"Yeah," she says. "But somehow, standing here talking to you . . . I feel better. Comforted."

Shit. That's when I know *why* she's hanging around me.

"There's just a warmth radiating from you," she goes on. "I can't explain it. It makes me feel good. It makes me think I can do this, I can quit drinking. That I can move from where I am to where I need to be and that everything is going to be all right."

She's not going to have any problems quitting drinking, the smart-ass side of my brain says. The other side, the nicer side, the one that worries why I know she's going to die tonight, speaks out loud: "Hey, be extra careful when you go home, okay? Do you have a long way to go?"

"Oh, no," she says. "My husband and kids are picking me up."

"I'll wait with you until they arrive," I say.

"It's okay, you don't have to do that. It's a safe neighborhood. You probably have to get home. Your friend is waiting for you." She wrinkles her forehead toward Sarah.

"Sarah won't mind, she'll wait with us."

She smiles again and says, "That'd be really nice. Thanks."

So we go outside and wait for her husband and kids at the corner streetlight. Sarah stands close, shivering in the night breeze. If only I had the guts to put my arms around her, warm her up. But they just hang there, all awkward, perfectly useless limbs. I curse them in my head. Stupid arms.

"I'm Desiree," the nice mom says as we wait. "Do you guys come to this meeting often?"

"Sometimes," I say.

"First time," Sarah says. "Adam asked me to come." She puts her hand on my arm and I get instant goose pimples all over.

"I don't know why," Desiree says, "but you seem familiar, Adam."

"I hear that a lot," I respond. "I must have a 'boy next door' face. Familiar but kind of forgettable."

She shakes her head. "You're too tall and skinny to be the boy next door. I'll remember you next time." She waves at a BMW station wagon pulling up to the curb. She grins, relieved, like she wondered if they'd really come pick her up. I'm already sad about what's going to happen to her.

I watch the car pull away.

"Walk me home, Adam?" Sarah asks.

"Yeah," I say. "Let's go the long way."

I lead her in the direction Desiree's car is heading, keeping my eyes on the retreating bumper lights.

It happens quick. As the husband pulls into the next intersection, a car flies out of nowhere and smashes into the passenger side. The car doors cave inward and little bits of metal and paint spark upward.

Sarah screams but I don't. It's not that I don't feel it. It's just that I know—instinctively—it's all over anyway. Death is instantaneous. There's no fight, no wait. Desiree's shadow—the clown that was making funny faces at me just minutes ago—floats up and out, lingering above the car for just a second, and then disappears.

CHAPTER 1.5

He cleared his throat and said, Are you sure the Synod is ready for what I'm about to tell it?

Her Excellency gestured, impatient. Get on with it, she said.

He said, Look, I wasn't there. But if I were to imagine the story in excruciating detail, it would go like this:

The sky was a puckered scar of darkness on the night the Grim Reaper escaped Rome and boarded a boat headed for North Africa. She and her companion, shrouded and shaking, clasped hands tightly under their cloaks. Yet their steps were steady as they disembarked and fled to the home of a local priest, an elderly man faithful to an ancient faith, unafraid to chant the vows that would unite them, one flesh forever.

They held hands in front of a fire. They gazed into each other's eyes. Eyes lit by an eternal desire.

If the priest had any idea who he was uniting, he—

Her Excellency interrupted: Come now. It didn't happen like that.

Oh? he said. Well, if you know, Captain, why don't *you* tell the story?

Elder #2, rolling her eyes: Just tell us what you know.

The longer I live, the less I know, he said. Let that be a lesson to you.

Yet he continued:

Later, after her demise, her consorts would ask why she had been in Rome. Had her purpose in the Eternal City been one befitting the Handmaiden of Death?

And what of her companion, the one now united to her, in death as in life? Would he gladly fulfill her duties in the new world or would he succumb to the gentle tugging desire of his family to return to his duties in the Eternal City?

CHAPTER 2

Biology is actually my favorite class and I usually follow Mrs. Feldman's lectures religiously. Today her whiny voice is a mosquito hovering just above my head then suddenly shutting off. The silence is blessed and wonderful, a calm oasis in an otherwise turbulent sea, as I slowly

drift

pillows some pillows would

be sooooooooooooo

sooooooo niiiii . . .

"Mr. Jones! What is *wrong* with you?"

Her knife-sharp voice jerks me awake. "What?" *Act normal, Adam! Just be cool!*

"You were mumbling something," she says. "Do you have a problem with my lecture?"

"No!" The word warms the edges of my lips. "I'm sorry. I had a late night."

She drops the volume of her voice as if she doesn't want the rest of the class to hear. "Adam, any scientist will tell you sleep is essential. If a person is deprived of it for too long, they can literally go insane . . ."

She's still talking but the rest of what she says floats off into the air, wisps of smoke breaking apart until it's gone.

I'm walking down a hallway. Where am I? Oh. Right. School.

Did the bell ring? I don't remember leaving biology but class must be over because everybody else is also here, walking somewhere.

I head toward the cafeteria. Is it lunchtime? One of the clocks on the wall reveals that force of habit is propelling me in the right direction at the right time.

For some reason, this strikes me as funny. I think I'm laughing out loud because people start edging to the other side of the hall to get away from me.

God, Mrs. Feldman is right. This insomnia is going to drive me crazy. I have to figure out how to sleep without going to hell. Hell. That's right, hell! Hell. Hell. Hell. Hello. Hello!

Hel*lo*, Sarah . . .

Sarah's standing on the other side of the cafeteria, talking to Dominick. *Why* is she talking to him? We hate him. He hates us. He's a Cool Kid. We are not. At least, I'm not and Carlos isn't and Jeremy isn't. Sarah could be, if she wanted. Who knows why she hangs out with us three losers.

Dominick bends close to talk to her. His shadow is all slimy and wet and oozy and getting all over her like . . . sperm or something. As I approach, it rises up, black and menacing, to stare at me.

I crouch to crawl under a table. Then I stop. You can't hide from people's shadows. So I straighten up, a little too fast, and almost lose balance. As soon as I'm righted, I face them. Try to keep my cool. But I can't help it, my shadow growls at his. Yes, my shadow is a dog, a German shepherd. Domesticated, a herder, but still a predator. And Sarah's one of my people. I have to protect her.

I head toward them, then suddenly pitch forward instead, jaw catching the edge of a table. For just an instant, I'm falling forward in pitch darkness.

I won't, I won't, I *won't* go to That Place right here, right now . . .

I jerk myself awake, babbling at the top of my lungs, but somebody clamps an oxygen mask over my nose and mouth, cutting off the flow of words. The ceiling is rushing past and three people are running alongside me, one of them—Sarah—shouting my name: "Adam!" Two medics wheel me down the hall, strapped to a gurney.

I grab the oxygen mask and lift it. "Sarah?"

Her shadow's a river, rapids lifting and breaking beside us. She's crying and scared, the river swollen and too full, ready to flood its banks. "I'm sorry, Adam," she whispers.

I lift my head and watch her figure grow smaller as paramedics wheel me into an ambulance. The principal's head looms in the doorway until the paramedics block him from sight. "Sorry, sir, we need to get out of here."

I think I should be worried but a deep sea–blue feeling of peace flows through each limb. I'm floating on a cloud in an endless blue sky. I'm—

"What the . . . What's happening?" I ask as they begin attaching things to me.

"You blacked out," one of the guys says. "Checked your blood pressure. Shame on you, you didn't eat breakfast." He wags an index finger at me.

"Do I have to go to the hospital?" I ask. My father will kill me. Things like hospitals, doctors—they're not for us, not for the Jones family, no sir. *Your time comes when your time comes,* Dad always says, *and there's nothing you can do to stop it.*

"You went a little crazy in there," the other one says. "You may have had a seizure. Cafeteria's a bit worse for the wear." He grins at me. Friendly. "You too. Wait till you see the shiner you gave yourself." His puppy shadow notices mine. They wag tails at each other.

The first paramedic glances at the second one, unbelieving. "You on anything?" he asks, voice flatlined, no sympathy but no judgment either.

"No."

"No Mollies? No X?"

"No?" I don't mean it to sound like a question but it squeaks out.

"Acid? Steroids?" His nose flares with suspicion, little nose hairs trembling with indignation.

I get this reaction from some people. It's not BO cuz I've smelled my pits. I've also checked my teeth (crooked), hair (dark, straight), clothes (on the ragged end but nothing unexpected for a kid my age). Slightly below average in looks, too tall and skinny for anybody's comfort, but basically normal. Still, no matter how much I'd like to scootch under the radar, I'll never be able to. Some people get suspicious as soon as they meet me.

I clear my throat. "No. I have insomnia. I can't sleep. That's all. I don't do drugs. I don't drink. I'm clean as a whistle."

"*Clean as a whistle?* What kid talks like that?" The friendly paramedic grins at me. "What are you, fifteen or forty-five?"

"Fifteen," I say. "It's a phrase my dad uses."

"I was joking around, kid." He puts a hand on my arm.

"History of seizures?" Paramedic #1 is back on track. "History of mental illness?"

"Um. No. And no." I wonder if I'm lying. "So . . . what exactly happened in there?"

"You went berserk," Paramedic #1 says. "You attacked tables and chairs. It scared half the school. You were screaming something about a demon? You failed to calm down until we subdued you. We've given you a sedative and now we're going to take you to the hospital to check you out." He stares at me. "Something's wrong. What aren't you telling us?"

"Hey, chill out," Paramedic #2 says. "He's just a kid."

"Can I call my dad?" I ask.

Paramedic #2 locates my cell phone in my backpack and hands it to me.

The phone rings and rings and rings. *C'mon, Dad, pick up. When do I ever call you? Never. Never! So you must realize it's an emergency, right? Pick up the damn phone.*

He doesn't. My dad, never there when I need him. Except in my dreams.

CHAPTER 3

The doctor doesn't find anything wrong with me, other than an excessive amount of caffeine in my urine. "Too! Much! Caffeine!" she says, speaking in distinct exclamation points. "You're going to end up with caffeine poisoning! And no wonder you're not sleeping! Lack of sleep can cause a psychotic break! Go home and take a nap!"

Well, I did get a nap. Here. Whatever those paramedics gave me knocked me out for about four hours straight.

I still can't reach my dad and the hospital won't release me without a family member—you know, being a minor and all—so I'm forced to call my crazy grandfather. I've never actually seen Grandpa leave his crummy little apartment so I have no idea whether I'm going to be stuck in the hospital until my dad comes back from wherever he is, whenever that is—could be days from now—but Grandpa just says he'll be there shortly. I can only imagine what "shortly" means. I wish I had a book or something. I have a stupidphone so there are limited options for amusing myself.

I hate hospitals. One of my earliest memories is waking up in a hospital bed. Someone started shouting, "Oh my god! Oh my god!" Then a bunch of people crowded into the room and poked and prodded me. I remember being wrapped in a blanket and being pushed out of the hospital in a wheelchair. I had some real difficulties for some time after that. I would have random thoughts that didn't seem like they belonged to me and I had to relearn how to walk. Whatever happened must have been bad. Neither Dad nor Grandpa ever talk about it. That's par for the course. We don't talk about shit in this family—the family consisting of the three of us. I think this happened around the same time my mom died. It feels like she was there before the hospital visit and then suddenly she wasn't . . .

I check the time and call Sarah while I wait. It rings and rings without voice mail picking up and then finally she answers in a small, scared little voice: "Hi, Adam."

"Sarah," I croak, voice careening over a cliff. "Hey."

"Where are you?"

"Waiting for my grandfather to pick me up from the hospital. Where are you?"

"Home."

"After my grandfather comes, I'll swing by." The thought of seeing Sarah gives me a warm rush, hot water spurting out of a showerhead on a cold December night before my stingy dad decides to turn on the central heat.

"Don't," she says quickly. "Just go home. Get some rest."

"I'm okay."

"No, no, you're not."

Fear slithers in between each word, boa heavy. Wraps itself around us, squeezes, squeezes, squeezes. I'm having trouble breathing.

"You're not okay, Adam, I'm not okay. That was not okay, what happened. It scared me."

I feel our friendship dying. I can already see the message chiseled on its tombstone: *Never quite took off.* I meant to rescue her from that creep but, according to the paramedic, all I managed to do was introduce my chin to a table at high speed and abuse cafeteria chairs while spouting nonsense.

"Sarah." Her babbling stops. "What exactly happened? Because I don't remember." I really don't, unless you count this vague darkness in the back of my mind, like a memory you don't exactly have but think you should have, of somebody asking me, *What day is it? Who's the president?*—like we're at the scene of a car accident. And I'm answering but what I'm saying makes no sense.

Her voice drops to a low hush: "You were—" A stop sign in her voice. Then she drives forward anyway, reckless. "You were seeing things that weren't there. You were—oh, I don't know! You were crazy. You were possessed. Like we needed to call a priest and have you exorcised. You acted like you were speaking to a demon. Do you believe in demons, Adam?"

Last week, I was hoping I'd get up the guts to take Sarah to homecoming. This week, she's telling me I might be possessed. Our romantic prospects seem to be taking a steep nosedive.

"I don't know," I say, because that's the truth.

"You wouldn't stop screaming." She pauses. "Adam, you need *help*."

The phone feels hot against my ear. We hang up and I hunch into my hoodie, wishing I could undo the last twenty-four hours.

* * *

My grandfather is a dinosaur. And by that, I don't mean he's old, although yes, like my dad, he is freaking ancient. You know how some people are going to be sweet and gentle when they go into that good night? Not Grandpa. When he dies, he's going to be a roaring tyrannosaurus rex that goes on a rampage, tearing apart the world around him and chewing up people into tiny bits with his shiny, sharp teeth in his enormous jaws until he finally crashes to the ground, flattening another dozen people.

He's glaring at me now with his mean little eyes in his gigantic tyrannosaurus head. "What'd you do this time, you little bastard?"

I jump up. "Nothing," I say.

"It doesn't sound like nothing!" he roars. Everybody in the waiting room stares at him, this giant old man with his shock of wispy gray hair sticking straight up from his head, ginormous liver spots dotting his face and skull. Ugly moles everywhere. "What are you, crazy? Running around babbling about demons?"

Grandpa's already barreling down the hospital hallway as he shouts. His enormous head on his little body bobbles back and forth with anger. People pop their heads out of offices, wondering what the commotion is.

"Did you already sign me out?"

"Signed, sealed, delivered!" Grandpa yells. He pushes a door open and we walk out into the bright fall day. "Now get in the car."

"What car?"

I'd sort of assumed Grandpa would sign me out and then I'd walk home and he'd make his way back to his apartment, however he got here. I'm totally shocked to see a Lincoln Town Car waiting for us.

I look at Grandpa with some concern. Has he lost it? How can he afford this car?

We roar away—apparently, the driver shares Grandpa's personality—and Grandpa glowers at me. When he's perturbed or angry, his eyebrows come together into this unibrow kind of thing. It looks like a lightning bolt imprinted across his forehead.

"Now tell me: what was all this crap you were spewing in public?" he says.

I glance at the driver, then back at Grandpa.

"Don't worry about him, he's deaf," Grandpa bellows. He leans forward and shouts at the driver, "Please confirm for the boy that you're deaf, Mr. Patel!"

"I'm sorry, sir?" Mr. Patel says.

"See? They're all deaf. Probably listening to crap music too loud, like all you young idiots. Now, tell me, boy, *what is going on*?"

I look at him desperately. Grandpa is not somebody you lie to.

"I can't sleep." It's sort of a relief to admit it to somebody, out loud. "I mean, of course I sleep. But I started having nightmares. I keep going to this cemetery. I think I'm looking for my mother's grave. And this . . . Thing . . . this black Thing tries to hug me and the next thing I know I'm falling and that demon Thing is chasing me."

"Good lord!" Grandpa shouts.

"I . . . I know that sounds crazy. They probably should have kept me in that hospital, right?"

"No, that's not what I was shouting about," Grandpa says. He sounds subdued suddenly. "Your father is a fool, boy. A fool. I suppose I'm a fool too."

"Excuse me?"

"He should have told you what this was about a long time ago. We argued about this, we did. And now we will argue again. I'm going to do something I should have done before. Your father will not like it but it has to be done."

He's alarming me now. "What are you going to do?"

"Don't worry, Adam. I promise not to do anything *too* rash."

I must look skeptical so he continues: "You have no idea how *important* you are. You're the last remaining descendent of a very ancient, very important, very rare family."

I snort. "You mean the ancient, extremely rare *Jones* family? Sure, we're really about to die off. Along with the ancient, extremely rare *Smith* family."

Grandpa jabs me in the arm with two knuckles. "None of your sass, boy!"

"*Ow*. That's going to leave a bruise, Grandpa."

"I may *seem* bat-shit crazy, but I'm not. And you're not going crazy either. You have a Destiny. And it's not to be a doctor or an engineer or whatever it is you think you're going to do with your life. Those dreams? They're part of your powers."

Silence fills the car. "You're saying I'm a superhero." My tone is flat because if I don't keep emotion out of my voice, I'm going to break into uncontrollable, hysterical giggles. I see the headlines of my own comic: *Dreamerman: Episode VI. In which Adam Jones, a.k.a. Dreamerman, passes out and wets himself in fear while confronting bank robbers! The bad guys heard muttering in back of cop car, "What a weirdo," and, "We would have gotten away if it wasn't for all the urine. Ugh!"*

"No. Something bigger than a superhero." The seat cushions make fart sounds as he sits back.

He's done talking apparently. I'm done too. I don't know how to respond. I mean, it's not that I disbelieve him. Entirely. I know I'm different. Special, even, though not the kind of "special" he's talking about. Still, it's sort of a relief to have somebody acknowledge it. Admit it's real. Thanks, Grandpa. You may be cracked. You may be totally loco. Completely coo-coo. But thanks. Thanks for confirming it runs in the family. I really am crazy too. I wasn't just imagining it.

I stare out the window, storefronts and apartments passing rapidly as we cruise down the street.

Grandpa comes inside for a little while but he doesn't stay long. "Are you okay, kid?" he asks, and when I nod, just so he'll go away, he says, "Then I better get back. Things to do. People to see."

Ha. I imagine a parade of famous people visiting his piss-pot apartment. John Lennon sitting in the corner with the cactus, gazing at the framed postcards from Bhutan through lavender-tinted glasses. Grace Kelly, leaning out the fire escape window, a thin trail of blue smoke trailing upward from her cigarette. Donald Trump sitting on the rumpled bedclothes in his expensive business suit. They all wrinkle their noses, wondering why it smells like boiled potatoes and bacon.

"No caffeine," he says. "Go to sleep. You're going to be dreaming all your life. You can't avoid it forever."

The apartment's empty as Mother Hubbard's cupboard. I rummage in the refrigerator for something to eat—beans and rice and oatmeal are all we have left—and turn the television on, not to actually watch anything because Dad's too cheap to pay for cable, but just so there's some noise in the apartment. I wish Dad would come back early from his business trip because I really don't want to be alone tonight.

He doesn't come back.

A more pressing problem presents itself: What am I going to do to keep myself awake tonight? And to prevent myself from thinking about everything I don't want to think about?

I slam a couple NoDoz again—despite the doctor's advice and despite Grandpa's parting words—and challenge Jeremy to a series of *Kill Sam* games for as long as—well, as long as possible. Like a good friend, he doesn't mention what happened at school. Still, he crashes at three—*Sorry, bro, some of us need our sleep*—and I spend the rest of the night pacing the floor of the empty apartment. My eyes close involuntarily a few times and I stumble against the couch or a bookcase.

I wish Dad would let me get a dog.

Around four a.m., I pull one of Dad's books off the shelves. Some of them are written in languages using alphabets I don't recognize. Some are fragile, handwritten on fragments of papyrus. Dad especially loves illuminated manuscripts—the ones monks spent hundreds of years transcribing by hand and which have all these strange fantastical illustrations of saints and crosses and mythical creatures in the margins.

I stare for a while at a scene I don't understand—a young girl using a golden cross to shield herself from a fire-breathing dragon. The dragon has an absurdly gentle look on its face, sad as it gazes at the girl. From its neck dangles a long golden chain with a symbol of a circle, broken down the top by something that looks like a fishhook or maybe a shepherd's crook.

The dragon's face starts to swim and it runs toward me, panting like a dog, and I reach out to pet it before waking suddenly with a peculiar feeling of loss and need. At least *that* felt like a normal dream. A proper *dream* dream.

Thank god, morning light has broken. Coffee, a hot shower, and a brisk walk to school with wet hair. Get me out of this stale, lonely place.

The early morning is crisp and cold, a hint of autumn in the air, the leaves turning yellow and red just before they fall off and die—the scent of living things beginning to decay as winter approaches. Despite the exhaustion and dread about returning to school after yesterday's fiasco, I inhale all that fresh air—the smell of winter coming, the earth going through its cycle of death before life returns—and I smile. Hopeful. Maybe yesterday's calamity will blow over quick. Maybe something even more gossip-worthy has happened in the meantime.

Or not.

"Freak." The voice is so soft, I almost miss it.

I glance up, caught. Dominick and his friends, waiting by my locker. A jock to my left—his shadow a bull moose bearing down, snorting, pawing the ground. Dominick on the right, a mountain of a young man, flesh straining and spilling out of his jeans. His shadow is small and twisted, flitting from floor to wall to locker and back. And then the guy directly in front. His shadow is thick, an anaconda, twisting around and over his shoulder. Tongue flicking out.

"Leave me alone." My voice is unsteady, uncertain, even though I mean what I say.

The anaconda sneers, lips pulled back, fangs gleaming.

"I mean it." Really really wish my hands would stop shaking. "Just go. Before it's too late."

The mountain snickers. The bull moose grabs my arm, slams me to the floor, and stomps on my head with his boot. I twist away, rolling across the sticky linoleum floor, but can't escape the boot. My nose is pouring blood and something hot and liquid drips out of my ear onto the floor. My vision narrows, black around all the edges, with only a pinpoint of light revealing the hallway's tiles.

And just like that, it happens. Have you ever seen heat shimmering off the asphalt so the air warps and distorts how things look? Suddenly, we aren't in the school hallway anymore. The four of us are standing in the middle of a deserted highway in the Sonoran Desert. Saguaros, straight arrows pointing to the blue blue sky. Cicadas whirring their wings together in endless song. Hot hot hot sand. The blinding sun.

A woman huddles at the foot of a nearby yucca. Her

skin is fish-white, burnt holes where her eyes and mouth should be.

She's here.

As She stands, the anaconda slithers off the asphalt and disappears over a small hill of sand. The bull moose's eyes flash panic. He hoofs it down the road, aimless, unsure how he got to this hot hell but hoping he can outrun this sudden apparition. He won't survive long. He's already frothing at the mouth.

She hobbles toward us. I look at Dominick, wondering if he, too, will back down. But his small, mean shadow glares at me. "Is She your secret weapon?" he spits.

No, I think, but do not say, *She's my nightmare.*

He jerks left then right then left, then darts around my back, grabbing hold of me from behind. I reach around and rip him off me—shadows are slippery but they're light, easy to grip and hold, rip, tear, shred—

"Adam!" Sarah shrieks. "Stop!"

I'm startled back to the crowded hallway just before first bell, students flattened against lockers, staring at me. The three guys who attacked me lie prone on the floor, knocked out or dead, I'm not sure which yet. And the principal of the school is bearing down on me, flanked by two security guards.

Sarah's so close, I see the startled whites of her eyes. Jeremy and Carlos stand beside her, faces twisted with surprise and fear.

I stumble over the guys on the floor. One of the security guards catches me, his arms locking under mine and gripping me against his chest so tight, I can't move.

CHAPTER 3.5

Her Excellency was astonished. She sat back, shook her head, and said, in as sardonic a tone as she could muster, And what happened next? Pray tell us. And don't spare a single detail.

He grinned, baring his teeth, and continued the story:

The Grim Reaper and her betrothed fled east to the desert. They honeymooned in a small hut, rust-red dust creeping in through all the cracks. They spent their nights clinging to each other, basking in the glow of passionate love. And so they woke each morning coated red, laughing at the way the land clung to them, seeped into their pores, soaked them in a strange ethereal glow, drenched them in deep happiness.

What in the world? Her Excellency asked. What is this drivel? What is this dreck?

What exactly do you think honeymooners do? he said. I thought I would spare the Synod the salacious details . . . unless you *want* them, that is . . .

No thank you, Her Excellency said, her voice high and pinched.

During the days, they hiked through the strange wilderness. Nights, they clung to each other in front of a fire. While she slept, the lover-husband wrote poetry.

This barren land
and you, my love,
and each day awakens
a new longing
for you alone.

But deep inside, they both knew the truth. It was something about which they did not speak.

CHAPTER 4

The less said about the horror show in the principal's office, the better. One of the guys has heatstroke. Another is severely dehydrated. One of them has burns on the soles of his feet. "And this is my fault how?" I ask, but they don't have an answer.

I point out, to no avail, that *they* attacked *me*. I'm the one with what I suspect is a broken nose, an aching head, and something wrong with my hearing in the ear that the bull moose slammed with his boot. Okay, yeah, one of those guys also has a broken arm and they all seem terrified and one of them can't say anything but "uh-uh, uh-uh" like The Wraith sucked all the words right out of his head. But still, why am I the only one in trouble?

They couldn't get ahold of Dad, big surprise. At least this time I don't have to get Grandpa to bail me out. But I am carrying a letter that says I can't return to school unless Dad comes to the office. I'm guessing this isn't good.

I text Sarah on the way home, just one word, *Sorry*, and she texts me right back. *It's okay, Adam, they hurt you first. It scared me to see you like that but it was three against one, whatever the principal says. We can talk about it later.*

Relief lodges deep in my stomach. I hadn't realized how stressed out I've been until the moment it lifts. At least Sarah's not completely, totally, 100 percent through with me. Maybe there's still a smidgen of hope.

A fat guy in a meticulously tailored suit is sitting on the steps right in front of the door to our apartment. His mouth is like an eagle's beak, his shadow shaped like a bird of prey. His small beady eyes dart this way and that, settling on nothing.

I stop and look at him. A smile—one of deep satisfaction—breaks out on his face. I shiver and feel the desire to scurry into a dark hole, mouse-like.

"Well, well, well," he says in an accent I can't quite place. He stands up—lumbers is more like it—and holds out his hand as if I'm supposed to shake it. Force of habit, I suppose, makes me take his hand. He grips it so hard, I wince. "Very good to meet you . . . ? And what is the name you go by . . . ?"

His voice trails off and I guess I'm meant to supply him with my name, but my eyes are caught by the silver medallion hanging around his neck—a circle, broken by a curved line that looks like a shepherd's staff. The dragon in the illuminated manuscript I was reading last night wore a similar symbol.

"What's that?" I ask.

His smile curves up, the sharp points of his mustache piercing his teeth. "Ah, of course, you would be drawn to the Broken Circle. It is the symbol for what we do." He unhooks it from around his neck and holds it in the palm of his hand, offering it to me.

My eyes are riveted by it, throat suddenly aching with unshed tears.

He's saying something.

"What?" I say.

He closes his palm over the Broken Circle medallion and suddenly I can look at him again, concentrate on what he's saying. "I said I'm a Finder. My job is to find people. People like you."

People like me? Just put a flaming-orange trucker hat on my head with the word *WEERDOUGH* emblazoned in neon pink. Yeah, I'm a freak, just like those assholes said.

"How old are you, my boy?" he asks.

"Fifteen."

"Shame."

My eyebrow crooks skyward. "Just so you know, my sources tell me being fifteen is only a temporary condition. Lasts about a year." I speak sotto voce, conspiratorial: "I've also heard that every adult has done it at some point . . ."

He shakes his head. "No. It's a shame you're fifteen, Adam, and you're just now going to learn your True Destiny." I swear, he speaks so I can see the capital letters.

Get lost, creepfest, I think very hard at the spot right between his eyebrows. "I'm going inside," I say.

His mouth parts, revealing a gap between his front two teeth and a missing canine tooth. One of his bottom teeth glints gold. "We thought you were dead. We thought you died during that unfortunate . . . accident . . . with your mother. Your father is a very naughty man, hiding you away like this." He tsk-tsks.

I close the door behind me and lock it, turning the dead bolt.

He shouts through the closed door: "Thank god you're

still alive! Thank god I found you! Now the world doesn't have to fall apart when your grandfather dies."

I call Dad again, hoping for a miracle. And I get it because this time he answers.

"Adam." Dad has one of those deep, mysterious radio voices, the kind you might have heard narrating horror dramas back in the 1950s. Which I totally listen to, by the way. One of my favorite ways to stay awake.

"Dad, where the heck are you?"

"What do you need?"

The fat man is standing outside our door, looking inside the window, straight at me, smiling. That smirk isn't going anywhere.

"There's a weird guy standing on the steps of the apartment," I say.

"Tell him to get lost."

Dad has this irritating habit of assuming I can take care of Big Problems.

"He's not going anywhere," I say. "He's huge. Besides, he says he's quote-unquote 'found' me. He says he's here to reveal my True Destiny or something like that. He's wearing a silver necklace with a broken circle."

"What?" Dad's phone begins to crackle.

I start to repeat what I just said, but he says, all in a rush, in that commanding radio voice, "Adam, keep the door locked. Whatever you do, don't let him inside. And don't go back outside. I'm going to be right there."

Dad's not one for "language," but I'd swear I hear the F-word roll off his tongue as he hangs up.

* * *

I stay in the foyer, watching the fat guy on the porch. He's looking at me, grinning his foolish face off. Dad sweeps up the stairs a few minutes later, black coattails flapping in the wind. Tall. Gaunt. Grim. Dad would look younger if his hair wasn't so straight, so black, with such a severe part. I'd swear his shoulders droop just a millionth of a fraction. Barely noticeable, but it makes my own heart drop.

He climbs the stairs, opens the door, and gestures with his arm for the gentleman to pass inside, glaring at him all the while.

"Your life is about to change forever," the fat man tells me.

"We'll see about that," Dad says.

"No, no, no," the man says. "I trust you understand what my visit means."

"This is all a big mistake," Dad says.

"Oh, it's a mistake all right," the man counters. "Yours."

They go into Dad's office and Dad closes the door firmly behind them. Although this meeting seems to be about me, apparently I'm not invited.

I wander around the apartment. It's not big. I'm able to cover the perimeters of the kitchen, living room, and my tiny-ass room in less than a hundred steps. I continue to pace. What does he mean, my True Destiny?

I think about all the crazy classes Dad's made me take all these years. Latin and Italian. Japanese cooking, where I learned how to make a mean teriyaki sauce, not to mention the art of sushi. Zulu jewelry–making. A drumming class. I always figured they were his way of trying to help me figure out what I have a passion for, what I might want to do when I grow up, my "destiny"—though I can tell you right now, Zulu jewelry–making is not it. (Not to lie: it'll come in handy if I'm ever homeless and need something I can sell on the street.) Anyway, the point is, I have this eerie feeling that everything Dad's given me, even all those things I didn't want, like those crazy classes, are about to be taken away from me. What kind of True Destiny is that?

They spend less than ten minutes inside Dad's office. Then the man tumbles out like Dad's chewed him up and spit him out, but instead of looking cowed, like Dad's the hawk and he's the mouse, he looks triumphant.

Using slow, deliberate motions, he touches my shoulder, closes his eyes, breathes in deeply, and releases the breath slowly. "Well now," he says. "Well, well, well. This suddenly became even more complicated."

He pulls the medallion from around his neck and holds it out to me. I look at the circle, broken by the shepherd's crook. I can't take my eyes off it.

"Take it, Adam," he says, voice hard.

I want to look at my father to see what I should do. But for some reason I can't. At last, I reach out and he drops the chain into my outstretched palm. My fingers close over it involuntarily. His eyes meet mine. He smiles, turns, and closes the door gently behind him. A kind of victory in the soft motion.

Dad sighs and gestures for me to follow him into the office. He sits at his desk—an ancient wooden thing that was probably built during the Civil War and is so heavy that nobody's dared remove it, so it's been here since the apartment building was erected. He props his elbows on the desk, rests his chin on his hands, and stares at me. His face is bathed in the pale green light cast by an old Tiffany glass lamp, its brass chain swinging gently, casting shadows on the pile of yellowing papers on his desk. The floor-to-ceiling bookcase behind him is missing random books, the empty, blank spaces like rotten teeth.

I have this theory about Dad: he seems younger than he really is because he surrounds himself with ancient things. I mean, what seems older, an old guy with dark hair that he combs over or a crumbling two thousand–year-old manuscript? Exactly.

"I suppose you're wondering why that man visited."

I fidget in the old wingback leather chair and pick at the stuffing spilling out of a crack in the armrest. My feet scuff the worn wooden floor. "Yeah, what'd he want?" I'm bursting with questions but I don't want to scare him off.

He shuffles and reshuffles the papers on his desk. "He was here to remind me of my obligations."

"What are those?"

He's silent again for a long time. Finally, he steeples his long white fingers and clears his throat. And instead of words, rocks fall out of his mouth.

"I must start training you to take over the family business," he says.

"Oh," I reply. Let me just be perfectly honest here and admit that I don't know exactly what Dad does. I *wish* he did something normal, like finance or trading or some such thing. But I think maybe he's, like, a voodoo god or something equally weird and scary. I suppose now would be the time to ask. Especially since I'm supposed to take over for him. Voodoo god Adam in training. I don't ask. Maybe I'm scared to know the answer. Instead, I follow up my brilliant "Oh" with the equally brilliant: "So what does that mean? Sometime after college?"

He looks terribly sad as he watches me with his deep-set eyes. Bits of energy spark off his bushy eyebrows. "I'm sorry, Adam, I had always wanted you to have a choice. But things are worse than I thought. You're not going to college."

I watch his mouth for some sign that he's joking but it stays flat. "I thought you set up a college fund! I thought . . . Dad! I've *always* been on the college track."

"The problem isn't money." He takes off his spectacles and wipes them. "Universities can't train you to do what I do. This is why I'm sending you to a special school, a boarding school."

A big black hole swallows up the whole universe. I jump out of the wingback chair. "You're sending me to a *boarding* school?"

"As soon as you finish, you'll join me in my work."

"No way!" I shout. "I want to stay in school *here*. With my *friends*." I forget for a second that my friends now think I'm crazy, that Sarah's a bit scared of me even though she knows it wasn't entirely my fault because those guys jumped me, and that the principal may or may not have expelled me yesterday, which I'll only be able to find out if I can convince Dad to accompany me so we can get the bad news in person . . . which is apparently not going to happen.

"I wish you could stay here too." Dad's eyebrows droop. "But we're in a contract and we can't get out of it. You're the sole surviving eligible member of the family, so you must go."

"God, Dad, this is total crap." Spit flies out of my mouth and lands on the spectacles he just wiped. He blinks but doesn't remove them. "You're always gone, you're always working, you've never cared about what I want, and now *this*?"

The words start spilling out of my mouth and I know I'd keep on going—*I hate you* is on the tip of my tongue—but Dad stands up, eyes flashing. His shadow swings angrily, a spiked mace above his head. He inhales deeply and suddenly, sucking all of the oxygen out of the room. The papers on his desk flutter, the thick velvet curtains ripple, and a fly crawling over his desk goes careening across the room. The air shimmers like a million dragonflies flying away. Just when I think I'm going to pass out or puke, or both, oxygen rushes back into the room with a clap.

"You should start thinking about what you want to take with you when you go." And with that, he dismisses me.

My hands shake as I stagger out of the room. I go to my bedroom, place the medallion on my desk, sit on the bed to play *Kill Sam* on my laptop. But Sam ends up killing me exactly the same way three times—a knife to the back of my head. My eyes keep wandering back to the medallion.

Finally, I unhook it and chain it around my neck. I know I'm choosing something. I wish I knew what. I wish I knew what the hell is going on.

Eventually I sleep. But She doesn't follow me into my

dreams. No, this time I'm alone on a tall mountain—just me, the trees, and the sky. When I look down, I see that the sea roils and rages below me in an ecstasy of green waves and what looks like sea monsters chomping at the bit, froth raging at their mouths. They're looking up at me, waiting. And when I look around to see if there's any way out, I realize that there's nowhere to go but down. Toward them. Toward the monsters.

CHAPTER 5

Sometimes when I'm in the middle of The Dream, I pretend my mom's with us, walking along beside us. Her face is freckled. Her nose is long and thin and she has a wide smile that stretches across her face in a way that might not be called exactly beautiful but is nonetheless beautiful because of how it makes you feel. At least, this is what I imagine her to look like.

I suppose I went to her funeral but I don't remember. I don't know where she's buried either. We have never gone to visit her grave site . . . unless that's what we're doing in my dream.

Even if I don't remember what she was like, I imagine she was good and kind and beautiful. And I wish she was still here. One of the reasons I've never brought my friends home to visit is that I can't imagine what they'd think. They've never met my dad but his shenanigans are legendary among them. Like the time he suggested I start going to AA meetings. "You can learn something from these people," he said, a statement that has been a source of endless amusement for my friends ever since. Or the time he signed me up for a dating class. I was twelve. The women in the room were all in their forties. Somehow, I was supposed to learn something from that experience too.

Last year, just before high school started, he took me

to a psychic convention in Manhattan. We visited a dozen booths. Dad would sit in the little psychic chair or on their couch and he'd close his eyes and most of the psychics pretended to read his mind—and I do mean *pretend* because they didn't have a clue what kind of person he is or they were liars or both. They kept seeing dice, or one of them said they saw a woman in his future, which is impossible, believe me. One psychic was real, though. She could see that Dad's shadow is an ancient volcano, like Mt. Vesuvius, constantly erupting, and she spoke breathlessly, keeping her head down, refusing to look him in the eye: "Sir, I don't know who you are but I'm afraid."

Dad smiled at her and said, "You're an honest one, aren't you?"

She kept her head bowed. But when he'd moved on, she grabbed my wrist, yanking me back. Lipstick bled into the wrinkles around her lips, and her green eyes looked haunted, like she'd just seen the atomic bomb dropped on her hometown. "Sweetheart," she said, "you're carrying death with you everywhere you go. It's a ghost inside you, flowing through the blood in your veins. It's a nightmare you can't escape. If you don't release it, you may as well go to the grave right here, right now."

She pushed me toward my father's quickly retreating back, calling out to me in a surprisingly low voice, "Honey, you don't belong here. I hope you make it where you need to be."

I stumbled after Dad, breathing one-two-three, so I wouldn't faint or pass out. *Yeah,* I thought, *she's right. I don't belong here at this stupid convention.*

Within a week, I had the first nightmare.

But that was still days away. That afternoon, we went to the main hall of the convention center, where a man from the Balkans was addressing a crowd of probably five hundred people. He started doing simple readings—how much money people had in their pockets, or whether they had a picture of a dead relative in their purses, that kind of thing. As the program progressed, he whipped the crowd into a frenzy, hypnotizing different volunteers into doing humiliating things like removing items of clothing or kissing strangers.

I became more and more agitated, watching him.

When he asked for a final volunteer, Dad stood up. The instant he was on his feet, the electricity in the crowd flipped off. People under hypnosis snapped out of it and ran to put their clothes back on or take a seat.

The presenter was ticked. "Who are you?" he asked.

Dad stepped out into the aisle. "Looks like I'm your final volunteer."

The hypnotist crossed his arms and tapped his foot as Dad made his way onto the stage. They stood face to face and looked deep into each other's eyes.

Then it happened. The hypnotist's jaw went slack. In front of five hundred people, his eyes glazed over and drool ran down his chin. His shadow ran for the curtains and stood behind them, cowering.

His shadow was *hiding* from my dad.

It felt like forever that they stood there, even though it probably lasted less than ten seconds. The crowd shuffled nervously in their seats. Finally, Dad harrumphed and turned away. The presenter clapped his mouth shut, swallowed hard, and backed off the stage, keeping his eyes on Dad. When he was a few feet from the closest exit, he turned and fled, the door sighing on its hinges as it closed behind him.

Everyone stared at Dad like they'd just seen an Angel of God descend from heaven.

"What *was* that, Dad?" I asked as we left.

"When a person mistakes their ability for privilege, they sometimes use it against others," he said. "Most people are weak. And people who have power—even a little power—sometimes use it as a weapon. To control people. Or just for fun. That's what he was doing to the people he hypnotized. Power is seductive that way. You have power too, Adam. I hope you are never that kind of person, the kind who abuses it, who uses it against others instead of *for* them."

It was strange, what he said. It filled me with a sense of—I don't know—destiny maybe. It's hard to describe what I felt in that moment, but if you pushed me to the wall, I guess I'd say it felt like an Old Testament kind of anointment—Samuel coming to say the young shepherd boy David was going to be the next King of Israel. Something like that. Like maybe I had power, but I could be a good person and use my power for goodness instead of evil.

Most of that feeling is gone now. I feel powerless instead.

And then I wonder: maybe that hypnotist was abusing his power, but didn't Dad do the same thing when he turned the tables around? That's something I wish I could ask him but we just don't communicate very well using words.

Sometimes, Dad looks at me and my shadow rises up,

I feel him calling it up, and I know that unless I block him, I'll be naked in front of him; he'll be able to see my every thought. So I pull back, I hide my shadow away from him. Maybe I'm powerless, but I can keep my thoughts private at least.

When I finally started fighting back, he liked it.

The first time I grasped his shadow with my mind, it was like falling out of my head and into somebody else's memories and thoughts and dreams. I couldn't believe what was going on in his head. A war, but like no war I've ever seen on television—women and children huddled together in enclosures, soldiers setting fire to farmhouses and the land. Fire ripped across the earth, leaving a scorched, blackened wasteland in its wake. The earth split in two—an earthquake, perhaps—and gold spilled out of its insides. A torrent of people, like a rainstorm, battered a land so hot, you could see the heat squirming toward the heavens like small silver worms. A woman in a yellow dress, her back turned to him, shoulders shaking with sobs. A hand—it must have been his hand—reached out to touch her shoulder but she shrugged it off.

There was something familiar about that last image. Like I wasn't just seeing it in his head. Like it was my own memory too. I had this feeling that maybe the woman in the yellow dress was my mother.

I expected Dad to be angry when I fought back. But instead, he put his arm around my shoulders and smiled. He actually smiled.

"You have talent, my boy," he said. "And you're going to be just fine."

CHAPTER 5.5

An aide brought him water and he drank the whole cup in one long gulp before continuing:

> *The Grim Reaper and her lover-husband awoke one morning a week or a month or maybe a year later, unsure of how much time had passed. The red dirt was caked in their hair, their fingernails rimmed with it, like dried blood. They laced hands and did not speak. At long last, the lover-husband stood and held a hand out to her. "Escape cannot last forever," he said.*

Elder #3 snorted.

I assume my son shared these details with you, dear, *dear* John? Her Excellency asked.

No, it's all conjecture, my dear, he said. If you would rather ask your son . . . ?

> *"It should," the Grim Reaper said. Her fingertips grazed his young-old face, skin smooth and unfettered by the passage of time yet somehow ancient too. "What is wrong with forever?"*

"Darling," the lover-husband cried. He clasped her in his arms.

"We of all people should understand the inevitability of endings."

She laid her head against his chest, feeling safe within his strong, manly arms. She could hear his heart beating within his chest. The sound comforted her, even though it reminded her of the terrible secret she was keeping from him.

CHAPTER 6

Once Dad tells me what's going to happen to me, he wastes no time "making the arrangements." Apparently, I'm to be in my new school bright and early Monday morning! Which means I'm leaving Sunday. Yeah, you heard right. Sunday! Three days to say goodbye to the only life I've ever known.

But still, we don't talk about it. We don't talk about what it means to be part of a "contract" that you can't get out of, like, ever. Or what I'll actually be learning to do at this boarding school. What this mysterious "business" of my father's is. When all's said and done, I'm guessing his business isn't exactly legal. That it's not something you small talk about at polite parties.

The next morning, Dad comes running out of his office at breakfast time, all excited, saying we have to leave right now, there's something ultra-extra-important he has to do immediately.

You might think that this ultra-extra-important task involves getting me school supplies, or some new clothes, or something school-related, but no. Because Dad only spends money on or gets excited about one thing: old, rare books.

"I just heard a report that a bookseller in Manhattan

may have a real find," Dad says, the breath wiped out of his voice. My impossible-to-excite father is *that* in love with books.

All over the city, prestigious book dealers recognize him on sight and take him to the back of their stores to show him items that aren't even on display for "regular" customers. He never bargains. They pass him a piece of paper with the price and he either hands them an envelope of cash or walks out.

I used to think, *There goes my college tuition,* every time he came home with a new book. Now that college is apparently off the table, I don't know what to think.

"And I need to be the one to get it, son. Other people searching for it would not handle it properly. We have to go now and get it before anybody else—" He stops as if the thought that somebody else might get to this book before he does is too difficult to bear. "I thought we'd combine a visit to your grandfather so you could say goodbye."

I groan audibly, not caring what Dad thinks.

He chooses to ignore the real meaning of my groan. "The bookstore stop will take only a minute, I promise," he says, "and then we'll have lots of time to visit with your grandfather."

I have to laugh. *Good one, Dad.*

So we go to this strange old storefront in an alley a couple blocks from Grandpa's place. It's not your usual book dealer's place. The sign says they sell liquor and cigarettes and "groceries," which probably means a couple of sad-looking oranges and packages of chips.

I get a horrible heebie-jeebie vibe as soon as we walk in and this older gentleman with bluish-silver hair scurries toward us. He slinks to a stop and holds out a hand.

Dad doesn't take it. He doesn't smile—or grimace, which is what Dad's smile actually looks like. His eyes flit to the man's feet, where his shadow is sliding around like Peter Pan's, trying to escape.

"And how may I help you, gentlemen?" the man asks.

"I'm looking for a particular book," Dad says. "A book I've been told I might find here."

A swath of hair falls over the man's face into his eyes. He sticks out his lower lip and blows the hair out of the way. "And which book would that be?" His weasel grin suggests he already knows, and he knows Dad knows he already knows, but he's going to play this game to the letter.

Dad leans forward and whispers in his ear.

The man's whole body springs upward in one sudden jolt and then he's gesturing for us to follow him. We pass through a swinging door into a back office, then down a short passageway. The man gets out a huge key ring, with probably a hundred keys on it, and unlocks a door, the keys jangling in a loud and satisfying way.

We step inside a small, crowded storeroom. The man squats in front of a safe, hiding the combination lock with his back as he twirls the dial to unlock it, glancing back at us, furtive, like we're trying to spy on him. It opens with a muted pop. The guy pulls out a package wrapped in heavy cloth, then carries it over to a small table, his motions slow and reverent.

Dad leans in, peering over the man's shoulder as he

slowly unwraps the cloth, then elbowing his way forward until he's standing just in front of the book.

They both breathe in at the same time, deep intakes.

"One hundred percent authentic," the man says. "A verified summary of the original book."

Dad opens the cover, delicately riffles through the pages, and shuts it carefully. "This is a very good copy," he states, admiration in his voice.

"Some people think it *is* the original," the bookseller says.

Dad barks a short, gruff, "Ha."

"The original is impossible to get, absolutely impossible. There's only one copy in the world and god knows where it is, although I've heard—" The bookseller looks nervously behind himself, then leans in and whispers, as though somebody might be listening, even though it's just the three of us in this tiny stale storeroom. "I heard that the original surfaced in Rome last month."

A swarm of snakes slithers crassly in and out of his mouth as he talks but it's the symbol adorning the book's cover that catches my eye. A half-circle nestled inside a complete circle, like an eye, pointed shards of wavy light radiating away from it. I shudder involuntarily. Unlike the Broken Circle medallion dangling from my neck, *this* symbol makes me want to run far, far away.

Dad squints at the symbol on the book, his nostrils twitching.

The man observes him noticing the symbol. "Ah," he says, "I can see that your son is already well on his path to enlightenment and perhaps that has made you a *true* seeker then? If that is the case, I can—"

That's when Dad puts out his hand, with the same gesture he uses in my dream right before he tells the woman in rags to stop, before She disappears in a pool of black liquid.

But the bookseller doesn't disappear. He freezes, his tongue poised in the middle of his mouth, almost as though Dad has grabbed it. Sweat pops out on his brow and his eyes bulge. His shadow slides out from under his feet and begins to rise through his body and then out his mouth, floating toward the ceiling like smoke.

I have this sudden sick feeling that I want to get out of here, that even if I wanted to stay, I should go, I should get the hell out of here and fast, but my knees are locked and I'm just . . . I'm just watching.

"You fool!" My father's voice booms and echoes in the small room. "Do you not understand that somebody could have tried to kill you for this book?"

"Dad," I whisper. Because somebody *is* killing him for this book and it's my father.

The bookseller makes odd gasping noises. He shrinks a million times, suddenly on the wrong end of a pair of binoculars.

I know that feeling of your soul choking your throat as it leaves your body. You see everything for just a few minutes, your whole life, whatever has happened to you, even those things you don't remember. Later, when you know your shadow's back in place, it's hard to settle things again. You realize there were things you knew just minutes ago that have now receded back into the dimness. It leaves you with this terrible feeling of losing something you had, but you don't quite know what it was, and you know it was incredibly important and more precious than, well, than *anything*. But at the same time, and I don't even know how to explain this, you're a little relieved to have forgotten.

"Dad," I say again, louder this time.

"Go on, son," he responds, eyes trained on the bookseller. He's getting bigger and bigger, a mountain chain rising from the ocean floor. "I want you to get out of here." When I don't move, he utters a single word: "*Now*."

I run down the narrow passageway, through the dusty grocery store, and out to the street, where I wait for him, heart beating fast. The whole world looks uncertain, as if a gauzy film covers everything. I imagine this is the way drunkenness feels, and while I'm imagining that, I also start imagining what it would feel like to be an enormous mountain just tumbling endlessly into the raging sea. Because the thing about being a mountain is that you're big. You're so big. You're bigger than big. But the sea can still claim you.

Dad strides out two minutes later, the tails of his coat flapping behind him. "Come on," he says, "time to go to your grandfather's."

"Did you kill that guy?" I ask, except it comes out as, "Did you buy the book?" Wondering if my wobbly legs are going to hold me up.

Dad pats his coat pocket. "Paid twice what he was asking for," he says. I almost pass out with relief until he adds, "But he won't do any more business in this town."

"Why? What happened? Is he . . . okay?"

He puts one hand loosely on my shoulder. "He's fine. Nothing that a stiff whiskey won't take care of."

"I could use one myself," I say, wanting to just sit down in the street and weep with relief.

He laughs. Dad has one of these skeleton-y laughs, a big bunch of bones shaken in dry dirt. "Not on my watch."

"So what's so important about this book?"

He bares his teeth in what, for my father, passes for a grin. "*The Book of Light* contains the most important secret of the universe. The thing everybody wants to know."

What is the secret everybody wants to know? Knowing my dad, the secret he believes everyone needs to know is how to speed-read ancient texts without suffering papyrus cuts on your index finger.

When he opens his mouth again, I think he's going to tell me. Not the secret itself but the thing everybody wants to know. After a pause, he says, "Listen, son. In our business, *The Book of Light* is forbidden. Even an unverified, plagiarized summary of the original like this bootleg copy is banned. The knowledge it contains terrifies the men and women who run the Synod."

"Okay," I say uncertainly. "Who, um, who is the Synod?"

"Oh!" Dad looks surprised. "Oh, the Synod is made up of the men and women who regulate our services and makes sure no member is . . . uh . . . breaking the rules. They have been searching for this book for generations so they can destroy it—along with all the knowledge it contains. So this book is not something you should mention to anybody at school. All right?"

"But . . . why would they ban books?" I ask. "I thought we lived in the land of the free and the brave and free speech and all that crap."

He looks annoyed, but he still answers: "They're scared of the ideas inside it. But the most dangerous ideas are those we try to suppress. If the Synod would let us make copies of this book and read it, we'd know what our enemies are up to. Words aren't magic; it's what you do with the knowledge they give you that makes them powerful."

"But what about the thing he said in there? About the original surfacing in Rome last month?" I don't know what I was hoping to hear Dad say—but he suprised me. Because even if he's right about what he says next, how could he say it after everything he's *just* said about censorship?

Dad shakes his head and slips into Italian: "Why do you think I went to so much trouble to buy it, even though it's only a copy? If this book falls into the wrong hands, in Rome or anywhere else, it will be a disaster of epic proportions."

CHAPTER 7

My grandfather lives in a studio apartment in Hell's Kitchen that doesn't even have its own bathroom. I always make sure I don't have to use the gross toilet out in the hallway. I don't think Grandpa uses it either. Actually, I think he might pee on his carpet instead. It sure smells like it.

Usually, he gives me twenty bucks or something, and I feel bad about taking it because it seems like he could really use the money—I mean, the only food I've ever seen in his apartment is a big tin of oatmeal and not even any milk or sugar to put on it—but Dad kicks me in the foot when I start to refuse so I always take it.

"I suppose you're looking forward to going to this useless little school?" That's how he greets me as we head inside.

I'm startled that Grandpa is on my side about this but it still feels like a trick question. I don't answer.

I'm sitting on the only available chair in the apartment. Dad's standing at the window, looking down on the street below, and Grandpa's sitting bolt upright on his sagging little bed, the way he always does when we visit. I hate being here.

"If the school is so useless," Dad says, in an extraordinarily controlled, measured voice, "why did you call the Finders and tell them about your grandson?"

"*You* did this?" I choke. "I have to leave home and go to boarding school because of *you*? This is what you were talking about outside the hospital, wasn't it!"

"Hospital?" Dad asks. "What hospital? I thought we agreed to stay away from hospitals, John!"

Grandpa turns his glare on Dad. "Abaddon, the boy fell apart at school screaming about demons so they rushed him to the emergency room."

Dad's head rolls back and he looks at the ceiling, exasperated or maybe he understands or both, I'm not sure.

"I've gone along with your lame-brained plan long enough," Grandpa says. "What did you think would happen? Did you think we'd magically find some family member that the Synod overlooked? Or did you think we'd just pull Adam out at some point, like a rabbit out of a hat, and say, *Ta-da! We have someone who can take over our territory after all?* Did you think that would stop a civil war from happening? Or were you hoping it would start one? Because it could."

Dad clears his throat. "I suppose I was hoping for a miracle, yes."

Grandpa slams his hand down on the bedside table, making me jump. "Adam," Grandpa practically shouts, "I agreed we should keep you secret from the Synod, that nobody in our business should know about you. But things are different now. Everybody else who could have done what you're going to do has died. In the past twenty-five years, all my brothers and sisters, all my nieces and nephews, my only child your mother—they've all died, under mysterious circumstances. Tragic accidents. Things that never happen—happened. My whole family—gone, just like that."

I look from Dad to Grandpa. "I didn't know we had family." I always thought it was just me and two cranky old men.

"Well, we don't now," Grandpa growls. "It's just you, me, and this fool." He jerks his hand toward my father. "The Synod is ignoring the fact that our clan is under attack. They know this, we know this, *everybody* knows this, but nobody wants to talk about it." He looks at Dad. "Speaking of which, Abaddon, have you warned him yet?"

A panicky feeling lodges somewhere in my throat. "Warned me about what?"

"We haven't spoken about it yet, John, no," Dad says. There's an unspoken *Back off* in his voice but Grandpa just wades right in, where men and angels fear to tread.

"This is completely irresponsible of you," he snaps. "The boy needs to know what he's up against. You can't send him off to school half-cocked like some gun that's going to backfire."

Dad sighs. "I know, I was just . . . waiting."

"Until *what*? Ten minutes before he says goodbye?" Grandpa starts chewing on something ferociously, probably his tongue because I didn't see him put anything in his mouth. I expect blood to start pouring down his chin at any moment.

Grandpa turns into a dragon, rapid-firing questions at Dad, flames leaping out of his mouth: "When are you going to tell Adam what happened to him when he was four? When are you going to tell him about his mother? When are you going to tell him we can trust no one? *No one.*"

That sliver of panic burns its way down my esophagus, through my stomach, and rages into my intestines. I have to get out of here. But Grandpa and Dad are locked into this, whatever *this* is.

"And when, for god's sakes, when are you going to tell him that we have enemies? When are you going to tell him that his life is in danger? That there are people who want to kill him?"

Dad's growing by the second until his enormous frame fills every corner of the room and I can barely breathe. I want to warn Grandpa of the danger he's in but he's practically apoplectic by now.

"Talk to your son, man!" Grandpa shouts. "Tell him what he needs to know!"

He snorts up a big mouthful of air and starts to cough as though he's going to choke. I'd pound on his back but I'm too busy dealing with my own feelings. Except then he falls over on the bed and starts to writhe. He stiffens and his mouth foams as his body jerks.

I look at Dad, panicked. "What's happening?"

Grandpa lets loose a long, low groan. He slumps and lies there, face pressed into the mattress, suddenly very still.

"Is he dying?"

"No, son." Dad has gone quiet on me. "You'd know if he was dying. You'd feel it. It's in your blood to feel it."

He's right. Of course I'd know. Just like I always know. Like I knew about Sarah's sister a couple days before she died. Like I knew about that woman at the AA meeting. Like I know about perfect strangers I pass on the street.

I don't think I've ever exhaled as deeply as I do now. So,

Dad understands the burden I carry. Apparently, he carries the same burden.

"What kind of school *is* this?" I ask finally, after a long moment of silence. "What is the family business?"

He looks uncomfortable. Like we're about to have the S-E-X talk. "Uh," he says. Literally at a loss for words. "Didn't I . . . you mean . . . I've never told you? You never . . . you haven't figured it out? Surely you know what I do."

So I make a joke. Sort of. "Are you in the Mafia?" I ask. Thinking about that guy earlier, the one he almost killed.

His shoulders relax and he chuckles a little.

"No, wait, wait, wait, I've got it," I say. "You're really Darth Vadar, aren't you?" Now I'm thinking about the way he can make people stop breathing just by looking at them, as if he's using the Force to control the air they breathe.

He smiles. "You've read the books I've given you over the years. And you've looked at the titles of the books in my office. Maybe even sneaked a peek or two?"

My memory sweeps the shelves of my room, lined with books I've deliberately stayed away from. *The Egyptian Book of the Dead. Death and the Afterlife in Ancient China. The Book of Graveyards. Mummies: What They Took with Them and Why.* Yeah, I've wanted to read them, but I've been afraid to. Afraid to be anything like Dad.

"Those books are irresistible to people like us," he says. "Our version of porn." He laughs awkwardly. "I've tried not to burden you with too much information but you've gone with me on business trips. Surely you've noticed my obsession with death. All those trips to cemeteries. How do you think I make money, anyway?"

"Dad," I say, feigning shock, "you're a grave robber? That's the family business?"

He seems at a loss for words.

"Kidding," I say. "I get it; you've been *dying* to talk to me about it all these years."

He looks relieved. Like he thinks I do get it. Like he's not going to have to explain wet dreams to me after all.

"It's just that we've done so much work together," he says. "You've learned how to summon souls. You've learned how to block me when I've tried to summon your soul."

Is that the sick game we're playing when Dad tries to separate my shadow from my body and I won't let him? Or vice versa? Summoning each other's souls?

"I know I've never given you the scientific explanation of what we're doing," he continues, "but you've picked up on it instinctively."

"Right," I say. "Instinctively." And, not to be outdone, I add, "As if I was born to do it."

"Exactly!" he exclaims with as much gusto as I've ever seen him put into something.

Out of nowhere, Grandpa starts speaking, voice muffled against the mattress: "You're the last of us. The last of our clan. Do you understand what that means? It's really important, Adam, more important than anything—you have to stay alive. You can't let them kill you. Trust nobody. *Nobody.* Assume everybody you meet is lying to you. You got that? *Everybody!*"

He sits up to stare at me.

I look at Grandpa. Does that include him? Cut my eyes over to Dad. Does that include Dad? Are they lying to me too? Yeah, maybe. Maybe they are. After all, they've lied to me all my life, or at least for as long as I can remember.

"I don't think you need the training at this school," Grandpa grunts. "You're smart, you're a natural. But we need you credentialed and official, so that there's no question when we hand everything off to you. So that nobody tries to challenge your claim to our territory, when you become the Patriarch."

He inhales air up his nose so forcefully, it sounds like half his brain is being sucked up those nostrils along with snot and air and whatever germs are floating around in this horrible apartment.

"You'll meet enemies, Adam," he says. "You'll meet people who want you to fail. People who will work—work hard—to make you fail." He shakes a finger in my face. "That school is crooked, but it's the only way you can take over the business. We just need you to survive, get through it. Keep your nose clean. Keep your ass wiped. For god's sake, don't get expelled. Do you hear me?"

I follow Dad down the stairs and out the front door into the busy city streets, into one of those safe spaces where anything you say is lost to the crowds and noise and wind, and nobody who overhears anything will ever think twice about it, even if what you say is absolutely the craziest thing in the world.

"I don't know where to begin," Dad says.

"How about beginning with the most important thing of all: is somebody really trying to kill me?" I feel like I might hyperventilate just asking the question. I try a meditation trick that I usually find soothing, even at night when

I wake up in the graveyard instead of in my bed, but it's barely working now.

I mean, I already know the answer to this. Because surely She is trying to kill me. But the real question is whether somebody else is also trying to kill me, if I have *another* enemy out there, and if I do, does this enemy at least have a face?

"Well," he says finally, after an interminable pause, long enough for me to lose a few hundred heartbeats off the rest of my life, "if people knew about you, they would try to kill you."

"That makes no fucking sense!" I sort of shout this a little bit, probably due to stress.

"Language, son," he says mildly.

I glance around the crowded street. Nobody even paid attention to my outburst. A drunken man is sitting on the sidewalk, slumped over, but as we approach, he presses himself into the wall, giving us space to pass by. People do that all the time for Dad, just make room for him, even when they don't look at him.

"Yeah, but . . . I mean . . ." Apparently, I can't figure out how language works anymore. My words are broken bits of the alphabet, strewn randomly on the sidewalk behind us. "What?"

"I've tried to protect you by keeping your existence secret from—well, from the other families who do what we do. I let everybody believe you died when your mother . . . died. As far as they're concerned, that's still true. I hope I haven't made a mistake."

I stop and stare at him. He makes an impatient hand gesture for me to continue walking.

"Adam, nothing will happen to you because nobody knows who you are. But promise me this: don't tell a soul where you're from. People will jump to conclusions about who you are, what family you belong to. It'll be dangerous for you. If they ask where you grew up, say you moved around a lot. I hope it's enough to protect you."

"All you're doing is making me wonder if I'm supposed to be afraid of my own shadow."

He laughs. "Never fear your own shadow! You never need to be afraid of the darkness, Adam. What you must fear is the light."

Well, that couldn't be any more cryptic. And it sure is the opposite advice I'd imagine any other father giving his son. I imagine being on my deathbed and screaming, *No! My dad said not to look toward the light! No! No!*

"Why can't you hide me again—somewhere else?"

He shakes his head. "I could do that, yes. But they know about you now. So they'd get the Synod involved and there are things I don't want the Synod to know."

I start to shiver and I can't stop. We're standing in the middle of the sidewalk, people flowing around us like we're rocks in the middle of a river.

Dad grasps my forearm and looks me in the eye. "Have I ever left you alone in that darkness? Have I ever left you to fall forever?" I stare at him and he repeats himself. "Haven't I always come to find you? Have I ever abandoned you?"

And that's when I know. My nightmare *is* real. Dad really does walk through a graveyard. I'm walking behind him but he doesn't know I'm there. My father is there when She takes me. He joins me in that endless fall. It really is him, he really is that light, and he really does come to rescue me. Night after night after night.

We're both breathing hard, staring at each other. And then we turn and we start to walk, fast, fast fast fast, all the way home to Brooklyn.

CHAPTER 7.5

And so the Grim Reaper and her lover-husband returned to Rome, to the Eternal City, to face the Synod's verdict. Would they be allowed to choose their own destiny or would it be made for them?

They stood, heads bowed, as Her Excellency expressed the Synod's deep frustration and anger.

"You have behaved like spoiled children, eloping to carry out this unsanctioned marriage," she said, her face grim, like a goblin's. It was one of the remarkable things about Her Excellency—how precisely like a goblin she looked. "Marriage among soul guides is a weighted decision, not one to make alone. Each alliance must be carefully calibrated to determine which families can bear to lose a member of their clan, along with that member's future progeny."

Upon hearing these words, the Grim Reaper fell to her knees. Her bosom heaved.

Oh, please! Elder #5 yelled. Do we really have to listen to this rubbish?

Pardon me, he said. I thought you wanted details. Or am I offending your artistic sensibilities? Did you want the story or did you want great literature?

This is ridiculous. He is talking about his daughter, Elder #4 said. Can we not command him to stick to the facts?

You creeps are the ones who wanted details, he said.

Her Excellency jumped in, chuckling as she spoke: I don't think we have much of a choice, he is having too much fun with us. But really, sir, restrain yourself. So I look exactly like a goblin, do I?

He smiled, a glint in his eye. I'll restrain myself as much as possible, madam.

She was young, freckled, her red-brown hair tumbling past her hips, her eyes a deep, blazing sapphire. Her lover-husband's eyes burned with pride as he gazed at her startling and fierce beauty.

"Is there no room for love?" she cried, falling to her knees and ripping her bodice. "Are we not allowed comfort and happiness during our short sojourn on earth?"

CHAPTER 8

The subway rocks gently and lights flash on and off as we tunnel deep beneath the city's streets. I'm heading to Coney Island with my friends and trying to find the right moment to mention boarding school.

Sarah's sitting next to me, so close I can smell a faint fragrance of strawberry-scented soap and mint gum. I always try to position myself so that it seems natural when I sit next to her. Jeremy and Carlos stand beside us, holding onto straps for balance.

Their shadows swim beside them, closely attached, almost a second skin—the way shadows usually cling to the young and the healthy. Jeremy's shadow is bunchy and colorful, a big bunch of balloons. Carlos's is always active, darting here and there, like he's playing soccer and dribbling a ball past defenders.

I watch Sarah's face go green, then white, then yellow in the flashing lights. Today, her shadow is a brook of clear, cold water, running zigzag down a mountainside, pooling among rocks, singing to the forest. She looks up at Carlos as he recounts some triumph on the soccer field, laughing at the punch line, her face free and open with light.

I love looking at her.

I start to feel homesick, nostalgic even, for my friends. I'm both enjoying them and missing them at the same time. Jeremy and Sarah start laughing about the haunted house they rode together the last time we went to Coney Island, just before school started. It hits me that I won't be with them again until Thanksgiving or maybe even Christmas, and whatever I might or might not say to Sarah about how I feel won't matter. She'll probably get together with Jeremy. The thought makes me queasy but it's not like I'll be here to stop it. They'll be taking the same classes, studying together, hanging out on weekends.

I can't help imagining them kissing behind the school and then, *bam*, Sarah's in a wedding dress and Jeremy's in a black tuxedo. I'm standing next to them, the best man, trying not to cry. They head off on a honeymoon, fifteen years old, driving away in Jeremy's mother's SUV, his blond head barely visible above the giant steering wheel, cans clanging behind them. I wave and cry and cry and then I'm forty-five and unmarried and thinking about the fact that all this happened because my stupid father made me go to boarding school.

Deep down, of course, I know it's my own fault if Sarah ends up with Jeremy—or anybody else.

The train takes a right turn. Sarah's hip touches my leg and rainbows flutter over my head. A burst of sunlight streams through her hair and little angels start singing arias while I fiddle with my shoelaces.

We clatter and rock in the tunnel. Carlos shouts over the rumble: "So when are you coming back to school, Adam?"

I squirm. Time for the big reveal. "I'm not. My stupid dad told me I have to go to some special school or something."

"Does that mean you were expelled?" Carlos asks.

"We never went to talk to the principal. My dad just decided to send me somewhere else." The great thing—possibly the only great thing—about those little incidents at school is that they make explaining the switch in schools easy.

"So what does 'special school' mean?" Jeremy starts to laugh. "Is it special or 'special'?"

"But you can hang out with us on the weekends, right?" Sarah actually sounds hopeful. My heart lifts for just a second before it crashes. Little bits of it scatter like broken glass throughout the car.

The words catch in my throat: "It's a boarding school."

"You're moving away?" Now she sounds dismayed. "When are you leaving?"

I shrug and try not to sound too miserable. "Tomorrow."

In the silence, the train couplings creak loudly.

"And you were going to tell us when exactly?" Jeremy's voice is loud with accusation.

Now I'm a bug pinned to the wall. "I'm sorry. It happened so suddenly. I've been trying to talk my dad out of this but he won't budge."

"At least we'll see you on vacations," Sarah says finally.

Yeah, I can catch up with them at Christmas, but everything will be different. I won't know the inside jokes. They won't know any of the friends I make at school or the things I experience there.

Maybe I should run away. I picture myself with a long beard and dirty clothes, a large backpack slung over my shoulder as I hold a tattered cardboard sign that reads,

ANYWHERE BUT HERE, right thumb up as cars whiz by on the freeway. It almost sounds romantic until I think about walking for miles and miles, sleeping under a highway bridge in the cold, the smell of pee and the thump of car wheels keeping me awake.

I guess I'll pass. I mean, I can't even grow a man beard yet.

We have a great time at the beach and then everybody goes on carnival rides. Everybody but me. Yeah, okay, maybe I'm lame, but I'm terrified of scary rides. Talk crap all you want but I have my reasons. Good reasons.

I rode a roller coaster last year for the first time. I'd always avoided them before. As soon as we crested the top curve and started hurtling toward the ground, I saw Her. Waiting at the bottom. Empty eye sockets. No mouth. One claw reaching out for me. A split second more, She would have gotten me. But we started going up and She disappeared—only to reappear at the next plunge. In the cars in front of me, people's shadows lifted like hair in the wind as the cars plunged in rapid descent and I could sense She was calling them too, only they were oblivious.

It's so easy to die and people don't seem to realize that. They don't seem to care. It's like they live their life ignoring the fact that they're going to die. I just don't understand how anybody, anybody in their right mind, can ignore this fact.

At least the Tilt-A-Whirl doesn't involve falling, so Sarah and I ride it together—the endorphins making us all laughy and buddy-buddy. At one point, she actually puts her hand on my thigh as the ride whips us around. I practically have a heart attack.

"Sorry," she says when the ride is over. "It's silly, I know, but I get scared."

I want to say something cool, something that will cement our friendship, take it in a different direction. But the only thing that falls out of my mouth is a frog-like croak.

She glances at me.

"Let's go find the others," I say, and then want to shoot myself in the head. Here's my chance to be alone with her before I leave and I suggest . . . the opposite?

"Okay," she says.

But when we turn around, a creepy guy dressed in a cape with stars and moons embroidered all over it and a hood shadowing his face is standing so close, we bump into him.

"May I reveal your fortunes, oh dreamers and sleepers?" he asks.

I don't trust people until I can see their shadow. His is missing or hiding. "I don't think so," I reply.

"Are you certain? It's free, absolutely free."

"No thanks," I mutter. My mouth's dry. I don't know why. I get a bad feeling. *Get out now.*

But just at that moment, Sarah takes my hand. She smiles at me and squeezes gently. "Let's do it," she says.

Sarah is holding my hand.

I look down at her brown fingers, laced with mine. "Okay," I say.

"We'll do it," she says to the man in the hood.

"Oh, delightful, delightful!" he cries, oddly excited.

"Nothing is going to give me greater pleasure today! Nothing!" He turns around and skips down the boardwalk. "Follow me, children! My crystal ball is over this way!"

"Maybe we'll find out our true loves." Sarah giggles, I'd like to think nervously.

"Maybe." I try to sound nonchalant but my voice squeaks a little.

"Have you ever done this before?"

"Never," I say, hands breaking out in a sweat. Am I lying? Does that encounter with the psychic count as getting my fortune told?

We follow the fortune-teller through the park to an old hippie VW van half-shrouded in a thick purple tent. He disappears inside, gesturing for us to follow. Sarah pulls the cloth back and allows me to go first. As soon as I enter, I start to back up, but she's right behind me. We bump into each other and she pushes me forward, laughing. "Don't chicken out now."

The fortune-teller whips a towel off a crystal ball with a flourish. Rubs his hands together. "Ah," he says. "Ahhhhhhh." He looks up at us. "Ahhhhhhh."

I don't even realize how much I'm fidgeting until Sarah squeezes my hand again.

"I don't normally do this," he says, a strange relish in his voice, a rising excitement. "I want you both to look into my crystal ball. When you are looking deep inside, at the mists and then at the clouds beyond and then the deep blue sky, let everything you've ever known in this life fall away."

Nobody ever said fortune-tellers were normal. We both stare at the crystal ball. He's right: deep within its swirling mists are clouds and a blue sky. I stare at it so intently that I begin to feel a little dizzy, a little sleepy. I jerk myself awake. But not for long. I feel myself swaying on my feet, a warm feeling flooding my body, Sarah's hand entwined with mine. And I start to let go.

I find it absurdly easy to let go of the things in life. I tick them off one by one and then let them swirl away into the mists of the crystal ball. After all, there's not much. My dad. My grandpa. My three friends. That's it.

"Nice work, young man, you're taking us there," the fortune-teller murmurs.

I have enough left in me to wonder where "there" is, his voice floating toward me, the words resting gently on billowing clouds.

"Limbo is a dangerous place. What's drawing you to it?"

I can't look up from the crystal ball but his words register somewhere. "What?" Then the next thing I know, I'm staring at the cemetery, in horror. Rain drips off a tree and plasters my hair until it's soaking wet. My shoes slurp juicily through mud.

I look instinctively for my dad, hoping he's already here. But it's the fortune-teller standing beside me, his hood off, and I recognize him now: the bookseller I thought Dad was going to kill to get a plagiarized copy of *The Book of Light*.

"You." I back up. My feet slip in mud.

"Ha! Yes." He's dripping with both glee and sweat, drops rolling down his forehead, dark wet stains under his arms.

"You don't want to be here with me." I'm trying not to panic, looking to the left, to the right. Where is She?

He grins again. "I can't believe it! You did it! You *did* it! You know how to get to Limbo and bring along somebody who's still alive. Do you know what this means? *You know how to get to Limbo.* There are people who deal in these types of realities and they would kill to find you."

"I'm serious." My voice soars and cracks. "Get out of here before you get killed!"

He grabs my elbow. "I'm not going anywhere without you."

A sudden wind shakes huge drops of water from the trees. They plop onto the muddy ground, soaking the tips of our shoes and splattering our shirts. The sky darkens, a cloud of black smoke curling out of the rusty metal bars covering the opening to a mausoleum.

"Shit!" I yell, and yank my arm out of the bookseller's grasp. "Run!"

Too late. She's here, stepping out of the black cloud of smoke, arms held out to embrace me. The bookseller screams as She reaches out a long finger and touches his shoulder. In one swift movement, She grabs the two of us and envelops us

and now we're falling

and falling

the endless dark . . .

Her lips pull back, revealing the dark hole of Her mouth, the bookseller's screams echoing in the long tunnel of my endless nightmare

Where is the light? Where's my dad?

Dad, where are you?

Sarah? The thought momentarily jerks me out of my fear.

"Where's Sarah?" I yell into the cold and dark.

The bookseller keeps screaming as though he's lost all words.

The world freezes momentarily. I have to get out of here and not for my own sake, for Sarah's, because I have to make sure she's okay.

I yank the bookseller with me. My conscience won't let me leave him here either.

Every other time, I've fallen endlessly until my dad comes to rescue me and then I wake up in my bed, or wherever I fell asleep, alone. This time I was wide awake when I came here. What does that mean?

I stumble. Reach for Sarah in my head. One thought. One name. *Sarah.*

Where are you, Sarah? Where are you, beautiful girl?

We hit the beach so hard, our legs stagger across the sand and plow through a pile of litter. Flat snow-cone cups, lollipop wrappers, and empty popcorn boxes fly toward the sky as we fall flat on our faces.

The bookseller's face is gray. His mouth pops open as if he wants to say something but the only thing that comes out of his mouth are these gasping noises. "What the hell was that?" he finally wheezes.

I scramble to my feet and shake my finger at him. "You leave me alone. Or else."

He turns over so he's reclining on his elbows. He takes a deep breath and closes his eyes. Then his body begins to shake. Laughter starts in his nose and catches in his throat. "You don't even know your own power." His laugh crescendos, a wave breaking over the beach, and now I see his shadow, a ferret, digging with its front paws to create a dark hole in the ground so he can hide.

I kick sand in his face, hoping he'll swallow some of it and choke, before turning and running toward his van, toward Sarah.

"You can't save her," he calls after me. "It's already too late."

I turn back to yell something but he's on his knees, puking his guts out.

She's inside the tent, lying on the asphalt, asleep or in a trance. She's shivering and her lips are blue, like she's been starved of oxygen.

I reach out and shake her gently. Caress her hair. Hold her face in my hands. "Sarah. Oh my god, Sarah!" I begin to rub her cold arms aggressively and shout, "Sarah! Wake up!"

When she doesn't respond, I plug her nose and begin to blow air into her mouth. "Sarah! Wake up!" *Breathe.* One, two, three. *Breathe.* Boy, this is a shitty way to get your first kiss . . . not that this counts as a kiss or anything. One, two, three. *Breathe.*

She shudders, shivers, a bird, feathers ruffled in the wind. Opens her eyes. "What—? What's going on? Adam?"

I jerk a hand across my face to wipe the tears away, grab her hand, and pull her out of the tent. "We have to get out of here!"

She follows me without question but as soon as we're

in the parking lot, she turns back, like Lot's wife, the one who was turned to salt when she looked back at Sodom and Gomorrah. I'm afraid she'll melt or freeze or something terrible. And then I'm the one practically turning to salt when I see the look of longing on her face.

"Why'd you take me away from that place?" Her shadow's a lonely, lonely wind whistling through the treetops on a moonlit night.

Oh, Sarah. Oh, beautiful girl.

"When he put us in that trance . . . I saw my sister. She was . . . I don't know, she looked different. But Adam, *it was my sister*. I mean, she had blond hair, not brown, and she was a lot taller, but it doesn't matter—it was her. She was laughing. Playing the piano. She didn't play the piano, we don't even have a piano, but somehow—impossibly—she was playing the piano. Adam, do you know what that means?"

I don't know what to say.

"It means . . . it means maybe she's still alive, somewhere. Not on earth but somewhere else. She's learning to play the piano. She's . . . she's not gone. At least, not forever, not the way I thought—"

"Sarah," I interrupt.

"I just had this feeling that she's not really dead. She's just living in a new body. I wish you hadn't taken me away from her, Adam." She sounds frustrated. "I wish I'd had more time with her."

"Sarah." I take a deep breath. *Don't hate me, Sarah. Please don't hate me.* I open my mouth to tell her that whatever she saw, it probably wasn't real. Or even if it was real, it probably wasn't what it seems. It wasn't good. Whatever that bookseller/fortune-teller is . . . is rotten. And wherever she went when we fell into that trance is a trap. She wasn't even breathing when I found her. What if I'd come a minute later?

"What is it, Adam?" Trust and hope pooling in her eyes.

It breaks my heart to see how much she wants this to be true, whatever it is. And if it is true, what does that say about the place I go to when *I* dream?

Hell. I already know it's real. I just don't want it to be. Maybe her place is as real as mine. If so, she's lucky. At least hers is happy.

"I'm glad what you saw made you happy," I say, closing my mouth.

We track down the others. "Dude, how'd you get so dirty?" Jeremy glances from my mud-splattered shirt and shoes, then up at the bright sunny skies.

"Long story." I don't offer any more and they don't ask. But Sarah prattles on and on all the way home. She even tells Carlos and Jeremy what she saw in the fortune-teller's ball—she seems to think it was just a vision, not that she actually went somewhere, or almost died doing it—and they seem to be happy for her, happy in a way I can't be. Me? I feel sick inside. Something's really off, I just don't know what. Still, I should have told her. I should have.

CHAPTER 9

When I get home, Dad tells me to go pack. He doesn't say *what* to pack. Actually, that's not completely true. He hands me *The Book of Light*, its cover with the horrible eye-like-a-sun symbol hidden under a brown paper bag book cover. "Pack this."

I get a shivery, gross feeling as soon as the book touches my hand. Nevertheless, I flip it open. The inside cover page contains only a title, in Latin: *A Summary of The Book of Light.* It doesn't list an author or a copyright or any publication information. I turn to the first page. Also Latin. Surprise, surprise. Finally those Latin classes Dad made me take will come in handy.

The words are printed in very tiny letters and crammed close together, beginning on one side of the page and extending all the way across with no margin, as though the printer was trying to fit as many words as possible on each page in order to save money.

"So you think it's beneficial to me if I learn the secret of the universe?" I ask and don't hide my tone, a tone that, if he cared one ounce, which he does not, he would realize isn't sarcasm so much as a plea for some help here.

Even so, Dad ignores the question. "Don't let anybody at school know you have this book," he says. "Remember, it's banned."

I flip it shut.

He disappears into his office. I know from experience he'll be there all night and I'll eat dinner alone.

Sometimes I wonder if Dad even eats. I mean, of course he does. Occasionally. We go to dinner every once in a while, to these strange little Mongolian or Pakistani or Senegalese restaurants, holes in the wall located in questionable neighborhoods where the owner ushers us to a back room or maybe even a broom closet and we sit at a little table, all alone, in a room lit only by candlelight. They bring us strange dishes and I'm glad it's dark so that a) I don't know what I'm eating, and b) I can't see how dirty the floor is.

Once, pushing a plateful of purple baby squids to the side—at least, I think they were purple, and I think they were squids, and I *know* they were babies—I actually asked him why we went to these places.

He gave me a five-second stare. "You can't understand an individual human being unless you understand where they're coming from," he finally replied. "Food is a window into the soul of a culture, into the soul of a human being."

I got goose bumps. But despite what he said, Dad mostly picks at his food.

So when his office door clicks shut at five—which is when most normal people *leave* their offices—I sigh and go to my room to pack.

I pick out clothes for seven days before realizing I don't know how often I'll be able to do laundry. Also, I still don't know where the school is located. It could be in Siberia for all I know. I imagine trudging from my dorm room to the classroom in snowdrifts as tall as my father, the tip of my nose black with frostbite because all I packed were T-shirts. I end up in the hospital, dying of some romantic nineteenth-century disease, like consumption or something. My father weeps at the foot of my bed as I take shallow, rattling breaths, trying to stay alive. *If only I hadn't sent you to boarding school!* he howls, throwing his head backward in agony.

In the end, I toss in almost all the clothes I own. Mostly this consists of old T-shirts, ragged boxer briefs, sweatshirts, jeans, and old socks with holes in the heels.

Hope it's not one of those British-style boarding schools where young men are supposed to wear button-down shirts, slacks, ties, and dress shoes, because—well, I don't own any. I guess if it's a problem when I get to school, I can pry open my father's stingy fingers and buy new clothes.

I wonder briefly if I should pack a weapon but we don't have anything remotely weapon-like. Even our knives are dull.

I feel very lonely all night. None of my friends are answering texts and even though we were together all day, and they just found out I'm leaving, I can't help wondering, *Have they already forgotten about me? Are they all out having fun together my last night in town?* I should have arranged to meet up with them later. Of course, it's Sarah I really want to see. It'd kill me if she's out with Jeremy, tonight of all nights.

But she held my hand.

That would make me feel better except that all she did when we said goodbye was hug me. She gave Jeremy and Carlos the same hug goodbye. Probably the hand-holding didn't mean anything. She was just, I don't know, excited about having her fortune told. And I happened to be there.

At one point I linger outside Dad's office door, but I know better than to disturb him. I put my ear up to the door, wondering if I'll hear anything. The rustling of papers. A pen scratching on a notepad. The clicking of a keyboard.

Nothing. It's as silent as a grave in there.

CHAPTER 9.5

Her Excellency turned her gaze on the Grim Reaper. "Comfort! Happiness! These are but small matters compared to the fate of the world." Her tone was severe, as though she were speaking to a small child. "You are the head of your clan, a clan that suffered terrible losses during the Great Civil War—losses it has never recovered from in terms of numerical strength. And, in recent years, your clan has suffered unfortunate accident after unfortunate accident. You and your father are the only ones left! Did you not consider how your actions would affect the entire future of the Reaper clan? Are you so selfish you think only of comfort and happiness?"

I said nothing of the sort, you ridiculous man, Her Excellency said.

Elder #4 said, delicately, Your Excellency, I was there and you did say something along those lines. It was sixteen years ago . . . perhaps your memory . . .

Oh, shut up, Mildred, Her Excellency snapped.

Then Her Excellency glared at the lover-

husband. Though he paled, he met her gaze full-on.

"And you," she said. "Did you not even once think about your responsibilities to the Eternal City—Indeed, to the entire country of Italy? The two of you gave not a second's thought to the way your so-called marriage of love"*—the scorn in her voice scorched the hair on their arms—"could cause the destruction of the Reaper clan and create a ripple effect, destabilizing the entire soul guide world."*

The lover-husband bowed his head. "I am deeply sorry you feel that way, Mother," he said. "Laws can be changed. Alliances can be made. Is there no way the Reaper and Mors clans can be aligned?"

"Rules cannot be broken. Bent. Yes. Bent very far even," she said. "But you can't change laws willy-nilly. This so-called marriage of love has addled your brain."

CHAPTER 10

The old leather suitcase Dad gave me for Christmas one year is bulging, even though I don't feel like I packed very much. I grab a few of my favorite books and throw them into my backpack along with my phone and laptop and the banned book.

I'm ready. Oh wait, toothbrush. All right. *Now* I'm ready.

I lug everything into the dinky living room, where Dad's waiting at the door to say goodbye. He emerged from his office just a few minutes ago. He's haggard and unshaven, eyes a little bloodshot—not because he's been drinking but from lack of sleep. Is this a hazard of the profession? Will I *ever* get a good night's sleep? Or am I doomed to this crappy fear-of-sleep life forever?

"So where am I going, Dad? Are you ever going to tell me where this school is?"

"They change the location every year for security reasons," he answers. "This year it's on an island off Maine. But you can't tell your friends where it is, understand? The school will reinforce this need for secrecy, but I want to make sure you understand from the outset. No texting your friends on the way there to tell them where you'll be."

"Yeah, yeah, I promise." Because my super-bad, super-dangerous friends are going to come kill me and my classmates if they find out where I am.

"I would take you to school myself," Dad says, "but I can't risk people seeing you with me and figuring out who you are. I asked a business colleague I trust to travel with you. She should be here in a couple of minutes. At school, she's how I'm keeping my eye on you."

It all comes out in a giant thunderclap of emotion: "It's not too late, Dad. I don't have to go. I could stay here. I mean, you said yourself that people think I'm dead. So how many people know? Just that one guy that visited? We could move, couldn't we? Find another place to live? I don't want to go!" Sobs are shoving, pushing their way forward, my eyelids a dam, and finally I can't hold it back, rocks crumbling and water burbling, foaming, spraying out, soaking Dad's shirt.

He puts a hand on my shoulder. When I don't calm down immediately, he shakes me a little. "There is not a lot of reassurance in this strange business of mine, the one you are inheriting. Just when you think you know the rules, they change. You are going to have to learn—the hard way—to be brave. But I promise—I wouldn't put you in a situation if I didn't know that in the end, you will be all right."

When I fail to respond, his hand drops.

"Remember, Adam, you have powers. Don't be afraid to use them, to protect yourself and others." He rustles deep inside his pants pockets and pulls out a small, shiny black card. "Keep this on you at all times. Use it in an emergency."

I turn it over in my hands. It's the shape and size of a credit card, but it has no magnetic strip, no name, no information, no numbers. It's a perfectly blank card. It feels like plastic but heavier. "How do you use it?"

"Just like a credit card," Dad says.

Apparently, the only kind of emergency he can imagine is the kind where I'm going to need money. Cuz if I stabbed somebody with this, it's not going to do much.

"Trust me on this one," he adds. "It's all you'll need."

Can I trust him? He's been lying to me my whole life.

But then I think about how he comes to rescue me, night after night, when I'm alone in the depths with that hideous Thing—Her—in that endless fall toward hell. I look closely at him now, at his eyes.

"Trust me," he says again, and for just a moment, we're on the same page.

"Okay."

"If you have to escape something, if you need to leave suddenly, if you need to come home—I don't care what it is—you use this card, understand? It can get you anywhere in the world, no questions asked."

It sure doesn't look that special. I put it in my pocket. My first sort of credit card. A perfectly blank one, but still.

"Just remember," Dad continues, "everything has an end. Everybody, and I do mean *everybody*, ends up in the same place eventually."

Always look on the bright side of life, right? Thanks, Dad.

Somebody knocks on the door, a firm, confident knock. Dad smiles. "That must be her."

He swings the door open wide. A young woman dressed in a denim skirt, a black jacket, and boots stands on our doorstep, smiling. Her short hair is bright pink and even though I'm tall, she towers over me by at least three inches.

I look up at her awkwardly.

"You must be Adam then." Her voice is rich and raspy. "I'm Aileen Cu Sith." She looks beyond me to my father. "Good morning, sir."

Dad's smile has always seemed more like a grimace, but now his face breaks out in a warm grin. "It is good to see you, Aileen, very good to see you. Thank you for your help."

"Pleasure."

They shake hands and Aileen blushes—really, I swear, she blushes, and who the hell blushes when greeting my father? The only thing I've seen people do is try to avoid touching him when he passes. Then he places a hand on my shoulder. "I hope you enjoy yourself."

"Will I see you at Christmas?" I ask.

"I hope so," he mumbles.

What does that mean? Does he mean he's not sure he'll be here at Christmas and I'll be stuck in an empty boarding school? Or does he mean, *Despite everything I've said to try to reassure you, I sure hope you survive and you're still alive at Christmas*?

Fuck you, Dad.

I trail after Aileen out the door, heart frozen with an impending sense of doom.

Eyes follow Aileen wherever we go, not just men's eyes, everybody's, even old ladies. It's not the pink hair, it's something else, something in the way she carries herself. Her shadow is very confident, an ocean, alive and awake and powerful. She owns herself. Even if she did blush in my father's presence.

Aileen hails a taxi and we slide in together, our bags on

the floor beside us. She tells the driver to take us to Penn Station and we settle back for the ride.

"I love your dad's work." Aileen fiddles with the strap on her bag. "I studied his best-known cases as part of my research during training. I mean, hello, Mussolini? And Fellini? Not to mention all those popes! He's one of the best, if not *the* best, of all times."

"Oh good," I say. "That's . . . amazing."

"Your dad is a walking legend."

Does Aileen really know my father? The one who never leaves the house and spends most of his time locked in his office, probably singing lullabies to his latest acquisition—some old book nobody else cares about—as he lovingly strokes its stained leather?

She smirks. "You have no idea what I'm talking about, do you?"

"Noooooo," I admit, which feels kind of like a relief, at least at first. But it also puts me in a strange position. In my experience, which is not that great—I'm only fifteen, after all—when somebody knows something you don't know, they can use it against you. It gives them power. This is why I've always refused to dive in and see what's going on in my friends' heads. You know, read their souls, the way I've done with my dad once or twice. I know you're just getting a snapshot about what they feel at that moment, not what they really feel, like reading a diary—it's real but not necessarily true all the time. But still, it gives you power over them. It lets you see things they wouldn't tell you or want you to know. The last thing I want is to have power over my friends. I just want us to be normal.

"So your father never told you what he does?"

"No, but it's okay, he's never explained sex either." And then I just about die. Because, did I just mention sex—to *her?*

She looks at me out of the corner of her eye. I shift uncomfortably, my face turning red. The silence is awful until I realize she's trying to hide a smile.

"When I was little, I used to tell people he was in finance or business or something like that . . ."

She laughs. "Not a bad thing to call it. You could easily say he's in the services sector . . . kind of like a financial advisor is in the services sector . . . but your father deals with *end*-of-life issues." The finality of the word "end" sinks into my brain like a stone through wet paper towels.

I mean, I'm not stupid. I've already figured out that whatever we do, it has something to do with the big D. My only question is precisely what it is we do. Like, do we KILL people? Are we professional hit men? Or is it even weirder and more horrible than that? When I *just know* that people are going to die, is it because I'm somehow *making* them die?

I sit on my hands to keep from squirming too much but Aileen apparently isn't bothered by long, awkward silences, kind of like Dad, and finally my hands fall asleep. I shake them out to get rid of the pins and needles.

"Don't worry about it," Aileen finally says. "Occasionally, there are kids who come to school who don't know what their parents do or what the school's about, so we have a special orientation."

Ugh. I'm already "one of those kids." Why didn't my father explain? Like, years ago?

* * *

The first leg of our trip is a train ride to Boston. We take window seats and face each other.

I flip open my laptop and plug in my earphones. Aileen does the same. I don't look at my computer screen or notice what tracks are playing. I think about my nightmares, the one in the graveyard and the other recurring one. The one with a woman in the yellow dress, riding an endless train. My mother, I think. A strong emotion I can't identify—loneliness, maybe, or homesickness—clamps around my heart when I see her figure, the fuzzy edges of her, the little I remember. The yellow dress, like sunshine or daffodils. Her freckles and the red-brown curls that were so soft to touch. A silvery voice, always with a hint of laughter in it. I remember peeking over the edge of her bed, the bedspread rubbing softly against my cheek. She lies still, fists clenched tight. My father kneels on the other side of the bed, eyes closed. He's breathing deep and he's here but not here, I know that much. His face contorts.

I jerk back to the present train ride, the one where a sexy young teacher with pink hair is sitting across from me. Aileen seems pretty absorbed, reading something on her computer and occasionally typing.

I start wondering how I should present myself when I arrive. I mean, to the other kids. Finally, I decide not to pretend that I know more than I do. Faking it only makes things worse when everybody realizes you're actually an idiot. I'll just have to be That Kid. If you can't change who you are, embrace it, right?

Then I wonder what my friends are doing, torturing

myself, imagining Jeremy and Sarah hanging out together. Without me.

Finally, I take out my phone. Aileen looks up from her computer. "You're not texting anyone, are you?"

"No," I say. "Video game." Like my stupidphone has video games. I turn the phone's sound off. Then I text Sarah, telling her I'm on my way to school.

She texts back a few seconds later, saying she's at some lame family gathering. *We should have had a party last night to say goodbye.*

That would have been nice, I text. *I'll miss you.*

I'm hoping she'll type something cheesy and romantic back but no.

So where's the school? Will we be able to visit?

I wish I understood what Dad is afraid of, who my enemies are, why the location of the boarding school has to be secret. Why would it matter for somebody like Sarah to know I'm going to be in Maine? Maine's a big state. Still, I stick with the script. Until I know what's going on, it's better that way.

In the middle of nowhere, I text. *We'll just have to wait until Thanksgiving or Christmas to see each other.*

Nothing will be the same without you, she responds.

Not quite *I'll miss you,* but it makes me feel a little better. For a few seconds. Because she's right, nothing will be the same, and because I'm not there, somebody (Jeremy or maybe Carlos) can step right in and take my place.

CHAPTER II

In Boston, we take a cab from one station to the next and get on another train. We ride it for what feels like hours and finally stop in Brunswick, Maine. The end of the line. It feels like the end of the world.

"Are you okay?" Aileen asks.

I nod. What else am I supposed to do but hide my real feelings about the situation?

I'm struck by the absence of noise as we step off the train and onto the platform: the usual hubbub of cars, the random guy playing a guitar, the horn in the train tunnels. And yet a strange sound, a sort of deep chirping, lingers in the air.

"I love the sound of frogs and the wind in the trees," Aileen comments.

Until she says this, I didn't know what it was. I like it too. It's comforting. As though assassins wouldn't possibly attack when frogs are singing in the trees. Obviously, they only do *that* to the tense vibrato of violins and rumble of the timpani in the background.

"So before we join everybody," Aileen says, "we should probably make sure our story is straight."

"Right."

"If anybody asks where you live, I met you at JFK and we took the train here, okay?"

"Where did I fly from?" If you plan to lie, you need to have answers for these kinds of details.

She thinks for a moment. "Tell them Rome. That will shut them up. Rome is in such . . . disarray lately. Flying from Rome could literally mean anything."

I search my head for something I might have heard about in the news that would clue me in to what she's talking about, but I come up with a big blank. The only thing I know about Rome is the Colosseum. I picture headlines proclaiming, *ROME IN DISARRAY! The cows have quit producing! "Madre di Dio, we have no gelato," says the minister of the interior, bursting into tears.* The newspaper article includes pictures of formerly sophisticated Italians dressed in rags with rat nests in their hair.

"And if they ask me, who am I?"

"You're Adam Jones, of course. And that's all anybody needs to know."

"Including me, apparently."

She grins. "Don't sulk about it, Adam. It's unbecoming."

A man who looks like he's about Aileen's age jogs toward us on the platform. His brown hair is cropped close but a bushy beard hangs halfway down his chest, his ears are studded with earrings, and tattoos run from his wrists to his neck.

"That's Jacob," Aileen whispers. "Jacob Samael."

Jacob side-hugs Aileen, his face breaking out in a grin. He pumps my hand up and down, smiling so hard it feels like his face might break, and his shadow bounces around, an overeager puppy.

"You must be Adam!" Jacob's bushy beard dances when he talks.

"Yeah."

I look down at the symbol tattooed on the back of each of his hands—a perfect circle, like a clock, with the section between twelve and two broken inward by a curving, looping shepherd's staff. The Broken Circle. I finger my own version of it, slightly different but similar, hanging around my neck.

Jacob gestures to a group of teens standing nearby on the platform. "We were on a weekend outing to the mainland today so you'll get to meet a lot of your classmates!" he announces.

I'm beginning to realize that everything Jacob says is an announcement, but the excitement isn't fake—in fact, it's contagious. I'm still nervous, the fear is still here, but now I'm a little curious too.

"We picked up another new student earlier today! Rachel! She's already met the gang but I think she's going to be glad to meet you! It's never fun being the only new person in school!"

We jog over to the group as Jacob shouts, "Hey, guys, Adam's finally here! Time to hit the road!"

The group looks more like a menagerie than a collection of kids going to some special prep school. A couple of the guys apparently just stepped off a yacht. They're dressed in polos, pastel sweaters tied around their necks. Their slick grins gleam, walking toothpaste ads. One of them is talking to a kid who looks homeless while the other is talking to a girl in full-on steampunk getup right down to the goggles on her hat. Two goth girls are sulking and smoking cigarettes over in the corner, blowing smoke in our direction, the butts of their cigarettes stained with purple lipstick.

One guy is wearing a coonskin hat, with a crow perched on his shoulder. A real, live crow, no kidding. And he's talking to two black kids with long dreadlocks who might be Rastafarians except neither is wearing red, gold, and green—one is dressed from head to toe in cream-colored slacks and shirt, while the other is clothed entirely in black.

Jacob puts his fingers in his mouth and whistles, a piercing shriek. A guy and a girl come ambling out of the shadows. They're dressed all in black, with red bandannas tied around their foreheads.

As they pass, the guy suddenly shoves one of the polo-clad kids, shoves him so hard he almost falls off the platform onto the train tracks. In the split second when it's not clear if he's going to fall or right himself, his shadow leaps into the air, up toward the train station's roof. But as his body rocks forward and rights itself, his shadow rushes down and latches back on.

He came so close. So close.

The collective sigh of relief is so strong, it's audible. I examine my future classmates a little more closely, not that I haven't been staring at them before this, but suddenly I realize a startling fact: I'm not alone. I'm so used to pretending I don't see things like that, I don't react—because nobody else I know sees shadows. But everybody here saw what I saw. *Everybody.* Fucking A.

"What's your problem?" the polo guy snarls at the Latino-looking gangsta kid. "Trying to kill me?"

I don't blame him for reacting that way, but I saw the gangsta kid's face right after he shoved the polo guy. He hadn't meant for it to go that far.

"All right, all right, you guys, break it up." Jacob noses his way between them. "Nobody's trying to kill anybody."

Aileen gently guides the polo kid away, one arm around him, as he says, "Everybody saw that, right? It came out of nowhere. I didn't provoke it and I expect there to be consequences."

"Now, Gabe," Jacob says to the gangsta boy, "the Angel and La Muerte clans agreed to leave the feud at home. We can't have violence at school."

Gabe looks surly but he nods his head.

"Sofia?" Jacob looks at the girl accompanying Gabe.

"You should hear those Angels, always making snide comments under their breath," she complains. "La Muerte always gets blamed but we don't start anything."

"Sofia," Jacob says again. His voice is patient and kind.

"Yes, okay," she replies after a short silence. "No violence at school."

"Good then!" And Jacob claps a hand on each of their backs and herds them down the platform and across a parking lot where a small bus is apparently waiting for us. They board and two dark shapes, lit up against the windows, make their way to the back of the bus.

I stick close to Aileen. Even though she's walking with the polo kids—Angels?—and they don't look like my type at all, she's my only anchor to the real world and I don't want to lose sight of her.

But when we all board the bus, she sits next to Jacob and I find a seat next to a girl who looks like she needs a friend as badly as I do. If I were placing bets as to the person here least likely to try to kill me, I'd put my money on her.

"Hey," I say.

She's a frightened rabbit and she hops behind the long curtain of hair falling down around her shoulders. So I decide to lay all my cards on the table, to coax her back out.

"I'm Adam. I have absolutely no idea what's going on. You?"

She doesn't say anything until we're bumping our way down the road. "I'm Rachel," she whispers. She sneaks a peek at the motley crew behind us. "I don't belong here."

Of course. The new kid *would* pick the other new kid to sit next to. Just my luck.

"Well, that makes two of us," I say. But then I decide to be hopeful. I mean, everybody here is so different from each other but they all seem to like each other—that is, assuming we can set aside the teeny-tiny incident on the platform where one kid almost killed another. And assuming nobody tries to kill *me*. In that case, we're all good.

We drive across a tall bridge spanning a bay. Lights wink below us, illuminating ships and cranes, and then we descend into what seems like complete darkness. The crow squawks intermittently.

After driving for an hour or so, we take a curving road, the bus's headlights lighting up the pine trees on either side. We pass an old cemetery and everybody cheers. The guy with the crow starts singing loudly, *"Hot-crossed souls, hot-crossed souls, one a penny, two a penny, hot-crossed souls!"*

The bus erupts in raucous laughter. One of the boys in a polo shouts, "Only two pennies a soul? No wonder you Crowleys are so poor! Or is that all they can afford down south these days?"

Crow guy laughs and yells, "We have organic souls down south! We don't poop plastic and diamonds like they do in LA!"

Everyone laughs again. Then somebody starts singing a song about a skeleton and a sheep dog. Between the pine trees and the bus full of laughing, yelling kids, and the overzealous teacher-cum-camp-director Jacob, it feels like we're headed to summer camp, not school.

Rachel grips the seat so hard, her knuckles are white. I pet her awkwardly on the head, then pull my hand back because, after all, she's not a rabbit, whatever it may seem like she is on the inside. But she gives me a small smile. "I just wish I knew what I was getting into," she says.

Eventually, we drive into a town, the old brick storefronts cascading gently down to a narrow bay. We stop at the waterfront and pile out to board a boat. Rachel sticks close to me, for better or worse. We sit at the front of the deck, the sea air washing over us.

Waves slap the side of the boat. Moonlight reflects a silver path on the water, beckoning us onward, across the water and toward a dock on the eastern side of an island.

We stumble from the dock to a set of wooden stairs, both me and Rachel lugging our tattered luggage up the steps. The climb feels endless. From there, a wide path leads up through the woods toward a large farmhouse.

The girls follow Aileen into the farmhouse and the boys trail through a small field to a large barn, which has been converted into some sort of dormitory. We pass through a common room on the ground floor, furnished with leather couches and a couple of wood billiard tables.

"Adam, here's a key to your room," Jacob says.

I climb the stairs, find my name on one of the doors, and lug my stuff inside. It's small, with a built-in bunk and wardrobes on either side. Bookshelves line the bunk's interior. A small desk with a lamp pushes up against the window and a door leads to a small bathroom.

I throw my suitcase against the wall, close the door, and crash on the bed. I don't even take off my clothes. The black card Dad gave me digs into my thigh a little but I ignore it.

I pull out my phone, the glowing light comforting in the darkness. Even though I'm exhausted, I'm even more afraid to go to sleep here than at home. What if I wake up in the cemetery and Dad isn't there? What'll happen then? I think back to the carnival and wish I knew how I got myself out of the dream, away from Her. It seems like a fluke.

I send a message to Sarah: *Made it. Exhausted. School here seems weird. Wish I was with you guys.* My phone beeps and a message pops up: *Undeliverable.*

I look at the bars on my cell phone and groan. Unfreakin'-believable. No cell phone coverage on this Podunk island? How am I going to get through this semester? And what if something does happen? I can't even dial 9-1-1 for help.

How am I going to play *Kill Sam*? How am I going to stay awake? What if I have an emergency? SHIT! I am completely 100 percent stuck here.

I let the phone clunk to the floor in frustration and roll

over in bed. A piece of paper crumples against my head. I turn on the lamp and read it.

DEAR ADAM JONES:

Welcome to the School for Soul Guides! We are excited to partner with you in your journey to becoming a successful soul guide. Please join us for breakfast promptly at 7:15 a.m. tomorrow morning.

Principal Armand Ankou

The note flutters as it falls to the floor.

Questions pound against my head. What is a soul guide? Is a soul actually something you can locate and teach and guide? Or am I missing the point?

Despite all the questions, and despite my best efforts to stay awake, I drift off to sleep.

CHAPTER 12

When I wake with a start, the room is still dark. I grope around, turn on a lamp, and check my watch: 5:20 a.m.

Following the sound of voices takes me to the first floor. The blond preppy guy who almost lost his shadow on the train station platform last night is perched on a stool next to a metro-punk guy in a tight black T-shirt and skinny jeans. Steam rises from their mugs.

The metro-punk guy nods toward a large carafe of coffee, sugar, and a jug of cream—full cream, not half-and-half. "If that doesn't bring joy to your soul, there's an espresso machine behind the bar."

He holds out his hand and we shake. He has a firm, friendly handshake and a frank smile. Tattoos sneak down his arms. Jimi Hendrix peeks out from under one sleeve and Bob Marley from another. I already like him.

"I'm Sean, one of the Dullahan clan. This killjoy is Zachary, he's an Angel."

Zachary eyes me from head to toe. "So you're the 'lost' boy. They told us to expect you."

"I'm Adam Jones," I say. "I didn't think I was lost."

Both of them look at me curiously. Zachary barks, "Clan affiliation?"

"Of the . . . uh . . . Jones clan?"

"There is no Jones clan," Zachary replies in that "duh" voice.

"Dude, he's a lost kid," Sean says. "He probably doesn't know who he is."

"Where are you from?" Zachary sounds like he's accusing me of something.

"I've moved around a lot," I lie. My stomach cramps. It's already beginning. Before yesterday, it would have been hard to believe either of these guys would want to kill me, but I'd rather be safe than sorry. "You know, military kid."

Zachary stares at me hard. I shift from one foot to the other. "Our families aren't *in* the military, Lost Boy," he says.

I'm getting peeved at Zachary's tone. "I suppose if you know so much, you must be Peter Pan. Oh, wait, Peter Pan was a lost boy. I guess that makes you Wendy."

"Ha! Good one, Lost Boy." Zachary flops back down on the couch, his attention immediately diverted from me to Gabe. His stare turns to a glare. "Hey! What are *you* looking at?"

"I'm looking at you," Gabe says. "You want to make something out of it?"

Sean rolls his eyes. "Gabe, Zach, get over yourselves and your stupid little feud."

"Oh, because the Dullahan clan couldn't possibly understand feuds," Zachary says. "The Irish have *always* gotten along with each other." He appears to have perfected the art of sarcasm.

"Are you always this pleasant to be around?" I ask.

Sean laughs. "He's an Angel, he can't help it." He moves behind the bar. "Cappuccino? Latte?"

I don't usually drink much coffee but Sean seems to be nice. "Cappuccino, thanks."

He hands me a mug of coffee, perfectly foamed, light sprinkles of chocolate across the top. "You're really clueless, aren't you?"

"Yeah," I respond after a moment. "I mean, I know this is a school for soul guides. I know none of us are exactly normal." At least, they can see people's shadows, which I know, from experience, isn't exactly normal. Maybe, like me, they go places in their dreams. "But I don't know exactly what any of it means."

I start laughing and he joins in. He has a nice laugh.

"So what exactly do soul guides do?" I ask. "Do we offer advice for depressed spirits? Are we über gurus for the dead?" I try to laugh again but—and this is embarrassing—high-pitched giggles emerge from my mouth and float to the ceiling like bubbles.

From his perch on the couch, Zachary shakes his head. "Keep laughing, Lost Boy. You have no idea."

"Wait. Is that it? Is that what we do? We're like psychiatrists or spiritual advisors for people's actual souls?"

I look from one face to the other and all of a sudden nobody is yuk-yuking it up.

"Some people call us harbingers of death," Sean explains. "But that's not exactly right. When people die, we're the ones who guide their souls through Limbo to the other side. Modern day Charons, rowing people across the River Styx."

"Wait . . . What?"

"Pick your jaw up off the floor, man," Zachary says.

"So . . . when you say you're an Angel, you mean you're an Angel of Death?"

He smirks at me.

"I can't believe you had no idea." Sean shakes his head. "That's so wrong. Your mom or dad should have clued you in a long, long time ago."

A million questions flow like water through my head. They all circle back to the same question, though, creating a whirlpool that sucks me toward one inevitable thought: *I'm supposed to help people die? Me? Adam Jones?*

This must be the universe's idea of one big sick joke.

Morning light filters through the large picture window. I walk outside, onto the deck. A thin stream of smoke trails from the couch, followed by the scent of a tobacco pipe.

"Come. Sit. It's a beauty-full day!"

A small birdlike boy with thick dreads and mocha-colored skin lounges on the couch. He pulls a pipe from his lip and smiles. "Tomás." He slides to a sitting position, allowing me room on the couch. "My family is Eshu."

I sit down. "I'm Adam. I'm . . . uh . . . I don't know my family. Apparently, I'm a lost boy."

The rich smell of his pipe smoke wreathes us as we watch the sun break over the ocean, lighting up the mist hanging in the trees. Rollers break on the rocky shore and seagulls let loose their haunting cries. Lobster boats bob on the water.

I sip my drink.

Tomás points his chin at the sunrise. "It is a great day to be alive, isn't it? Every morning, the chance to begin again."

And you know what? Given all the ways my life has changed, I have to admit—it is definitely good to be alive.

As the sun rises, other guys join us on the deck. Sean jumps one of the goths and they start wrestling. Soon everybody's throwing cushions. Tomás smokes in the corner, watching and making jokes.

We all stop when the clanging of a ship's bell breaks through the camaraderie.

"Breakfast!" Zachary roars, and charges up the hill toward the main house, leading the cavalry.

The rest of us follow more slowly. In the light of day, the farmhouse looks huge. It spreads across the top of the hill and engulfs what looks like an earlier, smaller barn. Clearly, this place was built in pieces over the years.

I follow the other guys into the old barn. It's been converted into a cafeteria equipped with long, rough-cut plank tables, benches, and a random assortment of odd chairs. Lamps hang from the rafters and light the room. One of the plank tables groans under the weight of a buffet containing every kind of food, from eggs to pickled fish to strange fruits and stinky cheeses.

"Eat up," Sean tells me. "It's gonna be a long morning." His own plate is piled high with French toast.

I get bacon and eggs and slide into the seat of an empty table just as the girls file into the room from one of the farmhouse's many wings. Then about two dozen adults, ranging in age from twentysomething to seventysomething, wander into the dining room. They all have a strange look in their eyes and walk as if their bodies are here but their minds live in another reality. I know this look all too well—I see it on Dad's face all the time.

Tomás sits next to me. "Are you from the Eastern Seaboard, Adam? You look and feel like you're part of the Reaper clan."

My dad's words keep running through my mind. *Don't tell anyone where you're from.*

"I was born in St. Louis," I lie.

"St. Louis?" Sean says. "That's Dullahan territory. I should know you." He screws up his face. "You're not one of my funny cousins, are you? The ones my dad always said have one screw loose and an extra gene just to make everything stick together?"

We all laugh.

"I'm pretty sure I'm not a Dullahan," I say. "No Irish blood in me." But even as I say it, I wonder if I'm telling the truth. I have no idea what my mom's background was. She did have red hair, I think. That's Irish, isn't it?

"As long as you're not a Reaper," Sean says.

"What's wrong with being a Reaper?"

"Everybody hates the Reapers," Sean says. "Even Reapers hate Reapers."

"If there was anybody left to hate," says Tomás. "They're all dead now . . . well, except the Patriarch and his Caregiver."

"Well, they are totally hateable," Sean says.

Zachary sets his plate down beside us. "Are we talking about the horrible, hateful Reapers?" He bites a carrot in two, his teeth vicious and quick. The cracking sound makes me jump. "They're gonna die off. All I can say is, good riddance."

My stomach is lurching all over the place. Am I a Reaper?

"I'm sure the Synod is searching high and low for any possible Reaper connections," Tomás says. "They'll find somebody."

"Don't know who they'll find," Zachary says. "Or *what* they'll find, more like it. My dad says the Reapers are totally incestuous, never married anybody but each other. Oh, and some Eurotrash."

"Then they'll find some fifth cousin with too many toes and goggle eyes, probably," Tomás says. "That'll kill all the upstarts who want a crack at the Reaper territory."

The look Zachary gives Tomás could curdle the milk still inside a cow. "I'm not sure you would understand all the intricacies of territories anyway. Your family has that unfortunate island mentality."

Tomás laughs. "Is that the best you can do, Zacky boy?"

"I just don't see why you're defending the Reapers."

"I'm not defending anybody. But if the Reaper clan dies off, it'll set off a territorial war like you've never seen," Tomás says. "Believe me, that would be a disaster."

"How come?" I ask.

"Everyone wants a piece of the Reaper territory."

"Do you?"

"Shiiii-yeah," Zachary says.

"The Reapers control the entire Eastern Seaboard," Sean says. "Which makes them richer than God."

"Before the Civil War, soul guides fought each other for souls," Tomás says. "It was a bloody free-for-all. As part of the Civil War treaty, the Reaper Matriarch brokered a peace deal to assign territorial rights. She tricked the Dullahans, Cu Siths, and Ankou clans out of half their lands, which is why the Reapers control such a large territory today."

"The Reapers are money-grubbing, power-hungry assholes," Zachary says. "And now they're all dead. Met their end in a series of unfortunate 'accidents.' One by one by one. Like dominoes. Karma, that's what I say."

"Yeah, payback's a bitch," Sean chimes in.

"That, or somebody's trying to spark a civil war between the clans," Tomás says.

"Shut up, Tomás," Zachary hisses.

Tomás clamps his lips down so hard, he winces. Probably bit his tongue.

Everybody starts shoveling food into their mouths quickly. When Zachary finishes, he gets up for seconds but then sits back down at a different table.

As for me, I sit in silence, a sick feeling in the pit of my stomach. Am I a Reaper? Do I belong to the clan everybody hates? From everything my grandfather and dad said—and everything the guys are telling me now—it sure sounds like it.

So. I'm a Reaper. And if people find out, they'll hate me. Or they're going to want to kill me.

CHAPTER 12.5

The Mors Patriarch and his wife, Leader of the Synod, Her Excellency, beseeched their wayward son and his lover-wife to choose the Mors clan. "We are facing a grave threat within our territorial borders," the Mors Patriarch said. "The rise of La Luz."

La Luz! That primordial immortality cult! That ancient archenemy of all that is sacred to those whose burden it is—

JESUS! Her Excellency cried. SPARE US THE THEATRICS!

Madam, he said, you asked me for the story. I am telling it.

The lover-husband and lover-wife walked the streets of Rome. "It is impossible," the Grim Reaper declared. She opened her arms wide as though embracing the world. "Why must every choice we make be a choice for death? No matter what we choose . . ."

"We chose love," the lover-husband reminded her.

"Perhaps we made a mistake," she said.

"The world has a solution for this problem."

He cried out, "Divorce?"

"It is not one accepted or legal among our clans but it exists among non-soul guides," she said. "We did not ask permission to marry; we do not have to ask permission to divorce."

They were walking in the Parthenon—

The Parthenon is in Greece, said Elder #5, icily.

Oh hell, you're right. Pardon me, they were walking in the Colosseum.

He stopped and held her beneath an arch, arms tightening around her waist. Already, life stirred in her belly. They sensed it. He was silent and still, waiting for her to speak.

"My love," she answered his unasked question. "Come home with me. Choose me. Choose the Reapers."

CHAPTER 13

Soul *(n): The part of a human that passes from life through Limbo into the world beyond. The soul is the whole person, alive or in the afterlife. Human beings have a spirit but they are a soul.*
Spirit *(v, n): The life force that animates your body. Directly connected to the brain, which controls thought and emotion. The spirit animates your body but, unlike the soul, it isn't the person itself, just as the physical body isn't the person.*
—From *A Soul Guide Dictionary*

I'm finishing my bacon when Aileen gestures for me to join her outside. I say goodbye to everybody, clear my plate, and join her. Rachel, the new girl with the rabbit shadow, is standing beside her.

"I'm going to take you to Principal Armand Ankou's office," Aileen says. "It's time for orientation. Then you can join everybody else for school."

I nudge Rachel, who's chewing her fingernail and staring out to sea. "So you're a lost kid too."

"Yeah, who knew?" She rips a hangnail with her teeth and her finger starts to bleed.

"Geez, get out much?" I say.

"Nope," she replies. "Foster kid. With habits to match." She holds up her hands facing out so I can see all her fingernails, bitten to nubs.

Now she has me laughing.

"Let's get this funeral started, shall we?" Rachel says to Aileen.

"You're a cheerful one, aren't you?" Aileen quips.

"I thought the bedside manner was appropriate," she says. "Given what we're doing here."

I'm liking this girl more and more. Her shadow is looking less and less like a rabbit and more like a tiny tiger, gripping something in its teeth.

"I see you've been talking to some of the girls. And you, Adam? Have the guys filled you in on your destiny here at the School for Soul Guides?"

I shrug. "Yeah, I guess so. It's still kind of confusing."

"Well, hopefully Principal Armand can clear up any remaining questions."

We follow Aileen into the farmhouse, then up and down several sets of stairs, tracking our way through the house's many additions. Finally, we squeeze into a small corridor, walk up two steps, and stop outside a short, narrow door.

I wish I could puke up the eggs and bacon I just ate but I'm not sure I can find my way back through the labyrinth in time. I swallow it, bile stinging the back of my throat.

"Listen, you two," Aileen says. "Some of what he's going to tell you may seem shocking. You can choose another mentor if you'd prefer, but in the meantime, if you have any questions, come talk to me."

We nod, both of us mute.

Aileen knocks on the door and a deep, scratchy voice calls, "Come in."

We stoop to enter a small attic room. An elderly gentleman is sitting behind a desk. He stands as we enter. He's so tall, he has to stoop to avoid hitting his head on the low ceiling, and so large that his presence fills the room. His skin is mottled brown and white, his eyes startlingly blue in his wrinkled face, beautiful but icy, like jumping into a glacier-fed lake on a hot summer day. On the surface of it, he looks like a kindly old man, but when you see the way his shadow hides behind him—as if his own shadow is afraid of him—you know better than to cross him.

"This is Principal Armand," Aileen says. "Principal Armand, these are the two lost kids, Adam Jones and Rachel Smith." She winks at us and closes the door behind her as she leaves.

Principal Armand motions to two chairs facing his desk. "Have a seat." He sits back down and uses his knuckles to tap a short rhythm on the wooden surface. "I'm sure by now you are both wondering what you'll be learning in this school, perhaps even what it means to be a soul guide."

We nod like little bobble-headed dolls. Why, yes, we are wondering.

He leans forward, resting his chin on his hands. "Have you ever thought about what happens to people when they die?"

Silence fills the room. He looks at each of us in turn. "Well? Adam? Rachel? Have you ever had questions about what happens after death? Do people cease to exist? Do they go on to a blissful state of nothingness? Are they reincarnated? Do they go to heaven or hell?"

I think about my other recurring dream—the one I'm

not about to die in—the one with the woman in the yellow dress on a train. She has freckles and kind of looks like Rachel, if you want to know the truth, and I think she's my mother but I'm not sure since Dad doesn't exactly keep any pictures of her lying around the apartment.

Principal Armand nods like he can hear me thinking. "Of course you have. Well, this school is all about what happens to people right after they die. And by right after, I mean *immediately* after. As in, the first few seconds all the way up to forty-eight hours postmortem."

"So what happens?" Rachel asks.

"As far as we can tell, who we are—what we refer to as the soul—has always been and will always be, just like the conservation of energy in physics. But our souls become attached to our physical bodies, which makes it very disorienting to die. To get a soul from this life to what we assume is the next life, we need a guide. A good guide is able to disentangle even the most obstinate soul from life, guide it through Limbo, and start it on its journey to the next world. We call it 'breaking the circle.' That is, our job is to break the circle of a person's going round and round in life and shepherd them safely along the narrow passage that leads to the next world. This is what you will be learning to do."

He points to the medallion hanging around my neck. "That's the Broken Circle. It symbolizes what we do." He straightens and starts waving his arms. "In school, you will learn about things that you didn't know existed and how to do things that normal people only dream about in their wildest fantasies."

I imagine careening through mountain peaks on a magic carpet, wearing a purple robe decorated with a moon and stars, as I smite the earth with my magic wand, or soaring up into the solar system and landing on a star where I unpack a picnic lunch; I gobble down my food—little sandwiches and cakes and a thermos of coffee—staring at the earth far beneath me.

"And no," he says, "this is not a school for magic, although magic does exist. Magic is not something for humans to mess around with. It was not intended for our use. We soul guides use *science* as our tool."

Rachel is sitting very still. "What's Limbo?"

"Limbo is the space between life and the next world. To become a competent soul guide, you will learn to communicate with souls, travel in Limbo, and help souls find their way to the other side. If a soul does not traverse Limbo, it stays half-connected to this world and half to the next. This is an unfortunate state of being and causes much anxiety and frustration both for the stuck soul and for those in close proximity to it."

"Do you mean ghosts?" Rachel asks.

He purses his lips. "That is what people call them. But they are not ghosts. They are simply souls who have become corrupted because of their inability to move on to the next life."

I raise my hand.

"Yes, Adam?" Principal Armand places his index fingers in a steeple formation over his lips and waits for me to ask my question.

"If a soul gets stuck in Limbo, is it stuck forever?" In

one layer of my brain, I'm still thinking about the dream of the woman in the yellow dress on the train. My mom. If she is my mom. In the dream, the train just goes around and around and around a circular track, never arriving at a destination and never stopping. But in another layer of my brain, I'm thinking about myself. About the endless fall.

Principal Armand frowns. "Yes. Well. There are ways to guide these stuck souls across Limbo, but only very accomplished soul guides should attempt it. I know of no living soul guide with the fortitude for it."

Rachel and I look at each other.

"So we're here because we're related to spirit guides or whatever you call them?" I ask. "That's what we do. What our dads or moms or other relatives do."

"Yes. This school is exclusively for the offspring of *soul* guides. Psychopomps, as the ancient Greeks called them. The real deal. You will learn all you need to know about your family's line of business over the next three years. Each year, you must pass a final examination at the end of the school term. If you don't pass, you can't continue. We are not about to let incompetent soul guides loose on the world."

Rachel lets out a quivery sigh. "So you're training us to be the Angel of Death."

Principal Armand sits back in his chair and uses his pinky to play with his lower lip. "Well, I don't know what your lineage is. The Angel of Death clan oversees the western territory of the United States. Other clans oversee other sections of the US. I am part of the Ankou clan. The Ankou was understood as the collector of dead souls in Breton cultures. He is the one who drove a cart and stopped at the house where a person had died, to cart their soul away. The Ankou clan oversees Louisiana. But . . . neither of you were assigned to a family when you were sent here."

"Why not?" Rachel asks.

"I don't know," he says. "I want to know where you're from so I can figure out what clan you belong to."

We sit in silence. I'm not going to tell him anything. Rachel's back is ramrod straight. I'm guessing she's not telling much either. Still, he starts with her.

"Rachel, where are you from?"

"I don't know. I'm an orphan." She folds her arms. "I grew up in foster care."

"Interesting." His eyes bore into her.

I've seen my father do that. It usually takes a minute and when he's done, the other person looks dazed. But Rachel just stares back, holding her own.

"And Smith is the surname on your birth certificate?"

She shrugs. Her unease is palpable. "Yes?"

He snorts. "Impossible. Adam's last name isn't Jones either. How did you come to be an orphan?"

"I was left in front of a hospital emergency room when I was a few days old. At least, that's what they tell me."

"Where?"

"Minneapolis."

"Minneapolis!" He shakes his head. "That's Pesta territory. Pesta, the Norwegian Personification of Death. I'm intrigued by the mystery. Direct lineage is a *requirement* to be a soul guide—so you have a clan affiliation. It may be

Pesta, it may be something else. In any case, the Finders don't make mistakes."

"Finders?"

"They are the people responsible for locating lost kids. Children who were lost never had their birth reported to the Synod. It is a violation of the treaty we all signed. Nevertheless, it happens more often than you'd think. Some misguided parents don't want their offspring to become soul guides."

"What if *I* don't want to become a soul guide?" Rachel asks.

"Ridiculous." His nostrils flare ever so slightly. "There is no other conceivable job for you. Unless you fail and then we put you to some other menial use. But you *will* be part of our world."

"So why don't you ask the Finders what clan we're from?" I ask.

"Ah, for reasons they haven't chosen to share, they are keeping your identities secret, even from me. Usually paperwork—birth certificates, etc.—accompanies students. You two have none."

His blue eyes lock on mine. "And you, Adam? Adam *Jones*. Don't tell me you're an orphan too." The biggest crabs I've ever seen fall out of his mouth. One attaches itself to his nose and pinches, hard. He wrinkles his nose like he smells it.

"No," I say.

"Well, where are you from? Who are your parents?" He sounds impatient now, his stare a proboscis. He stabs, cool but sharp, smiling the entire time—releasing paralyzing venom directly into my bloodstream. The poison spreads slowly through my body, muscles going soft and watery one by one. I'm a jellyfish. Slowly, I start to slide off the chair, barely keeping erect by pressing my feet hard against the dark wood floor.

He continues to probe, feather-light fingers tickling their way through my life.

First, he finds those things I keep skin deep, toward the surface—the things I don't want anybody to find out but if they do, I'm okay. Like, wondering whether my friends really like me or only put up with me.

But then he tunnels deeper. Did my mother love me? Will I ever feel normal?

He keeps pushing the needle. I swim in the icy waters of his eyes, floundering, and then he reaches the place where the real fears begin: those nights in my room, all the lights on and yet darkness surrounds me. I lie on my bed with vertigo, trying to keep myself awake, trying to keep myself there, in Brooklyn . . . but I can't . . .

I find myself in a familiar place, walking through a muddy graveyard, only this time it's Principal Armand at my side, not my father, and I'm panicking and he's surprised too, and I'm worried because what happens when Dad arrives and Principal Armand sees my father and then knows who I am and—

Rachel touches my arm, concerned. Those panting, grunting sounds must be coming from me.

A bony figure beckons to me. Black liquid laps at the desk, my shoes. The faceless woman reaches for me, drags me into the dark night, the endless fall.

Rachel grabs my shirt, hauls me back into my seat.

In the darkness of my mind, Principal Armand watches the light approaching—my father, coming to rescue me.

But he can't find out who my father is. He can't see that spark. *I won't let him.*

And then I'm surprised by the sudden warmth welling up from deep inside. My father, a hidden sun—but still with me, the way he always is. I grab onto that spark. Focus. What was it he told me just before I left? *Remember, Adam, you have powers. Don't be afraid to use them, to protect yourself and others.*

Gripping my armrests, I stare back at Principal Armand, sucking all the fear toward a flat line of nothing. I keep a picture of me falling in the darkness and the light of my father in the forefront of my mind so that the principal thinks he's still gaining on us, then circle back around, filling the gap between him and me with powerful emotions neatly packaged and ready to explode when he probes them.

He reaches for me. But the traps I laid hit him by complete surprise. I lash out at the small dark pearl in his mind, with all the strength I can muster. At the same time, I sneak inside, a dog slinking through a hole in the back fence—hiding behind the trees and bushes in his mind, until I'm deep, deep, so deep he can't dislodge me.

We're in a dark, cramped space. A young child huddles against a pile of wood, light piercing the darkness through cracks in the sides. The stench of swamp rot permeates the air. The child cocks his head, listening. Something—probably a rat—scrambles against the wood, kicking dirt up. He brushes his face to remove cobwebs and cowers against the wood.

And then it comes . . . the sound he was waiting for. The heavy tread of footsteps. Gravel crunching as someone passes by, stopping at the side of the shed, covering the cracks that let in the light, plunging the child into total darkness.

The door opens. Light floods inside and the child cringes at the sudden brightness, shrinking back from what's coming next. A pair of heavy work boots steps inside. Slow. Ominous.

The child screams.

Rachel hauls back and punches me in the face. "Stop it!" she shouts.

I careen off the chair and skid across the floor, wrist twisting as I hit the rough wood planks.

"Can't you see what you're doing to him?" she yells.

Principal Armand is lying on the floor in a fetal position, his back to me, shoulders trembling.

Rachel shakes the hurt out of her hand, pacing the room, hugging herself. "I quit," she says. "I quit this sick school."

Principal Armand's moans get louder and louder. The door crashes open and Aileen runs into the room. She slides around the desk and gapes at Principal Armand's body twitching on the floor. "What the hell?" She helps him sit up and he slumps over in his chair.

Blood drips from my nose. I wipe it away with the back of my hand. Bet my nose is broken. *Thanks, Rachel.*

"This has never happened in an orientation," Aileen says. "*Never!* What did you guys do to him?"

I can't look at the three of them, shame and anger

chained together and throttling the breath from my throat. I *think* I'm sorry for what I did . . . but nobody—and I do mean *nobody*—is going to root around in my mind or soul without my freaking permission. Take that, Principal Armand. Just try to do it again. I look him in the eye and dare him to try.

Aileen puts her arm around Principal Armand. He's mumbling, a confusion of words bubbling out of his mouth. She massages the back of his neck and whispers in his ear.

His eyes spring open. He wipes saliva off his trembling chin and points a thick index finger at me. "I don't know where you came from, boy, but you're not allowed to summon souls without permission. I could have you expelled."

Oh no. I haven't even been here for twenty-four hours and already my grandfather's prediction is coming true.

"He *what?*" Aileen glares at me. "He can't possibly have summoned your soul. He hasn't even been through the first year of training."

"It was worse than that," Principal Armand declares. "He didn't just summon my soul. He took me to Limbo. *My* Limbo. How the hell did you get there, you little shit?"

"I didn't know I was summoning his soul, Aileen," I say. "I didn't know I was going to Limbo. I was just protecting myself. He was poking around in my mind, trying to figure out who I am, where I'm from."

Aileen inhales deeply, taking in what I just said. Her lips thin, razor blades, as she glances at Principal Armand. "Sir, I don't know what happened here. It sounds altogether suspicious. Perhaps I need to bring this incident up to the Synod."

"Aileen, I was just trying to evaluate his abilities." Principal Armand wraps his voice up in just the right amount of tightness.

"I'm sure the Synod will be very curious about what you discovered," she says. "After all, they also want to know who these two are and what their abilities are. And I'm sure they'll be very curious to hear Adam's side of the story as well—whatever it is that happened."

They stare at each other. I see a lot in that quick exchange. Principal Armand is technically in charge but it appears that Aileen has access to power he doesn't want to challenge. Is it my father? Because it seems like he's sort of her mentor, or maybe her hero, or both, and I think maybe she's answering to him, not Principal Armand. Not that he knows my father is my father.

"It won't be necessary, Aileen." His eyes are rimmed red. "Neither one of us did it on purpose. Right, Adam?"

I look at him. His eyes narrow. My own narrow too. *I'm watching you*, his eyes say. *I'm watching you back*, mine respond.

Dad would want me to let this go. Grandpa definitely told me to keep my nose clean. Okay, I can pretend. For now. I'm good at pretending things. I've been pretending to be normal all my life.

"We're all good, Aileen," I say. "We're all good."

CHAPTER 14

As soon as the three of us reach the stairwell, Rachel sits down on the top stair, tears rolling off her cheeks and splashing on the floor. "Damn it, Adam, what was that about?"

"I was protecting myself," I say. I'm surprised by the bright red spots of anger on her cheeks.

"You seem like a nice guy. Don't let them turn you into an asshole." Her eyes are dark holes in a perfectly white face. "I survived the foster care system with only a shred of my dignity intact. Just a shred. But I have held onto it with everything in me. I won't let you guys take it from me. *I won't*. Do you understand?"

Aileen looks like she's working something around in her mouth. "Okay, Rachel," she says. "Let's talk. I'll come find you when we're done, Adam."

I wander outside, alone, scrambling across large boulders covered in thick moss and lichen. The ground begins to slope steeply away as the sound of the surf breaking on the rocks grows stronger. I reach the end of the trees and step out onto a rock shelf, the sun glinting off the Atlantic.

Seagulls take flight, screeching as they soar over the ocean. Large rollers break below, flecks of water splashing up into the sky. I sit on the edge of the rock shelf, turning that shiny black card Dad gave me over and over in my hands.

My phone still shows no coverage. So, I'm stuck on an island with a bunch of kids training to be Angels of Death, and adults who think reading your mind is a great way to get information.

I lick my lips and taste salt.

Training to take over Dad's business? I already see my future written on the wall. Growing old by myself, wearing grubby underwear, spending my nights in an office all alone to usher people from this world to the next. No wonder Dad never sleeps. Or eats. I imagine Sarah finding out and running away, screaming in horror, even as I call after her, *Wait! Don't go! I'm still the same guy you knew two weeks ago!*

As I watch yachts pushed and pulled by the waves far out at sea, I resolve to figure out a way to get Rachel alone so we can talk. Maybe I can help her understand why I had to do what I did. She and I are in the same boat. We don't know who we are or who to trust. Maybe we can help each other.

That afternoon, Tomás, Sean, and I drink three or four cups of cappuccino apiece as we play games out on the deck.

I'm pretty good at chess but Sean is a whiz. He beats us again and again in a rapid succession of very quick games. Before long, we concede total defeat.

And Tomás would kill us at *Monopoly* if he had any luck with the dice. Despite ending up with some of the crappiest properties, he bankrupts Sean in under an hour. I win only because I have Park Place and Boardwalk and Tomás lands on me twice in a row. He mutters something in Caribbean argot and starts mortgaging properties to pay me.

Right as I'm about to collect the money, Sean kicks the board. Money, cards, red plastic hotels, and a metal dog and car fly everywhere.

Tomás smiles, lighting his pipe and leaning his head back against the patio couch. He seems awfully relaxed. I'm so hopped up on caffeine, it feels like I'm levitating an inch off the cushions.

"Hey, what're you guys doing?" Sean yells into the barn.

A bunch of guys run out, Zachary in the lead, carrying an oblong ball that looks like an oversized football. "Rugby!" he yells.

We spend the rest of the afternoon tackling each other.

Olan Crowley, dressed in only a loincloth, his crow perched on his shoulder, is wily and fast, scoring several times before Sean gets a bead on him and brings him to the ground. The crow starts dive-bombing Sean, forcing him to take cover in the barn. Olan tries to catch his bird but every time he gets close, Sean charges from the barn and runs around the deck, laughing and waving his arms, riling up the crow all over again before ducking back to cover.

Olan finally catches his pet and puts him in a cloth-covered cage, while someone brings a vat of ice water and a pitcher of lemonade. We lounge on the deck and hydrate.

My T-shirt is ripped, my clothes are covered in grass stains, and my knees are scraped from getting tackled so often. It doesn't take long before I stiffen up. I've used muscles I didn't know existed and been pummeled from head to toe. But it's a good hurt.

When the bell rings for dinner, we head to the barn, where they're handing out sweet and slightly bitter lemon drinks in what appears to be a predinner ritual. I find out later they're shandies when I get a little light-headed and ask Sean what we're drinking.

I load my dinner plate with hot steaming lobster rolls and clam chowder and head to the table where Rachel's sitting, alone. She looks away when I sit down. I'd move to another table but Tomás and Sean sit down beside me.

Sean starts in right away: "Hey, guys, let's sneak out and row to the mainland, go see a movie."

"You just want off this island so you can call your girl," Tomás says.

"What girl?"

"Oh, right, too bad Liliana's AWOL." Tomás grins at him.

"Shut up." Sean's face gets really red. "She's not my girl."

"Who's Liliana?" I ask.

"Liliana La Muerte," Tomás sings. "Sean's been crushing on her since he was twelve."

"Shut up. I don't *like* like her," Sean says.

Tomás nudges my arm. "Yeah, he has it bad." He laughs. "But he will regret it, my friend. That Liliana is a loose cannon. She got expelled last semester."

"What happened?" I ask.

Tomás drops his voice to a whisper: "She flunked the final exams at the end of last year."

"Bullshit," Sean whispers back. "There's no way Liliana La Muerte would flunk her final exams. She's smart. And the teacher who gave the test was 'mysteriously' transferred somewhere else the very next day. My dad says there's something fishy about it all."

I look over at Rachel. She's busy shredding the lobster roll into crumbs. I imagine we're inmates surrounded by prison gangs eating dinner in the cafeteria. A three hundred–pound muscle man in the corner, racist tattoos all the way up his shaved head. A little guy who "knows how to get stuff" so no one messes with him on the other side of the table. Rachel, in an orange jumpsuit, tearing food apart and avoiding eye contact. This makes me nervous, worried for her, like maybe she's the person that could be picked on until she shrivels up and dies. But the tightness in her shoulders suggests another possibility, like maybe she's the quiet one with the big-ass shiv hidden up her sleeve and she'll cut you, cut you bad, if you look at her the wrong way.

Tomás nudges me in the ribs.

"What?" I say.

"You in or out?" Sean asks.

"Uh, sure, I'm in," I say, even though I didn't quite catch what I was agreeing to do.

"All right, we'll meet up at the grain silo tonight," Sean whispers. "I'll put a chair under the loft window so we can climb onto the roof. But be quiet—that roof might be pretty creaky."

"You're going to learn how to suck people's souls out of their bodies," Rachel says, her voice bitter, "and you're worried you'll get in trouble for sneaking out at night?" She gets up and hurries out of the dining room.

"I take it the lost girl isn't too keen on us," Sean says. "Or what she's supposed to do with her life."

"Um . . . no." I pick up both her plate and mine. "Listen, guys, I'll see you later. I'm going to go talk to her."

I catch up with her underneath an enormous craggy hemlock. She intercepts me with, "Look, it's nothing personal."

Logs fall out of my mouth. "I know it's nothing personal, Rachel, okay? At least not the way you mean it. But maybe it *is* personal. Maybe it's completely, 100 percent personal! You and I are the only people—the only ones here—who weren't raised to be this thing, this whatever-they-call-it, a soul guide. So couldn't we just, you know, be friends? Lay aside the hatchet and get along, maybe even be on each other's side? Because I don't know anybody else here who could be on my side the way you can. I don't trust any of them. I like some of them, I think some of them could become friends, but I don't know. You? I have to trust you. Don't you get it?"

She stares at me and I stare back and that lasts for a while until it gets uncomfortable.

"Okay," she says. "You're right. You're right. Okay? Let's be friends."

"Serious?"

"Serious." She nods and holds out her hand for a shake. I give her my hand. She takes it and I feel a tiger's paw beneath the human skin and fingers. A good tiger. Ferocious. She's strong and she'll do what she has to do.

I trust her already. No matter what Grandpa said.

CHAPTER 15

That evening, I unpack my suitcase while waiting to join the guys. It doesn't take long. I throw all of my clothes into the closet and arrange the books around my built-in bed.

I open the banned book. It's leather soft, and lighter than you'd think for a book that's supposed to contain the ultimate answer to the thing that everybody wants most.

I flip it open, at random.

One phrase stands out starkly: *Beware the Reapers and Angels of Death, the ones who take you to the grave, for their business is death and they cannot endure the light of life.* Ouch. I slam it shut and take care to hide it under the mattress. If I'm supposed to become the next Grim Reaper, why in the world does my dad think reading drivel like this is supposed to help me?

I check my watch. It's eleven. An hour to go.

I pull out a book of poems Dad gave me for my birthday last month, a collection of *jisei*, which I discover are Japanese death poems. Apparently, it's a Japanese *thing* to write poems on your deathbed, because supposedly people finally understand the meaning of life as death approaches.

I start reading.

Coming, all is clear, no
doubt about it. Going, all is
clear, without a doubt.
What, then, is all?
—Hosshin, thirteenth century

I think about that for a minute. What *is* all? When you're talking about that space between birth and death—that is, life—this thing called "all" seems pretty murky to me. If this poem is right, maybe that's a good thing—it means I'm not going to die anytime soon. If it suddenly becomes clear, I'd better be worried—it means I'm on my way out.

But how can you ever be sure of anything, even when you're sure of everything? How can you ever think you have a handle on "all"? Did my mother think about me when she died? Was I part of her "all"?

I'm fifteen. I'm supposed to "know it all." Hah! Turns out I know nothing.

One thing I do know: I'm not ready to die, even if I've just learned that I'm heir to the world's creepiest job.

Eleven fifty rolls around. Time to join the guys. I put on a sweatshirt and jacket and carefully open the door.

All clear. Somebody's propped a chair up against the wall at the end of the hall. The window is high, located where the doors to the hayloft used to be. That little Jamaican must be a spider if he got through that window. I have to jump from the chair to reach it, then haul myself up to get my butt on the sill. I sit half on and half off, legs dangling over the edge, panting.

I almost have a heart attack when I look down. This window is freaking twenty feet off the ground. At least.

For a minute I huddle in the window—too afraid to do anything at all. And then I glimpse something dark and shadowy disappearing around the corner.

Crap. Only thing to do now is go up and I better not fall because She's waiting for me. I close my eyes—gripping the top of the window—and breathe. In and out. In. Out. In. Out.

The old roof rail sticks out just above me. I crouch on the windowsill and lean out, holding onto the upper sill with one hand and reaching up to the roof with my other. I stand—everything but toes suspended in midair—and grab the rail with both hands. I swing my legs up, hooking the roofline with my heel, pulling myself up, bear-hugging the rail.

Panic grips me. Why did I do this again? Oh, right. Gotta be one of the guys.

Lunging with all my strength, I get my belly up and over the side of the roof, scrabbling on the shingles.

I lay on the slope, spread-eagled. I'm a crab, hugging the roof with my claws. Then I hear them whispering.

"Where the hell is he?" Sean's poking his head out of the window. "Adam, are you still alive?" he whispers loudly to the grass below.

"I'm up here."

His face blanches when he looks up and sees me. "You crazy shit."

"Aren't you guys coming up here?" I hate it that my voice is shaking. Maybe he won't notice.

"No chance in hell," he says. "We'll meet you at the bottom of the silo."

I crab walk across the roof. The barn shingles shine like tarnished silver in the moonlight. The silo, built into the side of the barn, isn't as tall as the peak. I shoot for it, sliding to the wall and stretching my legs out as far as they can go toward the rungs, rusty metal U's embedded into the wall.

Three inches short.

"You'll have to commit, Adam," Tomás calls.

Let my weight go out over the edge of the barn roof? My foot shakes, suspended over the roof rail. Something inside screams that I'm at the end of whatever rope fortune allotted me at birth.

"It's only ten feet, dude," Sean says. "You might break a leg but you won't break your neck. It isn't nearly as crazy as what you did climbing out that window!"

"I'll break *your* neck." *I can't do this.* "When I get down there."

But I can't stay here forever, not in front of the guys. I glance around, checking to see if She's nearby. When I don't see Her, I lean out and catch a rung with my foot. In less than five seconds, I'm on the ground. I grip the side of the silo, knees trembling with relief.

We all burst into nervous laughter. Then we can't stop laughing because we're trying so hard not to laugh.

"That was some sick climbing," Sean says.

"You must have a secret death wish," Tomás says.

"You are okay, Adam," Sean says. "For being a lost boy and knowing virtually nothing, you are okay."

Suddenly, I'm glad to be here, glad to be hanging out with these two.

We skirt the farmhouse, taking the wood stairs on the side of the bluff and entering the boathouse from a side door, the shadow of an old lobster boat projecting against the wall. Pulling the aluminum rowboat out the door makes a shocking amount of noise. We use Tomás's light to find the oars.

It must be high tide because the beach is just a few feet wide. We push off and jump in, holding our breath so we don't bust up laughing again.

The Milky Way's belted haze shines across the still waters. "What a glorious night!" Tomás leans back, stretching his arms out to rest on the boat's gunwales.

Sean takes the oars and starts us out into the bay. When we reach the mouth, Tomás directs Sean westward along the face of the bluff. We bob up and down outside the protection of the bay, the ocean smell clean and sharp and salty in the cool air. Water slaps the aluminum sides and hisses as it cascades off the oars.

Once we cross the bluff, Sean turns north. He hands the oars to me and I row for another half hour, watching the bluffs, now a silver arch in the distance as the moon crawls higher across the sky.

I stop for a second.

What, then, is all?

The waves are higher out past the protection of the shoreline. Tomás's skin blends into the darkness of the night and water, but the orange-red glow of his pipe lights up the whites of his eyes whenever he takes a drag.

"Smoking will kill you, you know." Sean's voice is half serious and half joking.

"Really?" Tomás sounds startled, as if he's never heard this before.

"I'll get you an ePipe the next time we're in town. A fuschia-striped vape pipe."

"Only if it has bright green LEDs on it," Tomás replies gravely.

They start laughing again and I can't help joining in. Tomás's laugh is infectious.

"You have to live longer than me, Tomás," Sean says. "When I die, you're the one taking me to La La Land. I'm not letting anybody from my family near my soul. The Dullahans are completely crazy! But the Eshu know how to live. How can you die if you've never lived?"

Tomás grins.

Sean pulls a flask from his jacket pocket. "To the Eshu. May they always know peace and find their way in the darkest hour! And may they learn that lung cancer isn't good for their long-term prospects!" He throws his head back, drinks deeply, and then hands the flask to me.

I take a small swig and immediately start coughing.

Sean grabs the flask back. "That's fine Irish whiskey you're coughing all over our boat. Stop it! This has to last until Christmas."

He hands the flask to Tomás, who takes a small pull. Sean screws the cap on and puts it back in his pocket. He points to a small island a short distance away. "You guys up for a little exploring?"

Tomás and I look at each other. I don't know about

him, but I'm starting to think about being deep under the bedcovers in a warm room.

"We probably won't get another chance," Sean says. "It'll be too cold or too windy to do this again until next summer. Don't stop now, we're almost there."

Tomás takes a turn at the oars but he's so small, it just looks funny. We start giggling and Sean takes over again.

We row up to a rock, level with the gunwales. Tomás hops out and ties the boat to it, heaving the rock into a crevice. I'm worried that with the tide going out, the rock will get dislodged and we'll be stranded, but Tomás and Sean don't seem that concerned. They scramble to the top of the small island.

I put my hand on a rock and it comes back slick with white goo. "Did you guys notice the rocks are covered in bird poo?" I call.

I find a different path between some rocks and join them at the top. We all snicker at the state of Sean's jeans, covered with white poo.

He groans. "How am I going to explain this to the guys who do our laundry?"

We start walking toward a stand of trees on the far side of the rock outcrop. But we don't make it very far before the feeling creeps up on me—the black chill from my dreams.

She's here.

For a moment I'm frozen. The moon and stars dissolve into pure darkness. I'm falling. Slamming into the darkness.

Tomás catches me with his shoulder and I come to, yelling something—I don't even know what, "YAAAAG!"

I think—and I'm flying back to the boat, my tennis shoes slipping on the rocks.

The guys are on my heels. We climb and stumble back to the boat. "Quick, man, quick!" Tomás yells. "Quick quick quick!"

I yank the rope free and we jump in. Sean takes one oar, I take the other. We row so hard, my muscles ache.

"What's going on?" Sean asks finally.

We're halfway back already. I focus on the water directly behind the boat as I pull the oars, afraid to look at the receding island, afraid of what I might see.

"What do you mean?" I'm breathless, but not because of rowing. "Didn't you feel the demon or whatever the hell it was on that island?"

"No." Sean stops rowing and the boat rotates in a slow circle because I keep going. "I ran because you did."

"Did you feel it?" I ask Tomás.

Tomás shakes his head slowly. "No, but you felt some bad juju, serious. Just keep rowing. Whatever it was, we don't want to mess with it."

"All right." Sean picks up the oar again but his heart isn't in it. He sighs. "I'm sorry, I thought Adam saw something like Principal Armand in the trees. I know that doesn't make any sense."

"You ever feel something like that before?" Tomás asks.

I nod but say nothing.

"I experienced a bad spirit like that one time," Tomás says. "During Carnival a few years ago. A stuck soul got loose, somehow made its way out of Limbo, and five people were murdered in our village."

Sean shudders and takes a pull on his flask. "All right, this isn't fun anymore. Let's get out of here."

What if She had gotten Tomás and Sean? Collateral damage. Two deaths on my conscience.

The boat bobs from side to side as we pull the oars out of the water one second and plunge them back in the next. Cold water hits my face. I taste salt water mixing with my silent tears.

CHAPTER 15.5

And so the lover-husband left Rome for the New World, for the crass, glittering lights of Manhattan and . . . the Reapers.

Ay. Therein lay the rub. He had thrown away his fortune, his inheritance, his respectability. And for what? For this family with a reputation as thugs? For this family with a Patriarch who went bat-shit crazy with grief and depression and had long ago bequeathed the clan rights and responsibilities and territory to his only daughter, decades before expected?

Did you? Her Excellency asked.

Did I what?

Go crazy?

Madam, he said with great dignity, I would posit that all soul guides go crazy with grief—either that or we turn our emotions off and become hard, cold, dead things that lack heart. The only question is what choice we make. Which choice did *you* make, oh captain?

Hmph, she said and turned away.

And so the two lovers started a new life in

the new world. And oh, they were happy! Oh, they loved each other. Every night was champagne and chocolates and truffles, not to mention their work together, the ushering of souls across the great divide between this life and the next.

It was as if they were made for each other. Imagine it, if you can. The beautiful Grim Reaper, young and full of life, skipping down the long avenue, cherry blossoms fluttering in the wind behind her.

Are there cherry trees in New York? asked Elder #1.

There should be, he said. There should be cherry trees everywhere.

Though the Mors son was dour of expression and lacked charisma, he made up for it in passion and intelligence and talent. It didn't take long before he was compensating for the Reapers' lack of numerical strength and then some . . .

Her Excellency had a tear in her eye. And did you accept your son-in-law? she asked. Did you feel he stole your daughter from you? Or were you glad to have him?

He has been my salvation, he said simply. All these years, I do not know what I would have done without him.

CHAPTER 16

There are more things in heaven and earth, Horatio,
Than are dreamt of in your philosophy.
—Hamlet

After a fabulous breakfast of Swedish pancakes lightly drizzled with maple syrup and powdered sugar and a bucketful of coffee—because I'm not gonna lie, I didn't sleep a wink last night after we got back; there was no way I was going to risk falling asleep and finding myself in the cemetery, not after the experience on the island—I follow the other first years to the "reading room." There are eight first years—me, Rachel, Tomás Eshu, Sean Dullahan, Zachary Angel, Emily Yamaraja, Gen Shinigami, and Sofia La Muerte.

It feels like I need to pry my eyelids open with a pair of crowbars. "Late night," I mutter to Rachel.

She scoots over to make room for me beside her on the sofa. "So you guys really made it off the island?"

I yawn. "Shhhhh," I say. Unnecessarily, I think. Rachel doesn't seem like the type to tattle. She may be less than thrilled with the life we've been thrust into but she's honest and real. She doesn't hide what she thinks. I totally like that about her.

"Was it easy?"

"Yeah," I say, and then take a good look at her eager face, her shadow a dazzling hopeful star dancing in the background. "But hey, I don't think you should try it. I saw something out there that you don't want to face alone."

"I've faced everything alone my whole life," she responds.

"Right. But this is different. Wait until Christmas and then just, you know, don't come back. Much easier than running away."

"You act as though we're not alone here," she hisses.

She's right. I don't feel alone, not anymore, not after becoming friends with Tomás and Sean. "You're not alone," I say. "I'm on your side."

She acknowledges this with a curt nod. "Don't you realize that if you become a soul guide, you'll never have a normal life? You'll be a complete and total freak."

The word "freak" echoes around the room and several people look up from whatever they're doing—mostly reading books.

"Your chances of having friends in the real world? Zilch."

Does she mean that I can never be with Sarah? "It's not that bad," I say. But I already know I'm lying. I mean, I was a freak before I arrived here and I'd bet a boatload of money that Rachel was a freak too.

The look she gives me would seriously shrivel raisins. "I see you've already drunk the Kool-Aid."

"No," I say, "it's just that my philosophy has always been, *When in Rome . . .*"

Speaking of being in Rome, I'm not really sure what I'm supposed to be doing. I keep waiting for a teacher to come in and tell us what to do but so far none of them seems in a real hurry to do that. And all the other first years look like they're already deep into something.

Zachary and Sean huddle over the same book, something that looks like it came off my dad's shelves. They talk in low voices and occasionally trace an outline of something on the page.

"That's just a myth!" Zachary exclaims loudly.

"Expand your worldview, dude." Sean's taken a page out of my old man's book (minus the "dude," that is). "There's more truth in those old myths than people want to admit."

Zachary snorts. "Next thing, you're going to start calling me Horatio."

"If the name fits," Sean counters.

"So." Sofia La Muerte—dressed completely in red, right down to the red bandanna slung around her neck and her richly, deeply red lips—plops down on the sofa beside me. "The girls have placed bets on which clan you're from."

"What?" Girls have never been curious about me. I don't think Sarah's even curious about me and she's the closest thing I have to a romantic interest.

"We've known the rest of these guys all our lives. I mean, *all* our lives. Our families go on vacations together, or we see them every year at the annual North American Soul-Reaping Reunion. But you're a great big blank."

"What about me?" Rachel asks.

"Oh, we already have you pegged as a Reaper." Her nose wrinkles in distaste.

"Do *you* think you're a Reaper?" I ask Rachel.

She shrugs. "It would be just my luck. Nobody likes the Reapers. Story of my life."

"Well, one of you has to be a Reaper," Sofia says. "The Patriarch's children all died in strange Reaper-like accidents. The only one left is his son-in-law. So they've been looking far and wide for possible candidates, anyone with the tiniest amount of Reaper blood who might be able to renounce their clan affiliation to be a Reaper instead. Where have you lived? Soul guides usually live in their territory."

"I've lived all over; I'm an orphan," Rachel says. "I didn't even know I was a soul guide until a few weeks ago."

My stomach clenches. I live in Reaper territory. Should I keep them thinking about Rachel to deflect attention from me? Because if I'm right, if I'm a Reaper, they'll all hate me once they find out. "What about me? What clan do you think I'm from?"

Now her curious stare turns frank as she examines my facial structure. "Well, I heard you flew here from Rome. Plus, you're a dead ringer for the Mors clan. But you're obviously not Italian. Not a hint of an accent and they send their soul guides to a school in Ethiopia anyway."

"Why does it even matter?" Rachel asks.

"Your clan is *everything*," Sofia says. "You're tied to your clan's territory and your clan is responsible for all the souls in your district. You can't enter Limbo anywhere outside of your territory, even if you want to. Except here at school. They do something to change the territorial boundaries so we can enter Limbo while we're in training."

Rachel mutters something under her breath.

"Well, guys, I'm outta here," Sofia says. "I'm going to the River Styx Simulation. Have you played it yet? It's this computer program that simulates journeys into the underworld. I'm super excited to try it. My cousin, who runs Mexico City, says it rocks."

Rachel and I twiddle our thumbs while everybody else starts doing something, apparently used to this directionless type of "school." Gen sits near us and begins playing the guitar. Sean and Emily confer, then they disappear briefly, reappearing clad in white gis. Emily has a black belt and Sean a brown. They move to a large room just off the living room and begin grappling.

Tomás's pencil is going a hundred miles an hour. "What are you up to?" I ask when he looks up.

"I'm doing equations," he says.

"Just random math? For fun?"

"No, I'm trying to figure out how to explain Limbo. Limbo doesn't exist using the current physics models of the universe. But we know it's out there so I'm trying to produce an equation that encompasses what we know is true. I like messing around with the latest theories."

Gen stops strumming the guitar long enough to say, "He's being modest. Tomás is a math genius."

"What happens if you think you have something?" Rachel asks.

"I write an algorithm and start testing it against simple known assumptions of the universe. Once I produce a model that encompasses Limbo, we can begin testing the model to help us understand the universe. Who knows, maybe Limbo is the missing factor that will unify the theory of relativity and quantum physics. In the future, physics departments can replace String Theory for the Theory of Limbotivity." Tomás grins as he scratches away at a new piece of paper.

"Can I join you?" Rachel sounds almost joyous. "I love math."

"Sure." Tomás pulls out a chair and Rachel leaps up to join him.

Gen's long black hair falls over his face as he picks at the guitar strings with slender, nimble fingers. "Tomás loves math. I love the blues. Music with soul in it."

He begins singing. "*Southern trees bear strange fruit. Blood on the leaves and blood at the root . . .*" He has a raspy voice but if you closed your eyes, you wouldn't be able to tell if it was feminine or masculine. "Billie Holiday," he says.

"So . . . this is supposed to be school?" I ask.

He looks surprised. "Yeah. Why?"

"I mean, you guys are just doing whatever you want to do!"

"Don't worry, you'll have plenty of opportunities to break your brain." He continues strumming.

For a few minutes, Tomás and Zachary join in from where they're sitting and they all sing in super spooky falsettos: "*Have you seen the ghost of John? Long white bones and the rest all gone. Ooooooh. Wouldn't it be chilly with no skin on?*"

Zachary laughs uproariously and slaps Tomás on the back.

"So if we can do whatever we want, what do you want to do?" Rachel asks.

I'm afraid to tell her the truth, knowing how she feels about it. "Chess," I say.

"Don't lie to me."

"I want to know more about summoning souls," I mumble.

She snorts.

"I want to be able to protect myself," I say defensively. "I've had some bad experiences."

Her brown-almost-black freckles look exceptionally bright against her white skin. "I've had bad experiences too, which is exactly why I don't want to throw myself into situations where I have to face them again."

"What do you want to do?" I ask.

"Figure out how the hell to get out of here." She sighs. "I was talking to some of the girls last night. They're actually kind of nice, even the scary-looking ones. So I guess as long as I'm stuck here, my first priority is finding out more about my family. What happened to my parents? And if I have a clan out there, why haven't they claimed me?"

"Somebody has to know," I say.

"Yeah, maybe they'll let me talk to one of the Finders."

"But what about after that? Once you know, what then?"

"I'm not sure. Everything else is pretty scary. I don't want to learn how to summon souls. I just want to get back to the real world."

"Maybe this is the real world," I say.

"Yeah, don't say that. Just don't."

Eventually, teachers begin to wander in. Principal Armand surveys the room, then strides over to the table where Zachary is sitting. He bends over to whisper in Zachary's ear. Zachary glances up and looks at Rachel and me before muttering something in response. My ears strain to hear what they're saying but I can't catch a single word.

Aileen saunters in and perches on the edge of the sofa near where I'm sitting. She's wearing jeans, a blue shirt that clings in all the right places, and black boots.

I keep my eyes on her face. On. Her. Face.

"Do you have plans today?" she asks.

Rachel and I look at each other.

"Um . . . I thought we'd be doing school," I say.

Aileen's silvery laugh echoes throughout the living room. "Duh. But do you have an idea what you'd like to learn first?"

We shake our heads.

"I'd like to get you started on a little light reading." She looks over to where Zachary and Tomás are wrangling over the finer points of something I can't even pretend to understand. "Zachary, get your ass over here."

Zachary and Tomás bump fists and Zachary hurries over. "What up?"

"Principal Armand said he'd like you to fill in the gaps in your learning by joining these guys," Aileen explains.

"I know, he told me," Zachary says. "Do I really have to?"

Aileen gives him a look. "It's up to you. Are you coming or not?"

"I'm coming, I'm coming," he grumbles.

She sets a brisk pace while we follow her past the kitchen. Half a dozen cooks are busy poking, tasting, opening ovens, stirring pots. We continue on through a study where the second and third years are bent over books and computers, studying, typing, talking in low voices together. A guy in the corner constructs a minature building of some sort while two girls in the center of the room are playing the tallest, largest game of *Jenga* I've ever seen.

"So I noticed everybody's doing normal things," Rachel says. "When do we start learning all the voodoo and hocus-pocus?"

Aileen throws back her head and laughs as though Rachel meant to be funny. "The only hocus-pocus you'll learn is the kind to avoid. The best soul guides are interested in just about everything. The better you are at math, for example, the better you'll be able to help a math professor navigate Limbo."

If my face looks anything like Rachel's, she's being confronted by two blank stares. Zachary sighs loudly.

"How do you think a math professor sees the underworld?" Aileen asks. "He sees it through the prism of his experience and interests. So to navigate that, you're going to have to see Limbo the way he sees it—as a math problem to solve."

"Really?" For the first time, Rachel looks kind of interested.

"Every soul's journey across the underworld is a problem to solve, a puzzle to put together," Aileen says. "Your job is to be good at solving problems. All kinds of problems. The more curious you are about the world, the more you know, the better you'll be as a soul guide."

I think of my father. Of all the time he spends reading, studying, learning. All those classes he's signed the two of us—or just me—up for. He's interested in so many different things and he's tried to create an environment so that I'll be interested in and exposed to a little bit of everything. He must be one helluva soul guide.

"So what if we really suck at something?" I ask. "Like math."

"Usually when people think they suck at something, it's just that they're not that interested in it," Aileen responds. "Most people's interests can be piqued in just about anything, if presented in the right way, or if they're given the freedom to explore. But rest assured, we probe all first and second years for potential weaknesses. If you truly suck at something, you're unlikely to make it to the third year."

"Oh. So we're expected to know everything in just three years? Know everything and be an expert in everything?"

"Only a newbie would ask that," Zachary chimes in. "Some of us are already experts in everything." He holds a hand up as if to high-five Aileen, but she ignores him.

"Hardly," she says. "The Reaper is a living legend and he'd be the first to admit he's a jack of all trades, master of none. These three years are just the beginning. You'll be learning all your life."

Zachary mumbles something that seems to have the words "shitty" and "Reaper" in it.

"So what you're saying is that we'll have to study the same boring-ass stuff we would study at a regular high school?"

"With one key difference. *You* choose what to study and when. Nobody's going to make you do anything."

"Literally everything we do or learn is a good thing?" Rachel's face is flushed.

"Yup. If you want to learn to cook, we'll make sure you learn to cook. If you want to build a yurt, we'll make sure you have the materials and instructions. There's nothing you learn that isn't useful. In fact, all of you will add chores to your list of things you need to learn. A soul guide cannot be exempt from cleaning toilets or doing laundry."

She opens a narrow doorway. It leads to a curving staircase vanishing into total darkness. She claps her hands and lights turn on. We descend into a huge basement, row after row of books disappearing into the dim darkness. It's like the New York Public Library down here.

"Wow," I say.

"I've never seen so many books anywhere in my entire life," Rachel says.

"Yes, we have quite a collection." Aileen's boots click on the scuffed concrete floor.

"What happens to this library next year?" I ask.

"What do you mean?"

"My dad said that the school changes location every year." I gulp, realizing I just mentioned my dad in front of Rachel and Zachary.

Aileen glances at me, letting me know she noticed my slip-up. "The library goes where the school goes," she says.

"All these books?" I ask. "That must take an army of people."

For the first time since I've known her, Aileen looks severe. "Resources," she says, "are not a problem."

Oh. Nothing like my cash-strapped public school in Brooklyn. I'm not going to lie, the librarian tried hard and she was super nice, but given the collection of books I had available to me in our apartment, tiny as it was, I knew the school's library was super lame.

As we follow Aileen into semidarkened rows, sensors click and lights turn on automatically. "Arms!" she barks, demonstrating how she wants us to hold our arms like baskets.

She begins pulling books off the shelves. Some she

puts in Rachel's arms, some in mine, some in Zachary's. Between the three of us, we must have at least fifty books.

"Why don't you find a comfy spot somewhere in the farmhouse?" Aileen says. "You can read alone if you'd like but I suggest you read them together and talk about what you're learning."

"You call this 'light' reading?" Rachel asks.

Aileen's brow furrows. "What's the problem?"

"Just wondering how many weeks you're giving us."

"Oh, there's no deadline. But I can't imagine you'll need more than a few days."

When she turns her back, Rachel and I giggle at each other and I guess I'm a little too loud because she elbows me to shut up. We stagger up the stairs.

Aileen pauses at the top. "I'll ask the kitchen to send up a snack." She taps her temple. "Brain food. It'll make studying easier."

We find a couch in a hallway that seems fairly isolated from the bustling activity of the kitchen and the classrooms. Strains of music drift out of our classroom, where Gen is clearly still playing the guitar. Somebody else is beating drums. Wish I could join them. It seems like a great way to spend the morning.

I pull the first book off my stack, a plain one with a gold-embossed title sprawling across it: *Demons, Genies, and other Human "Myths."* I sneak a peak at the title Rachel has open: *Real Magick.* Zachary is perusing *Sleepwalkers*.

It doesn't take long before I'm engrossed in my book. I look up only when a cook appears before us with a large plate of cookies and a carafe of coffee arranged on a platter with thick cream and sugar.

"Wow, I'm famished," Rachel says.

"Me too." Zachary gives us a grin. "Studying always does that to me. I go into a library, first thing I do is get hungry, even if I just ate."

We dig in. The cookies are still warm, chocolate chips dripping hot. I lick my fingers.

"You got a little chocolate on your face," Zachary tells Rachel.

"Oh, where?"

He leans forward and dabs chocolate on the tip of her nose. He grins again. "Right there."

"Ha ha." She wipes it off.

I'm looking at Zachary, trying to figure out if that was a dick move or if he was actually just teasing her in a friendly way. Or maybe even flirting.

Each of us makes it through several books before lunch. And I swear, I don't skim.

"Talk about speed reading," Rachel says.

"Yeah, what did they put in those cookies?" I joke.

Then Rachel and I look at the cookies with genuine fear. Or reverence, maybe. In my old life, that would have been a joke. But here, they really might have put something in those cookies that helps us read faster and absorb information easily.

"Dude, they're just cookies," Zachary says. "It's you that's getting through the reading. Because you're *interested* in it."

"What are you guys reading?" Rachel asks.

"I'm reading about ghosts," I say. "Souls that get stuck in Limbo. What happens to them?"

"Some of them just go away on their own," Zachary says. "Others become real problems. They're stuck in Limbo but they become more and more real and create all sorts of trouble. You might think a peace treaty is signed, but a ghost will steal it and then you're right back where you started from. Or an engineer will create plans for a bridge and the ghost will change the plans overnight. Plus, they screw around with people. People can get so messed up—you wouldn't believe how messed up—because of ghosts."

"I'm reading about magic," Rachel says. "Remember Principal Armand said magic isn't for humans? This book claims that soul guides who use magic never recover. It warps their souls. They become total monsters, Hitlers or Stalins, and that's when you see wars or plagues or genocides."

"Ugh," I say. "No magic for me!"

Rachel shudders. "Me neither."

"What's *Sleepwalkers* about?" I ask.

"Sleepwalkers are soul guides who accidentally enter random people's Limbo when they go to sleep. Onset of sleepwalking occurs between twelve and twenty. So any of us could be struck down by this affliction. Well, it's genetic. Runs in certain families. It's an aberration. And completely dangerous. I mean, going to a living person's Limbo? Bad idea. You might not get back out. And what if you bring things there with you and accidentally leave them behind? It can screw up that person's Limbo or even the whole system."

My chest feels like he's hitting it, hard, with a metal

hammer. Is that what I do when I go to sleep? Drop into other people's Limbo? I have a million questions I want to ask but I don't dare. One more secret. As if I don't have enough already.

CHAPTER 17

It surprises me, though I don't know why it would, that a dozen kids plan to go to the mainland to attend church. Sean is one of them.

"Really? Church?" I ask. We're chowing down on the best ceviche I've ever had, laying the lime-coddled fish thick across salty tortilla chips.

"I'm Irish," Sean explains. "I'm as Catholic as they come."

"Yeah, but you're a Dullahan." I search my memory for what I've read about the clan. "You think priests would feel good knowing that people die if you just *say* their name?" I snap my fingers. "And the whole headless horsemen thing. You guys are creepy. I bet the Catholic Church wouldn't think too highly of your chosen, um, profession."

"ADAM JONES," Sean declares, crossing his eyes. He grins. "Time to saddle that old horse."

I know he's joking around but it's hard for me to find death jokes funny. "C'mon, I'm serious. What do you think they'd think?"

He shrugs. "So what. I know more than they do, but it's not like I have all the answers. I still have faith that there's something bigger than us. Than me."

"Think of it as a field trip," Tomás says, coming to my rescue. "You can't separate most people's ideas of death from their religion. You can't escape Rastas on the islands so I study Rastafari."

Sean purses his lips and makes a motion with two fingers like he's smoking a joint. "Yeah, I'll just bet you 'study' Rastafari."

Tomás chuckles.

I groan. "Just when I thought I was getting a handle on things, you add religion to the mix? And smoking pot?"

Of course, Dad took me to a number of bizarre faith-healing, snake-handling, and speaking-in-tongues services as I was growing up. I had a feeling he was raised Catholic but we only went to those somber services once or twice. Despite that, religion feels like an entirely new thing to have to know all about.

To be honest, I think I've done pretty well. I've taken up fencing—something I never thought I'd do—and started learning the piano, under Gen's tutelage. I've made it through the stack of books Aileen gave me and I've read more history than I ever thought I'd learn in my entire life. Last, but not least, Rachel and I literally blew up half the science barn trying some genetic experiments she wanted to do. Just for everyone's general edification, you're supposed to add acid to water—not the other way around.

Fortunately for us, they shrug those things off around here. Tragic accidents? No big deal. As long as we're still alive, it's all good. As long as we learned something . . .

One of the cooks dongs the bell and we all wander into the dining room. Tonight's menu: enchiladas with a spicy tomatillo sauce, chile rellenos, gorditas, cole slaw, Spanish rice, and black beans. Man, they know how to cook here! I hope the school's next incarnation, wherever it is, has the same cooks. Or cooks as good as these.

I pile my plate high and sit down near Sean and Tomás. Rachel sits down next to me. Sean scoots over to give her room.

"Are you going to church tomorrow?" she asks.

"I wasn't planning on it," I say. "I thought I'd relax."

"I want to explore the mainland a little."

It occurs to me that this is a chance to use my cell phone. Maybe I can get a signal on the mainland. Call Sarah. Call Dad.

"Are you still planning to run away?" I ask.

She considers the question carefully. "Noooo," she finally answers. "I don't think so."

I smile at her. "It's better than you thought it would be?"

She shrugs. "Well . . . at least the food's edible."

I burst out laughing.

"No, seriously," she says. "One of my foster moms thought a bag of Doritos was a decent dinner."

It is frigid cold at seven a.m. when we pile into the boat. I think we're going to have the first snowfall soon.

The kitchen packed a basket and everybody's helping themselves to pastries while Zachary grabs the thermos and pours steaming milky-sweet coffee into mugs. We pass them down the line.

I settle into the prow of the boat with my coffee and a lemon-cream pastry that is out of this world. It's good—so very good—to be alive. Even if it is cold, the sun is shining and the air is crisp and everybody behind me is boisterous and carefree. In fact, I wouldn't describe the atmosphere in the boat as exactly churchlike. Invisible balloons and confetti dot the sky above us, people's shadows getting ready for the mainland. I wonder how many of the others will actually go to church. I mean, besides Sean, obviously.

When we get to the mainland, everybody scatters in different directions. Rachel and I walk with Sean to St. Francis of Assisi's.

"Aw, come on, you're really not coming to Mass?" he asks when we stop at the church gate.

"Next time," I say.

He shrugs. "It's your soul in jeopardy."

As we walk away, Rachel whispers, "I think Sean's a true believer."

"Maybe," I say. "Does it matter?"

"No, I just . . ." She trails off. "It's hard to reconcile that with what he's going to be doing for a living."

"You mean the fact that he's going to escort people to the world of the dead?"

"Yeah. Don't you think . . . I mean, there's nothing like that in religion." She rolls her eyes.

"Actually, the Angel of Death is straight out of Scripture," I say. "And you find a similar figure in practically all the major religions." I didn't know any of this crap a couple of months ago. Now, call me an expert in death.

"Yeah, I guess," she says. "I'm so sure the pope would be glad to know one—or more—of his faithful are soul guides."

I've sort of figured out Rachel has a problem with authority. I guess I don't blame her. After all, she's never had parents, and she's been shuffled from one home to the next.

"Maybe he'd be relieved," I say. "To know that God found a way to offer people safe passage to the other side."

"I assumed they would think it's a straight shot from here to heaven or hell," she says. I have this sudden vision of a chute, a large water slide, with dead people hurtling inexorably down toward the afterlife on the other end. "Do you believe in hell?"

I don't know what I believe. I guess I'd like to think that if there's a god—and I suppose I do sort of believe there's a god, even if I'm not sure what he or she is like—then I'd like to know that He had found some sort of solution that was better than hell. Because we all make mistakes, some of us worse than others. Could He possibly figure out a way to help us change and make better choices after we die? I don't mean reincarnation. Or maybe I do, if that's what it takes for a particular soul to grow and change and make the right choices. Maybe some people only need one life. Maybe others need more time to figure things out. The universe is a big place.

Ah, hell, what do I know? I'm just an agent.

"I guess I just think I only know one part of the picture," I reply. "I can't pretend to know more."

We walk downtown, looking for a place to hang out. Seagulls circle overhead. The air is fragrant with the smells of fish and salt and seaweed drying on docks.

Rachel stops outside a café and points out a newspaper with the headline, *Rome Teen Claims He's Human Clone.*

We walk inside and crouch down next to the magazine rack to read the story about a government bust of an underground science lab. They found several teenagers locked in cages—like lab rats. One of the teenagers claimed they had all been cloned approximately fifteen years earlier.

"What are they smoking in Rome?" I say.

"I don't even know what to believe anymore," Rachel says. "The truth about life is turning out to be different than anything I ever thought."

"So who do you think is behind all of this weird stuff in Rome?"

"You haven't been reading the USGNN?"

"What the hell's that?"

"The Underground Soul Guide News Network?" She grins at me.

"Uh . . . no."

Her look is withering. Apparently, I've been falling down in the game. I swear, something about Rachel feels like the sister I never had, the one I'll always fight with but who'll be on my side no matter what.

She leans over and whispers two words: "La Luz."

The sky darkens, sunlight sponged out for a few seconds. *La Luz. The Light.*

My skin breaks out in goose pimples and I feel instantly cold and Rachel and I both start shivering uncontrollably.

"What's La Luz?" I whisper back.

"An immortality cult." Her voice is low. "They've been popping up all over the place lately. Rome. New York. Mexico City. Beijing."

An enormous dunce camp is stuck to my head. How

could I have been so oblivious? "So what are they doing? I mean, what are they trying to accomplish?"

The question lingers in the ocean breeze. Rachel shrugs. "I don't know, exactly. According to ancient legend, La Luz was a city where the Angel of Death wasn't allowed to enter so nobody could die. If La Luz really has the secret to immortality, what would happen if they learned how to go to Limbo? They could put a kink in the whole system. Everybody in the world could become the walking dead."

We put the newspaper back in the rack. I'd like to buy some coffee but I don't have any money so I just inhale the delicious cinnamon coffee smell. I try not to look too conspicuous, but I notice this one huge guy at the counter staring at me as he makes espresso for a customer. A big man, curly mustache, dressed in a plaid shirt. A lumberjack making espresso. That's Maine right there.

Rachel heads outside where she spots a pay phone.

I turn my back on the strange coffeehouse dude and take out my cell phone. Uh-oh. Thirty-eight text messages, dating back to the day I arrived.

I open the first ones from Sarah with a sinking heart. They start out friendly: *Hey! How's the new school?*

And then worried: *Adam, can you just let us know you arrived and that you're okay?*

And then slightly pissed: *Okay, okay, thanks so much for keeping in touch.*

And then they stop.

My other friends have texted too and they are also in a similar vein, though most of them drop off before they get to the pissed stage.

I call my dad first because, well, that's what you do. To be honest, I'm sort of surprised he answers.

"How's school?" he asks.

"Weird."

He laughs uncomfortably.

"It's a good weird," I add.

I look around the coffee shop. Most people are texting on their phones or staring intently at laptops. I glance at the guy making espresso. He glances at me. I hunch over and speak kind of low: "Who am I, Dad?"

"You're my son," he responds automatically.

"No, you know what I mean. What clan do I belong to?"

He sighs. "That's a difficult question to answer."

My heart sinks. "It's the family everyone hates, isn't it?" I don't even want to say the word "Reaper." But in my heart, I know. My dad's the Grim Reaper. And I'm next in line. I imagine myself years from now, all alone in the dim kitchen of our little apartment in Brooklyn, shaky old hands slowly peeling an apple with my giant scythe, black robe hanging from my skeletal frame. Will I get a standard-issue scythe or is it custom-made with my name embossed on the handle?

"Thanksgiving is coming up. I've sent money to Aileen to pay for a train ticket home. We'll talk about it then."

That's such bullshit. I'm so mad, I hang up on him. And then I'm just angry enough that I get the courage to call Sarah.

It rings and rings and then goes to voice mail. Normally, I wouldn't leave a message—I'd text or something, or maybe just let her see that I'd called—but I have to say something. My voice shakes a little as I begin, "Hey, Sarah . . . I'm really sorry I've been AWOL. I don't have Internet access or cell phone reception at the school—it's strange, I know, but it's just the way it is. Listen, Sarah." I pause. Then I pause some more. "I just wanted to let you know I've always liked you. I mean, *like* liked you." Shit. Did I just say that? Now my voice is *really* shaking. "I mean, I understand if you don't feel the same way about me. Especially since I haven't been in touch for so long. I don't expect you to answer. I just wanted you to know. Okay. Bye now."

I have to sit down as soon as I hang up. What the hell did I just do? It came from nowhere and it's too late to undo it. God. My face burns. Who leaves a message like that on a girl's phone? A loser, that's who.

The internal groans quicken, big bullfrogs voicing their displeasure. To ignore my shame, I dial Jeremy. He answers on the third ring, sounds kind of sleepy. "What up, man?"

"Hey," I say. "What are you doing?"

"Sleeping in. A regular Sunday-morning thing for me, if you haven't forgotten."

I glance at the clock on the wall. Oops. Hadn't realized it was only nine.

I choose to ignore the dig about forgetting his habits. It hasn't been *that* long. I've been at school, what, a month? "Yeah, well, sorry I haven't been in touch," I say. "We're out in the boonies. No cell reception. No Internet."

"Oh. Sucks for you."

"Yeah." I swallow around the lump in my throat. I want to ask specifically about Sarah but don't dare. "How is everybody?"

"Dude, it turns out Carlos is some kind of soccer star," he says. "You should see him. He's killing it on the field. They've put him up to varsity and he's only a sophomore."

"Wow."

"You should call Sarah."

My heart skids down an icy trail and smashes into a wall of snow at the end. "Why?"

"I don't know," he says. "Something happened with the two of you at Coney Island . . . She says it changed her forever. I don't know, it's like . . . it's like she's going to church now, except she's not. Like she got religion—but it's not any religion I've ever heard of. I can't explain it. I just—you should call her, that's all. I mean, you were with her, right? You probably know better than any of us what she's talking about."

I look at the phone and wonder if or when Sarah will listen to that voice mail. If I've already been a loser, I might as well be a total loser, right? I send her a quick text:

I'm sorry, Sarah. If you're not too mad . . . Listen. I don't have cell phone or email access during the week. But if you want to talk to me, I can talk any Sunday you want. Some kids come to the mainland for church so I can catch a ride with them. Oh, yeah, we're in Maine. So I'll be at this coffee shop on Main Street in Belfast. 10 a.m. Every Sunday. OK? If you can come, great. If not, I mean . . . I understand. I'm really sorry. I meant what I said in my voice mail. Adam.

When Rachel comes in rubbing her hands, her cheeks red from the cold, the homesickness fades. I wish I could be in Brooklyn but I guess I'm also glad I'm here. This is the world I'm in. Maybe Rachel's right. Once I become immersed in this life, I won't be able to go back to my old life, at least not in the same way. It's not like I can be honest with Sarah or Jeremy about who I am or what I'll be doing with my life. I'm already regretting the text.

"So who'd you call?" I ask.

"None of your beeswax," she says with a grin.

"You have a boyfriend—or a girlfriend—I don't know about?"

"Wouldn't you like to know?"

We both laugh.

"So who'd *you* call?" she asks.

"My dad. Some friends from home."

"And where is home, Adam?"

I shrug, then give her a sheepish look. "I promised my dad I wouldn't tell anybody."

"You mean because then everybody would know what clan you belong to?"

"Yeah. I don't even know my clan but I have my suspicions. What about you? Do you ever think you'll find out what family you belong to?"

Her eyes are large in her delicate face. "I hope so. It's the only thing I want. To have a family. I mean, why haven't they claimed me?"

"The Finders haven't told you," I point out. "Maybe they haven't told the clan either."

"Maybe. But why not?"

She has such a lonely, longing look on her face that I just sling my arm around her shoulder and say, spontaneously, "Hey, Rach, it's okay. We'll create a new clan. You and me. The Smith-Jones Clan. With, I don't know, a legless grasshopper for our mythic figure. The legless grasshopper that prefigures death. It'll scare the hell out of people."

"Ha." She puts her arm around my waist and squeezes so I know she appreciates the gesture.

On the boat ride home, just before we reach the spot where cell phone service cuts out, I get a text from Sarah:

> *Me too. I've always* like *liked you too, Adam. I'm sorry I got mad. I'll try to come some Sunday really soon. OK? I'll text to let you know when. Hope you get this. xo*

My face burns. She likes me too. *xo. xo!* My face breaks out in a grin and I look at Rachel and I just want to hug her, hug her hard, but of course I don't. I peer out over the ocean water instead. I'd text Sarah back but my cell phone signal cuts out at exactly that moment.

That's okay. Let's leave it as it is. *She likes me! xo!*

Maybe I can convince Tomás and Sean to steal a boat again, row out just far enough to get a cell phone signal, so I can text Sarah back. Something sweet. *She likes me!*

Sean catches my eye from the other side of the boat. Two seconds later, a football is sailing over the heads of everybody on board. I catch it with a flourish and throw it back. It feels like I'm the one sailing over everybody's heads. It feels like I could sail around the world.

CHAPTER 18

A few weeks later, Sofia and Gabe La Muerte invite everybody to join them in the barn after dinner to celebrate Día de los Muertos. We're supposed to bring pictures of loved ones who've crossed to the other side, along with their favorite food or drink or things that remind us of them.

I don't even remember my mother, of course, but she's the only person I know who's died.

I think about my dream with the woman in the yellow dress riding on the train. I ask Aileen for help locating a toy train and a piece of yellow fabric. I might be mourning my mother or I might be mourning an imaginary woman who haunts my dreams, but it's all I've got.

It's still better than what Rachel has.

"Are you going to come?" I ask her.

"I won't make an altar—I don't have anybody to remember—but I'll help you make yours."

"Thanks," I say. Then: "It's for my mother. I don't really remember her. She died when I was four or five. But—I miss her. At least, I miss the idea of her. I think about her all the time."

"I think about mine all the time too. And I never knew her." Rachel is not the sort of person to invite pity. But still, I feel for her.

We stack wooden benches and tables around the circumference of the room to clear a space in the middle, leaving two tables in the center. Sophia drapes each table in bright pink–and-green Mexican blankets. In the corner of one table, she places a large candy skull, a bouquet of orange flowers, and a plate with a tamale and Spanish rice on it. She arranges pictures around it—an icon of the Virgin of Guadalupe and a framed photo of an elderly woman. She hangs a rosary off the picture frame and lights a candle in front of it. Then she carefully pours a shot of amber-colored tequila and places it next to the candle.

"This is my little grandmother," she says. "Abuelita. She died five years ago. I miss her."

I'm surprised to see that most of the school is there, students and teachers, though the Angels are conspicuously absent. People claim spots on the two tables. Before long, we've created a bizarre pattern of pictures and miscellaneous items across their surfaces. People pour libations of various kinds in mugs and goblets and shot glasses. Pink, blue, and yellow sugar skulls dot the tables.

"Where did you get these skulls?" I ask Sophia when she passes by.

"Oh, I asked the kitchen staff to create them," she says. "Aren't they great? Very traditional, just like we do in Mexico." She holds out a short candle. "Would you like one?"

I take it. "Thanks."

"Who's your altar for?" she asks.

"My mother. I don't remember her."

She smiles. "You can honor your ancestors even if you've never met them."

What does it mean to mourn somebody you never really knew, or at least as much as any four-year-old can know their parent? What was it like for my mother to die, knowing she would never see who I would become? Would the pain of that lead somebody to cling to life and make it harder for them to move across Limbo to the other side? I think it would. I imagine my mother tried to resist. I imagine she tried to stay. To be with me.

Or maybe that's just wishful thinking, because I want to believe my mother would rather have been with me than to die. But then, I'm more scared of death than anybody I know.

I look around at the altars other people are constructing. My toy train and piece of yellow cloth look meager compared to the things others have brought. Tomás has created an elaborate altar to his great-grandfather, which includes a spiced rum drink, rum-soaked raisins, and a bottle of rum. "My pop-pop liked rum," he says.

Gabe stands at the front of one of the tables and clears his throat. The buzz dies down. "Normally," he says, "this is done at our loved ones' graveyards."

He holds a large bowl of bread and a bottle of tequila. "This is *pan de los muertos*," he says. "Bread for the dead. I'll pass it around and everybody who wishes to take some can. And tequila if you wish to drink for your loved one."

I take one of the sugary rolls. Rachel does the same. She grabs two shot glasses and pours them to the brim with tequila.

We all light the candles in front of our altars.

Somebody turns off the lights and we all stand in shadowy darkness. Even in the candlelight, I can see other people's eyes rimmed red. Principal Armand, standing all the way on the other side of the table from me, wipes his eyes with his sleeves.

Maybe it shouldn't but it surprises me, I guess, to see grief here, among soul guides. And seeing Principal Armand openly crying makes him seem a little more human. Though after seeing him as a child, locked in the shed . . . huddled against the pile of wood . . . honestly, that made him altogether human.

Suddenly, I feel funny. Woozy, even, though I haven't touched that tequila yet. The room starts to fade and it's not just the candlelight. A flicker of a face. The woman on the train. I feel—

Rachel grabs my elbow. "Steady there, cowboy," she whispers.

"Thanks," I whisper back. "I almost fainted." I look at her and something about her face is . . . familiar. The freckles. She and the woman on the train suddenly seem like the same person and I'm overwhelmed with a desire to hug her. No, a *need*. Like she *is* the woman on the train. Like she *is* my mother. I put my arms around her.

She pats me awkwardly on the back. "What is this for?"

"I don't know. I'm glad you're my friend."

She extricates herself from my embrace and elbows me. "Don't say things like that too often, people will think you're going soft." But I can tell from her smile that she's glad we're friends too.

Gabe starts chanting in Spanish. The words are similar to Italian so I understand just enough to know he's saying a prayer for the dead.

People hold their libations high. I carefully take the shot of tequila in hand and Rachel does the same. A few drops spill on the piece of yellow cloth.

It burns all the way down my throat, past where I thought my throat ended and into my chest. The burning is a kind of relief. At least I feel something where the ache of my mother's absence should be.

I begin to cough and Rachel pounds my back.

"Lightweight," Sean whispers loudly from across the table, and everybody around us giggles.

CHAPTER 19

I guess life seems charmed for a while. Long enough that I even start to sleep and I don't end up in the cemetery. I have no more episodes. Everything is just peachy.

It doesn't last long, of course. I get a bad feeling one night after dinner on my way to the barn. It comes and goes quickly, the clenching of the stomach, and I hurry to reach the light pooling out onto the porch.

Inside, evening festivities are already in progress. Tomás and his cousin Agwe are playing darts in the corner, and Zachary and Emily are playing pool. When I walk in, Zachary looks up and says, "Just the man I was looking for! I was telling Emily here that we can demolish you and Sean at a game of pool. You in?"

Sean shrugs so I say, "Okay."

As I take up the cue stick, I look back outside. I could swear I see a black shadow passing across the moon but it's gone before I can even blink.

I stay up with the last of the revelers, playing pool until the girls have gone home and Sean's fallen asleep on the sofa, his mouth open, snoring gently. Tomás puts a finger to his lips, then uses two fingers to pinch Sean's nose shut.

Sean snorts and his eyes fly open. "You. Guys. Are. Not. Funny." He stomps off to his room as Tomás and I howl behind him.

Then I head to my room and the black Thing I've been trying to ignore begins to press against my thoughts again. I open and close my door quickly, locking it, as if that could keep Her away.

I brush my teeth and lie down on the bed, leaving the light on. Panic oozes in around the edges, yellow, slick, and ugly. I try to calm down, breathing deep, following the techniques they taught me in meditation class. *One. Two. Three. Breathe.*

Dark clouds and the cemetery flash before my eyes and then . . . And then a young woman with dark eyes and long, curly black hair cascading down her back stares at me across a meadow surrounded by snowcapped mountains. The sun and the blue skies are startlingly bright. A Spanish-style hacienda in the distance. An adobe, like the kind you see in New Mexico. She's holding a horse by the mane. When she sees me, she pats the horse on the rump and it runs away. She advances toward me, slow, keeping her eyes on me all the way. Her shadow is like that horse, skittish and ready to run.

Wouldn't it be amazing if this could be my nightly dream? Then I'd be taking Ambien every day and night, instead of popping caffeine pills. Could this girl be real? I sure hope so.

"Who the hell are you?" she calls. "You're not supposed to be here. This is my—"

Her words are cut off midsentence, her mouth a perfect round O. My stomach drops about a million floors as the familiar rotten-vegetable smell reaches me. I whirl around to see wisps of black smoke spinning around Her fish-white face as She floats toward us. The vast blue skies of this world suddenly collapse into low-lying clouds and mists of heavy rain across a blackened sky.

I turn back around to the beautiful girl. She looks like she's ready to fight but her shadow is about to get the hell out of here.

"You should leave," I say, my voice shaky. "It's dangerous."

She glares at me. "Fuck no," she declares. "This is *my* Limbo. I belong here. You and that Thing—whatever it is—don't. I'm going nowhere. But you? You and that Thing? Get out. Get out now."

Suddenly, I'm back in my room, sitting straight up. *What was that?*

I start taking deep breaths to calm myself. Was that girl real? Was she really so amazing that she expelled me from her Limbo? I hope She left too. I hope the girl wasn't left alone facing Her.

I get up and decide to go back downstairs. Somebody's bound to be awake and I can hang out and hold onto this lovely feeling, the face of the girl, her indomitable spirit, the way she controlled everything in her space.

Out in the hall everything is quiet. The moon is shining in through the loft window, the one I climbed out of. It's irrational but I start thinking that if I got out of that window, She might be able to get in. The chair's still sitting there so I climb on it, jump, and grab the windowsill, pulling myself up to see if I can lock it. I hear a loud bang right before the window slams open, hitting my face.

I jump backward, tumbling off the chair.

A foot appears in the window, followed by a pair of

legs, and then a head with long, dark hair. A girl. Not one of the other students. She balances on the edge of the windowsill and looks down at me. "Are you going to help me down from here or what?"

I recognize her immediately. Golden-brown skin. Dark, curly hair. A gold ring in her nose. Her shadow a band of wild horses swimming across a rushing river.

It's the girl. The one I just saw. The one who kicked me—and hopefully Her—out of her Limbo.

I see the shock of recognition in her eyes too. And then a sudden decision, resolve. She grabs the top of the windowsill and pulls herself inside.

How in the world did she do that? I mean, that window is super high off the ground. No way she came that way. And having used it to climb onto the roof, I can't imagine reversing that journey.

I must be staring because she stares back until I look away. "I need to hide," she whispers.

We slip inside my room and I close the door behind us.

"Sorry to barge in on you." She slings a backpack onto the floor and collapses on the desk chair. "I'm Liliana. Liliana La Muerte."

"You're Liliana?" I blurt like an idiot. No wonder Sean's been crushing on her since she was twelve. "What are you doing here? I thought you were expelled."

"Yeah? So?" She stares at me, long and hard, until I drop my eyes and look at the floor. It's wooden. The floor, I mean. "Who are you?"

"Adam."

"Okay, Adam. Thank you for letting me into your room."

I finally get enough courage to look at her again. Her shadow prances around the room, nervous about being cooped up.

"I'm sopping wet. Can I use your bathroom, dry up, maybe sleep on the floor?"

"Sure?" I don't mean for it to come out as a question. I just—I can't believe she's here.

"And yes, I was expelled. But it wasn't my fault. I passed my Limbo test." Her eyes bore into mine. "Somebody's lying. Somebody doesn't want me to become a soul guide. Probably lots of people. I'm not exactly welcomed by all soul guides. Bastard child, you know. Unclaimed by my paternal family. So, nothing I'm not used to, but I never expected dirty play here at the school."

"Really? You've felt like an outsider all your life and you thought things would be different here at school?"

"Youthful idealism," she says. "Stupid of me, I know."

"So who are you hiding from?"

She sighs loudly. "Everybody. But specifically, tonight, at this exact moment, I'm hiding from that dangerous Thing that somebody let loose on the island." She keeps staring at me.

"What dangerous Thing?" I swallow the confession. It tastes sour around the edges.

"You tell me. I was sleeping in the boathouse—that's where I'm hiding out while I figure out how to prove I'm right about corruption here—when that Thing showed up. A dark spirit of some kind. So I decided to make myself scarce. I'm going to impose on your hospitality until it goes away, okay?"

My tongue cleaves to the roof of my mouth. "That Thing is probably coming here, to my room," I confess. Only it comes out as, "What if they check our rooms?"

"What, you going to narc on me?" Her look has enough venom to poison the heartiest of souls.

My heart bottoms out in my stomach. "I'm not a narc. I was just asking."

She leans forward, legs spread slightly, one hand on each knee. "Well, stop asking then."

I peer into her beautiful brown eyes, gold-flecked, and even though it's clear she doesn't trust me, not one tiny bit, I can see all the warmth and humor that sparkle somewhere back in there, deep, deep inside, and I think I fall in love with her a little bit, maybe. Can she hear the beating of my heart? Drumbeats on the wind. "I wouldn't narc," I say. "No matter what."

She yawns. "I know. You're not the narc type." This girl can flip a switch so fast, it'd make me tired if I wasn't already exhausted. "Listen? Mind if I use *el baño?*"

I fidget while she uses the bathroom. She comes out wearing these pink flannel pajama bottoms and a hoodie on top. I can't help noticing how cute she looks in them.

"Dibs on the floor." She unrolls a Therm-a-Rest. There's just enough space for her to sleep, her head at the desk, her feet at the bathroom door.

I give her an extra blanket, turn the lights out, and slide into bed.

We're silent for a little while. I wonder what would happen if they did a surprise check tonight. I imagine trying to explain Liliana's presence. Wide-eyed innocence.

Girl? What girl? Oh, that girl. You mean we can't have random girls spend the night? I thought that was how things happened here, strange girls popping in to sleep on the floor. How should I know better? I don't even know what clan I'm from. She was expelled? You don't say.

She speaks in the darkness: "So, listen? How'd you get into my Limbo?"

The little panic demon starts pummeling my heart again. She's going to figure out who I am. She's going to figure out what's wrong with me.

"I know you know what I'm talking about. You came to my Limbo. The mountains? The horse? The blue skies? How'd you get there? You're not supposed to go to somebody's Limbo unless they're dying and . . . I sure hope I'm not dying—unless you know something I don't. So don't lie to me. Am I dying?"

"Noooooo," I say.

"Then how'd you do it?"

"I don't know. It surprised me too. I just went to sleep and there I was . . ."

"Hey! You're a sleepwalker! That's dangerous!"

I reach down and grab her arm. "Please don't tell anybody."

"Ow. Let go."

I release her quick.

She rubs her arm. "I'm not going to tell anybody, asshole, okay?"

"Thanks."

"But." She settles back comfortably on her bedroll. "Maybe this is a skill we can use. Maybe you can help me prove I should still be here, in school. If you can get into other people's Limbos—"

"No way. I am not volunteering to go into other people's Limbos."

"I have some time to work you over." She yawns again and rolls over. "Look, maybe it's stupid, but I trust you're not going to kill me. So good night."

I lie in bed, staring at the ceiling, glancing from time to time at the beautiful girl sleeping peacefully on my floor.

Despite all efforts to prevent it, I fall asleep. When I wake up, I'm following Dad's long legs through the cemetery.

Feeling lightheaded, I do what I always do: trudge after my father. Wisps of black smoke curl around the grave and Dad shoves me behind him, muttering.

The figure dressed in rags turns her head toward me, burnt holes where she should have eyes and a mouth. Throws back Her head. Cackles hollowly.

Dad picks me up and starts running through the cemetery, graves whipping past us as She slithers in the air behind us, in hot pursuit, blackened arms reaching out for my shadow.

And then I'm falling in darkness. I slam hard into Her. Her serpentine body coils around mine, cool scales leaving a slimy residue. She begins to glow in the dark, Her mouth close to mine, stretching upward in a toothless grin.

"Adam!" The whisper is loud and harsh, fingers gripping me painfully in the darkness. "Wherever you are, get back to the here and now. Now."

I jerk to, cold and oily, covered in Her slime. Liliana's

huddled beside me, holding me upright. When she takes her hand away, she wipes it on a towel, leaving a smear of something shiny and gross on it.

"Somebody's trying to get in your room," Liliana whispers. "I'm going to hide in the bathroom."

I stagger over to the door. The hallway is empty. But just as I go to close it, something cold and dark slithers past me into the room.

"Adam!" Liliana yells from inside the bathroom. "Get out!"

We run out to the hall, slamming the door behind us. We slide to the floor, backs against the door. The doorknob rattles.

"Okay, let's make a run for it," she whispers. "On the count of three."

"Don't count out loud. In case She can hear us."

"She? That Thing is a *She?*" Her shadow rears up like a cobra, tongue flicking, ready to strike. "Apparently, She is following you around. I knew from the moment I saw you, I shouldn't trust you."

"Could've guessed that," I hiss, "from the way you were snoring peacefully on the floor of my bedroom."

"Shut it." She holds up a finger. *One.* We crouch into a kneeling position, backs still holding the door.

Two. The door feels like an icicle on my back. Who said hell was hot? They obviously never met my personal wraith.

Liliana grabs my hand. She jerks her head to the left, toward the back stairs and a door at the bottom, to indicate the direction we're going.

Three. We scramble down the hall, Liliana pulling me behind her.

My door bangs open, swings off its hinges. I look back for one second and out of the corner of my eye, I see Her, face bone-white. Fists clenched.

I run to the top of the stairs and glance back again. The hall looks empty now. Even though it isn't.

We jump down the stairs, two at a time. Doors crash open, and a cacophony of voices soars above the pounding of my heart. "Hey!" Zachary yells from somewhere. "Who's making all the racket? It's five effin a.m. Shut up!"

We slam into the door below. Liliana fumbles it open and we run outside. We duck into a small open space under the barn and crouch there, waiting. Listening to the other person breathe. I'm not sure exactly what we're waiting for or how we'll know when She leaves.

Let's just say you think someone, or several someones, including maybe something supernatural, is trying to kill you, what makes the most amount of sense—to stay holed up in your room and never come out again or decide you're never going back to your room?

I choose option B. I just don't know how I'm going to accomplish it.

By the time our invisible stalker stops Her heavy breathing and sniffing around looking for us, my muscles are cramped from being in the same position too long. Liliana groans as she stretches.

"So what the hell is that?" she asks.

"I don't know," I say. "But She's everywhere I go."

"You mean She followed you here? To the school?"

I shrug, trying to remain cool, like, *Oh, it's no big deal.* The effect is spoiled by the tears that spurt up in the corners of my eyes, tears that dry up almost instantly by her follow-up question.

"Who *are* you? What did you do?"

"I don't know," I say, stung into defending myself. "I also don't know why some people in this world apparently want to kill me, but they do."

My shoulders sag with the weight of what I just revealed. Crappity crap crap. My big freakin' mouth.

"I just want to be safe," I say.

Liliana shakes her head then leans over and socks me on the shoulder. Hard. "I've got news for you. There's no such thing as 'safe' in this life. What do you think you're going to be doing, kissing boo-boos and wiping runny noses? This is a hardscrabble, hooch-drinking, bootlegging type of life. Got it?"

"Does this mean I can't camp out with you in the boathouse?" I ask.

We hear voices from the main room downstairs and then somebody comes out onto the porch in the darkness and lights a pipe.

She pushes me toward the barn door and hisses, "Get out of here and don't tell anybody you saw me or you'll regret it. Believe me."

I do believe her. "Will I see you again?"

She crosses her eyes, which is totally . . . adorable. "Yeah. I've got my eye on you."

I watch as she disappears around the corner of the barn, and I feel lost and alone and . . . lonely.

And I still don't want to go back to my room. I sniff my pits. Uck. Nope, don't want to go back. Not even to take a shower.

But of course I do. Because nothing seems as scary during the light of day as it does at night, and also because I'm already That Kid—the one who doesn't know anything—and I can't be That Kid Who Stinks Because He Doesn't Shower, too.

CHAPTER 20

The soul already resides in Limbo, though it can be difficult for the spirit to untangle itself from life to see the world around the soul. To reach Limbo, soul guides must pull their consciousness there . . . When directing a soul through Limbo, soul guides must help construct a world that the soul's spirit understands.
—From *The World of Limbo*

I wish I knew exactly why Zachary keeps hanging around us. He doesn't need a refresher, that's for sure. It feels like he's spying, not that there's much to spy on.

This morning he greets me with a cheery, "You look like death warmed over, pretty boy. Having trouble sleeping?"

Okay, yeah, I'm back to not sleeping.

Rachel and I are sitting on a porch swing, trying to get through a few more books by the end of the week, while Zachary is attempting to balance on the fence that surrounds the farm. The air borders on frigid, but it's nice to be outside anyway.

"Looks like you're working real hard, training to be the best soul guide you can be," Rachel calls out. "It's giving me a whole new understanding of the phrase 'dead beat.'"

He jumps off the fence and wanders up to the porch, squatting down in front of us and chewing on a blade of dried grass. He grins at Rachel. "You have a lot of sass. I like that in a woman."

"Are you leering at me?" Rachel replies. "Because if you think for even a minute that I'd—"

"Oh, keep your panties on," Zachary interrupts. "I was just appreciating your style. So . . . who's in?"

"Who's in for what?" Rachel's mouth is puckered.

He sighs loudly. "Going to Limbo. Bet you Adam's too chicken."

He's right. Little chicken feathers sprout all over my back and arms. I rub my arms to get rid of the feeling.

"I didn't even know Limbo existed until a couple months ago," Rachel says, "much less how to get there."

"It's a cinch," he says. "We can go and be back in less than ten minutes. That is, if you're not too afraid."

"Have you ever been there?" I ask.

"A few times," he says nonchalantly.

"What's it like?" Rachel asks.

"It's different for everybody."

"If we all go, whose version of Limbo will we be in?" I ask.

"Mine, of course," Zachary says, his shadow gliding around us like an ice skater sailing across ice, smooth and confident. "Look, you guys have never been to Limbo and my version is already quite strong for my age. Only someone with a much more developed Limbo could override mine." He snickers. "I gave one of the teachers quite a surprise a few weeks ago when they took me to Limbo, expecting their comfortable snoozer of a Limbo, and we ended up in mine."

"What's your version of Limbo like?" Rachel asks.

"It's a rush. A carnival ride of happiness! It's impossible not to love my Limbo! If you like, once we've reached it, I can help you start creating your own version. C'mon! It'll be fun."

Rachel shakes her head. "No thanks. You're asking for trouble."

Zachary makes a face at her. "Well, party poopers can just stay here. How's that sound?"

"Fine, count me out," Rachel says.

"And how about you, chicken boy?" Zachary tucks his hands in his armpits and flaps his arms like chicken wings, elbowing me at the same time.

"OW, get your elbow out of my ribs."

"*Bawk, bawk,* you little chicken," he says.

"Did your mom drop you on your head too many times when you were little?" Rachel snaps.

Zachary puts one hand around her wrist. She shakes him off immediately. "You're cute when you're trying to protect your little friend," he says.

Somehow I know the gauntlet has just been thrown down. Even dancing around like a scared little chicken, Zachary's looking me straight in the eye. This is a challenge. Something more than double-dare. A game of chicken, ha. Zachary wants me to back out and lose face . . . or, better yet, accept the challenge and get humiliated.

The void of my dreams stretches out below me to infinity . . . And there She looms, winking ghoulishly at me. No. He can bluster all he wants. I *am* too chicken to find myself in the nightmare with Zachary.

"Look, Zach, you're right. We would have a blast in your world but it seems a little dangerous to me."

His lips twitch. "I've heard a rumor you think you're pretty hot stuff. Even, maybe, some sort of savant when it comes to soul work. But what I've heard is you're more like one of those *idiot* savants. I may have to hang around you newbies but I've got skills too." His shadow spits venom at us.

I glare at him.

"You're just a scaredy-cat who acts tough around the teachers. I know the real guy. The Adam who can't even pee without someone helping him unzip."

And there it is. I could ignore the verbal abuse. But Zachary is summoning up my soul. Or trying. He has some pull but he's completely weak compared to my dad.

I look at him with contempt. Blood finally boiling. Who does Zachary Angel think he is?

I lash out, vice-grip claws clutching at Zachary's soul, pulling it up to look at it, to gaze at his tiny, tiny black soul. Everything he is, laid out before me, a small nugget burnt at the edges: the fear, hurt, and anger he's feeling because I took his place as the gifted student.

He's in way over his head. I should stop, but I'm too mad. I reach out to grab that nugget, to twist it around and expose it. Make him pay.

I grab but something's not right. Shit! I've made the same mistake Principal Armand made with me and I've fallen into Zachary's trap. He has me in his grip and it's unbreakable . . .

Everything goes black. For a split second, I hear the

sound of the ocean and catch a glimpse of swirling neon lights. Then it is all sucked away into the hole I know I'm going to fall into forever.

Everything plummets away.

My heart speeds up and drops. Panic slams into me.

I'm floundering through pitch blackness. No stars, no light, just a black hole. Falling and falling.

Yup. This is my Limbo. And apparently, Zachary's version of Limbo is not stronger than mine, whatever he wants to think.

And then I feel it. Something cold and wet slithering past.

She's here.

She squirms close, lips pulled up in a grin, eyes closed. Not too old, not too young. The irises ignite in blue flame. She has the soul of a human—a female—but the body is dark leathery wings and long skeletal limbs and blue, blue flame.

I sense another presence, a small light, but it's weak and frail and every time it tries to get close, my soul grabs but She's faster and reaches it with sickening speed. Her talons prick the small light. It sputters in the sickening darkness. Zachary. I need to get him out of here before She kills him.

I leap in front of Zachary's light.

Her spiked tail snakes up from behind and whacks me. Blood spurts from the wound She gashes in my back.

She bites and tears at me with bony fingers.

I punch and flail. She wraps her tail around me and pins my arms to my side, facing me, mouth opening, opening, a gray vacuum sucking me toward her.

I don't want to die.

She whips her tail around me like a rope. Three times. Four times.

God, I don't want to die.

Please don't let me die.

Please.

Silence. Darkness.

Part of me wants to let go. Relieve myself of the crushing fear. The other half is too afraid for what will come. After.

God. Please.

I think I'm praying.

Please.

I want to live.

Then I feel a light. A strong light. Warm on my skin, like a small ray of sunlight or an extra-hot lightbulb.

"Dad?" I say into the darkness.

I thrash as the beast flinches and recoils away from the light.

A second light floats toward me. Something grabs my legs, even as the beast screams and squeezes me tighter, clutching me to its slimy chest.

I choke and gasp as the world closes to a small pinpoint of light and then even that is snuffed out.

I wake.

Still falling and falling, but the lights are with me this time.

My head hurts so bad. My arms and legs tingle. My body feels bruised, like somebody used me as a punching bag but somehow left no marks, and my clothes drip and ooze with slime or maybe, yuck, saliva.

Somebody hovers nearby. I open my eyes, expecting to see Dad.

"Can you move?" It's Aileen. She's leaning over me but doesn't touch me. Jacob is standing just behind her, his campy grin replaced by a grim smile.

I sit up slowly, realizing I'm on the porch near the swing, only somehow it's been ripped off its hinges. Deep gouges mar the blood-smeared wall. Zachary is sitting a few feet away, face in his hands. When he looks up, he's so pale, I'm worried he's going to faint. Rachel's beside him, her mouth open.

"Are you okay?" I ask first because I want to make sure She hasn't hurt him.

Zachary looks contrite but his shadow contorts into something resembling half fear, half sneer.

That's it for me. "You asshole!" I shout, wincing at the pain. "You did this to me," I add in a quieter tone.

Aileen touches my forehead. "You're burning up, Adam. You need to go to bed."

"No!" I try to shout, but my head hurts so much, it comes out as a loud groan. I don't want to go to my room, I try to avoid that place as much as possible, but of course they don't know that. "I want to know what happened to me. Did I make it to Limbo?"

"You made it to Limbo all right." She looks sympathetic. "But you've been there before. Did you ever have a near death experience?"

"Not that I know of," I fib, thinking of all those nights

when I wake up in the cemetery. "Okay, maybe," I say. My voice sounds faint and far away.

"Dude, I thought we were going to lose you." Zachary's face sags. "I thought you were going to die in there."

"Was that your plan?" I ask. "To get me to Limbo and try to kill me?" I wonder what happens if you die in Limbo. It can't be a good thing.

"No, man, I—" He swallows whatever he was going to say. But then his shadow giggles at me, nervous or maybe just bold, I'm not sure.

Aileen and Jacob don't seem to notice, probably because they're staring at me so intently.

I glare at him. "How did you guys get here?" I ask them.

"I fetched them," Rachel says.

"If she hadn't come to get us, one or both of you might not have made it out of there alive," Aileen says.

"You have a very strong Limbo, Adam," Jacob says. "When you go there, you're somehow attached to a demon or a fairy of some kind. Maybe a ghost?"

"I've heard of this," Aileen says. "But I've never seen it. What happened to you hasn't happened in generations. No wonder your dad didn't want you to go to school. He must know about this."

Zachary perks up a little at the mention of my dad, though maybe I'm imagining things because all he says is, "I'm sorry. I'm sorry I dragged you there." He looks at Jacob and Aileen and swallows. "I really mean it. I had no idea."

"We should probably tell Principal Armand about this," Aileen says slowly. She doesn't look thrilled at the prospect.

"Do it," I say. Little angry ghosts squeeze their way

through the spaces between my clenched teeth. "Make sure Principal Armand throws the book at him."

"Dude," Zachary says. "I'm sorry. I'm . . ."

I don't want to hear it. I turn away.

Aileen and Jacob glance at each other.

Zachary looks crestfallen. "It's okay. You should tell him. I deserve to be expelled for this." But even as he says this, his shadow creeps over and peeks at me from behind him, grinning and winking at me. You have got to be kidding me. Doesn't anybody else notice this?

One look at the rest of them and I can tell the answer is no.

Jacob clears his throat. "Adam, it may not be in your best interests for Principal Armand to know about this. Zachary's not the only one who will get in trouble. And you're already on his bad side."

"But I will talk to your dad, Adam," Aileen says. Her eyes are sad. "He needs to know this happened."

"I'm not going to lie to you, Adam," Jacob says. "I'm not sure you should ever go to Limbo again."

"Why not?" I have to clear my throat to get the words out.

"Every time you go, Adam, it will get worse," Aileen says. "Unless you can conquer the bond you have with that demon. Your experience of Limbo is so strong, I don't know if you'll be able to overcome it to see Limbo from another soul's perspective. That's essential, if you're going to be a soul guide. And besides, you could get killed in there. That demon is looking for you."

For a moment, I feel relieved. Never returning to Limbo

means never having to face Her again. But the relief is quickly followed by a crushing disappointment. Something about being here—in this school, with these people—feels right. I have never felt like I belonged somewhere more than I do here.

And besides, I *have* been to other people's Limbo. I went to Principal Armand's Limbo. I've been to Liliana's. Maybe to my mother's, if she's the woman in the yellow dress on the endless train. I'm pretty sure I started to go to Zachary's Limbo before I got sucked back into the darkness of my own.

If I can help people make it across Limbo safely, in a way that they don't have to experience something like that . . . that Thing that I have to face when I go to Limbo . . .

We lose so much when we die. To have all of that taken away, like my mother was removed from me, and have no one to help us to the next life?

I stare at the Broken Circle symbols tattooed on Jacob's hand. That's how you get people out of Limbo—you break the circle and let them drift out, out, out to the next world or whatever is beyond. We need help to do this. We can try to do it on our own but we're helpless. I want to be the help.

And maybe people don't really have to die. If I can be a soul guide, maybe I can bring those people back. Maybe I can help people live. Maybe . . . maybe I can bring my mother back.

Staring at that symbol, I realize that, even though Aileen and Jacob have just told me that I might not be able to be a soul guide, it's what I want more than anything in my life.

CHAPTER 20.5

And so the two lovers were ecstatic with their new life together. And they had big plans for uniting the warring clans of the new world, who were kept from civil war by only the thinnest of agreements made after our country's Great War, the war between the States. They wanted to see the fragile agreement transformed into a true democracy. Oh, those two, they had plans.

But the plans were interrupted.

Never have you seen a more besotted pair than those parents with their child. He was not a beautiful child. He had his father's big ears and grim smile (ironic, since his father was a Mors and not a Reaper at all), but the Mors have never been known for their looks. The boy had the same thin, skeletal body, and pale, pasty skin. Nothing like the beautiful mother with her lusty complexion, her head of rich red hair—

I thought she had auburn hair, Elder #2 said.

She did, he said. Sometimes!

She had red hair when *I* met her, Her Excellency

said. That's probably why my son lost his head. I never met my grandson. So the child did not take after your daughter?

Not in looks, no, he said. And he was sickly from the beginning. But they loved him. Then came the real disaster.

CHAPTER 21

I'm done with Zachary. The next day after breakfast, during which he weirdly keeps falling asleep at the lunch table where he's sitting with the other Angels, he follows us out to the bench under the big maple tree, a new study spot since we sort of don't want to go to the porch anymore. At least I don't. I know the staff has already cleaned it and not a single trace of my blood remains, but still, I just can't.

I face him, fists clenched. "Go play with yourself, Zachary."

"Adam, look . . ." he begins, and I think maybe he's going to try to apologize again, but I don't want to hear it because I don't believe it, not for one instant. He totally meant to do that to me yesterday and I was just lucky he didn't succeed. His shadow lurks behind him, hiding from me. Probably trying to hide the grin on its face. Fuck that. Fuck him.

"Shut up," I cut him off. "You had your fun, hanging around with the lost kids, probably making fun of us behind our backs. Now get out."

"Dude, I never made fun of you," he says. "I feel really bad—"

"Just get lost."

Rachel chimes in: "You almost killed him, Zachary. Just leave him alone." I shoot her a grateful glance. She acknowledges it with a quick nod.

"I could really help you," Zachary says. "You shouldn't just dismiss me like this."

"I'm better off without your help." I jump swiftly behind him just in time to catch a fleeting glimpse of his shadow as it runs to hide. A sneer on its ugly little face.

Zachary startles, though, and grips my wrist. "What are you doing?"

"I'm looking at your ugly little soul." I grit my teeth.

For just a second, his face is a windshield wiper clearing off a deluge of rainwater before the downpour returns, and I see something—hurt, maybe? Then it's immediately gone. He starts giggling, high-pitched, either nervous or hysterical.

"Shut up," I say. "What's so funny?"

"Nothing." But he can't stop giggling. "What do you know? Nothing, Lost Boy, absolutely nothing."

What do I know? My mind races through all the classes I took last year. World history, English, math, sex ed. "I know how to put condoms on carrots," I say.

Rachel snickers and I grin at her, glad she gets my sense of humor, but it's a mistake because Zachary takes the opportunity to attack, the back of his hand smacking me hard in the face, knocking my head back, a gush of blood pouring down my nose. The salty, rusty taste of blood down my throat.

I react instantly and the next thing I know, we're grappling, rolling on the lawn, his hand in the small of my back, my fingers hooked around his neck, ready to wrench his head off.

But Rachel didn't spend her life in foster care for nothing. She hurls herself into the fight, tackling Zachary and sitting on him until he can't move, his torso pegged between her thighs. Apparently, her very strong thighs. I pull my arm out from under his grasp and stand up, my lips twisted in a snarl I can't seem to wipe off my face.

"Truce?" he gasps.

"What do you mean, *truce?*" I yell. "You attacked me!"

"I'm sorry. I'm sorry for everything." He's speaking into the ground. Let the earth take his words. I don't want them.

I haven't told Tomás a thing, but he seems to know all about it already. I expect we'll ignore the topic, but then he launches into it almost as soon as we get back to the dorms after lunch.

"You're making a mistake, man." Words fall from Tomás's mouth like small stones, stinging as they hail against my skin. "Zachary really is sorry but now you're going to make a true enemy of him."

"I don't think he's sorry."

Tomás shakes his head. "Even if you're right, Zachary Angel comes from a powerful clan. You want to stay on their good side."

"I was already on his bad side before I ever stepped foot in this place." Of course, Tomás doesn't know that I'm a Reaper, and Reapers are on everybody's bad side.

"You need to calm down," Tomás says. "And I have an idea what might help."

He takes me to another room in the farmhouse I didn't know existed. It's floor-to-ceiling shelves are stocked with vinyl records. Old-school shit.

"I didn't know they even made vinyl anymore," I say.

Tomás grins. "Yeah, and the best part?" He points his chin toward an antique wooden table holding two record players. Gen's already there—surprise surprise—listening to something with headphones on.

"He lives here," Tomás whispers.

He goes to a section marked *F* and riffles through it. After a few minutes, he comes back with a record. The cover shows a black man dressed in swanky underwear, playing a saxophone.

"Fela, the King of Afropop," Tomás says. "If this don't put you in a good mood, nothing will."

I turn the cover over. It says Fela challenged corrupt politicians, was arrested multiple times because of his political activities, and died of AIDS.

We put it on the record player next to Gen. I sit in a wooden chair, put headphones on, and listen, the beats and rhythms making my feet tap. I feel light, bodiless, like I could just drift up to the skies and keep right on going beyond that.

Forty minutes later, the album is over. The needle scratches across the surface for the last time, then clicks as it lifts and returns to its resting place.

A thought loops through my mind, over and over, and it's not the feel-good stuff Tomás thought I'd experience. No. The thought that I can't get rid of is that it's such a tragedy that a man like this had to die.

But don't stop there.

Why does *anybody* have to die? Ever? Why can't we just keep going and going, forever? What a terrible thing to have to say goodbye to people you love. To have to leave behind such talents. For the world to lose those gifts.

I open my eyes. Tomás is gone, Gen is gone, and now that the music is also gone, it feels like a heavy weight is tying me to the earth.

As I tramp back to the dorms through a light snowfall, my phone beeps. I almost don't recognize it, it's been so long since that happened. I don't know why I even still carry it around or why I bother to keep it charged. But here it is, beeping.

I pick it up and notice about half a dozen messages from Sarah. In one she says she really misses me and can't wait to see me. In another, she says her entire life has changed since our encounter with the fortune-teller on Coney Island. In another, she says she's joined the most important group in the world, something she calls a "youth group that believes in life, eternal life, but here on earth!" In another, she tells me she isn't mad at me for dropping off the face of the earth. She understands, she says. More important, she says, is what she's learning from this group she's joined and what she'd like to share with me.

This gets me all worried.

But her last message is the one that makes my stomach clench with dread and excitement: "*Okay. Okay. I'm coming this Sunday. I'll take the all-night bus and be at that coffeehouse on Main Street in Belfast early in the morning. Believe it or not. You better be there. After all we've been through . . . and to know you like me too . . . I can't wait to see you.*"

That's, like, tomorrow. Urp. Panic mode sets in. Is this

for real? And then a worse thought: is this even a good idea? Why'd I tell her how to find me? What if something bad happens?

Liliana's lying on my bed, staring at the ceiling. The banned book rests on her stomach. She looks at me when I come in and shakes her index finger at me. "You so naughty," she says.

Apparently, Liliana also reads Latin.

I snatch it from her. "Leave my stuff alone." What was I thinking, hiding it under the mattress? That's the first place people look.

"And here I thought you were a goody two-shoes," she says. "Where'd the contraband come from?"

"None of your business."

"Aren't we friends, Adam?"

"I thought you were 'working me over,' *friend*."

"I am. Keep your friends close. But keep potential enemies closer." She laughs, like this is oh-so-funny. "That's why I'm here with you instead of hanging with Zachary."

I glare at her. Why in the world did I think her shadow was like air, that it flitted about like a fanciful fairy? It's heavy as lead and just as ugly too.

"I'm just kidding, Adam." She glances up at me under thick black eyelashes, her skin this gorgeous coffee—*Shut UP, Adam.* "I just had no idea you were so—exciting." She points her chin at the banned book, reaching over and resting her fingers lightly on my forearm. Goose pimples form immediately. I jerk my arm away. *Yes, I'm sulking, just in case you were wondering, Liliana La Muerte.*

"Obviously under the mattress is a terrible hiding place. And if Principal Armand caught you with this? I don't think the Synod itself could save you from getting expelled."

"Maybe I don't care."

"You should. If you're expelled, your life is over." She swings her legs over the side of the bed and sits up. When she does, her long hair swings too, cascading over her head. She looks at me out of these melty chocolatey-brown eyes and my heart does a loop-de-loop. Or maybe it just goes, *Urp.*

I decide to change the subject. To something more important. Like the question of Liliana and Zachary. "So you and Zachary, huh? I thought the Angels and La Muertes hated each other."

"Appearances can be deceiving."

"Well, speaking of deceiving appearances, I don't trust Zachary."

"Zachary's okay. It's not his fault he's an Angel."

"I don't care if he's an Angel or a devil." My voice rises involuntarily. "But I do care that he almost got me killed and I think he did it on purpose."

She snorts. "You're one to talk, Mr. I've-Got-a-Wraith-Who-Follows-Me."

I cross my arms across my chest. Half of me wants to grab her and smother her in my chest and the other half wants to push her out the window. "So what are you doing in my room again?"

"Same as last time," she says. "Your Thing is back. The lady ghost that follows you."

My heart lurches.

"I don't want to be alone," she says. "Safety in numbers, you know."

I look at her and I know the truth. She's not here to protect herself. She's here to protect me. Because she thinks I'm in danger. "Thanks," I say.

She narrows her eyes. "Somebody has to make sure fools and children don't die."

"What do you think it is?" I shrink down to my five-year-old self as I ask this.

"I don't know. But it's evil."

I let my breath out slow. Maybe we should sleep downstairs. Or in the boathouse. "What if it comes back?" I ask. "What do we do?"

She's busy pulling out her sleeping bag but now she stops and looks me full in the face. "We're not going to run. Not this time. We're going to face it. Because until you do, it's going to keep coming back."

"You'll be safer somewhere else." There. I said it out loud. I'm not a total coward.

"You think I'm the type of person to abandon a friend in trouble?"

"Am I your friend?"

"Yeah. I was totally kidding about the enemy part."

Just like that, a joyous chorus of angels are suddenly singing, "*Hallelujah.*" I want to jump up and yell at the whole barn that Liliana La Muerte is my friend. But I don't. I just go into the bathroom, brush my teeth, and then lie on my bed quietly.

Finally the barn is silent, everybody in bed. We lie there

in complete darkness. Just as I start to wonder if she's still awake, I hear her sigh.

"Are you scared to die?" I ask.

"No. Are you?"

"No," I lie.

Silence.

"Are you scared of that Thing?" I ask. "I mean, Her? My wraith?"

"No," she says. "You?"

"Of course not!"

Silence again.

"I'm not scared," she says, "but I'll hold your hand if you want."

My heart is beating against my chest. "All right," I whisper.

I slip my hand out from my blanket and she takes it in her cool, dry palm. Prickles inch their way up my forearm.

"You have goose bumps," she says matter-of-factly, as if she doesn't know she's the one who gave them to me.

We fall asleep that way, holding hands. My sleep that night is restless, full of half-dreams, and when I wake up, Liliana is gone.

I rinse my mouth out with mouthwash, then step out of my room as if I'm going to find her in the hallway. Of course she's not there. I stop beside Zachary's door and put my ear up against it, listening. It's silent inside. Then I tiptoe away, feeling like a stalker.

The back door at the bottom of the stairs is wide open. I descend, planning to just close it, but the newly fallen snow reveals several sets of footprints, shining brightly in the moonlight. I follow them a short ways into deeper snowdrifts, then wonder again what I'm doing. Am I looking for Liliana? Am I looking for Zachary?

On the way back, I pass a tree and the hair on my arms stands on end. She's waiting for me. As I pass, Her head turns to watch me. Maybe if I pretend She isn't here, She'll leave me alone.

I wait until I'm completely past before I break into a run.

Maybe it's because I'm running that I don't see Zachary standing silently next to the barn's back door. He grabs me around the throat, choking me with the crook of his arm. I react instinctively, my foot kicking backward, connecting with his crotch.

"What are you doing, trying to kill me?" I yell.

"Ugghhhh," he groans, crumpling over and falling on the ground. His head rolls back and his arms fling wide open, like the arms of Jesus, and that's when I see the blood seeping through his shirt where She must have swiped him with Her talons.

CHAPTER 22

The boat to the mainland is fuller than normal. Some of the kids are going to church, like usual, but half are there to see Zachary off. Even Principal Armand is coming. Aileen's accompanying Zachary back to California, where he can recuperate. Even though she told me last night that it looks worse than it is, that Zachary's going to be just fine, I could hear the uncertainty in her voice.

I know he's going to be fine physically. That's obvious. It looked like a lot of blood, but by now I know enough to realize we'd all sense it if he was in mortal danger. No, what we're all worried about is that he's been . . . touched . . . somehow. I wonder if Aileen and Jacob have told Principal Armand what happened when Zachary and I went to Limbo together.

I'm not seeing Zachary off, obviously, and I also don't want to tell Rachel about Sarah, so I just say I'm in the mood for some good coffee.

"Because this isn't good enough for you?" she says as she sips the cinnamon-flavored Mexican coffee the kitchen sent along in a large thermos. But she agrees to tag along without asking any other questions, which is only one of the reasons why I like her so much.

I tell her what's up after we disembark and we're some ways away from everybody else. "We're going to meet a friend of mine from New York."

"Oh no you didn't," she says.

"Didn't what?"

"Tell somebody from your previous life where you are?"

"Sort of," I admit.

"Fuck." That single word is all it takes to drop my pretense that anything about this is okay.

"I know it was stupid."

She glares at me. "You think?"

"It's going to be fine. We'll go and say hi and have a cup of coffee and then we'll explain that we're not really allowed to be doing this and we have to leave and then she'll go home and we'll pretend it never happened."

"Oh, it's a *she?*" The scorn Rachel puts into the final word is impossible to describe.

"It's not like that."

She knocks me upside the back of my head with the flat of her palm. "It's exactly like that, Adam, don't even think you can lie to me. I grew up in foster care, lies are child's play to me." She stops in her tracks. "We should turn around right now and go back to the boat and pretend we didn't even come here."

Honestly, that thought has also crossed my mind but I can't, I just can't. "No," I say. "I have to at least see her to tell her I can't see her."

"That'll go over real well." She starts walking. "Fine. Let's just get this over with."

I'm so relieved she's still coming with me. "You can be a real grump, you know that?" I say.

"Well, you can be a real idiot, you know that?"

I grin. "Yeah."

* * *

When we push open the door to the coffeehouse, I see Sarah waiting inside, her hair pulled back in a ponytail.

A little sun bursts in my heart.

Her eyes glitter warmly as I step inside. She runs over to give me a hug. My arms close around her slender waist and I smell that strawberry scent and my heart sinks even more, thinking about the gulf between us, a gulf I didn't choose but which I can't erase. But just under the strawberry scent is another, new smell that I don't recognize . . . something decaying . . . something rotting.

I step away.

Then Rachel says, "Hi." She lifts her hand in a sardonic little wave.

"Who are you?" Sarah asks.

"This is Rachel," I say. "From school. Rachel, this is Sarah."

Something is wrong with Sarah's shadow. It's halting, not the usual limpid flow of gurgling water. Like it's been dammed up somewhere. Something's wrong. I mean, deep down, not just a surface thing.

Sarah glares at me. I look at her face carefully. There's something strange in her eyes. "I took the train all the way up from New York City, not even sure if you were really going to be here like you said you would, and you bring another girl to have coffee with us?"

"Um. Yeah?"

She sighs heavily and heads to the line to get coffee. Rachel stops me from following her. "Is she your girlfriend?" she whispers.

"No," I whisper back.

"But you like her?"

"No," I lie. Then: "Yes. Yes." And I think about Liliana and wonder if it's still true.

She shakes her head and sighs almost exactly like Sarah just did. "You better tell her I'm just a friend."

"How am I supposed to do that?"

"Find a way. This is a bad idea but if we're going to be here, I'm not going to sit here and watch you fuck it up. Go get me a coffee."

"What?"

"You dragged me here under false pretenses, the least you can do is buy me a coffee."

"You don't think that'll give Sarah the wrong message? Anyway, I don't have any money."

"You are useless." Rachel gives me a five-dollar bill and shoves me toward the line, where I wait miserably because Sarah ignores me, even though I'm standing directly behind her. I get our coffees from the guy dressed like a lumberjack, the one who served me the last time we were here, his eyes instantly riveted to me, now just like then. Then I follow her to a plushy couch by the window.

Sarah tries to smile but it falters. She's either going to cry or hit me in the face, one or the other, so I don't sit very close.

"How's school?" I ask.

"It's okay," Sarah says. "It's nice to be a sophomore. To feel like I know what's going on, you know?"

"Not really. I feel like a freshman again this year."

"Why's that?" Her eyes look glassy, like she's not all there, or like she's on something.

"Oh, being the new guy and all. But it's cool," I add hastily. "I like it. I like my classes. I like my classmates."

"Oh," she says softly.

I look out the window at the overcast sky, the people meandering past on Main Street. I realize suddenly that I like it here, maybe better than I ever liked New York. I feel at home here. I mean, it's not Maine that feels like home. It's freckled, smart-ass Rachel, sitting here beside me. It's Sean, going to Mass even if the priest would be horrified to know what or who he is. It's Tomás, greeting the morning sun. It's Gen, obsessed with music. Maybe even smug Zachary with his boisterous ways.

"So I guess it's better than you thought it would be?" she says.

I stare at a patch on the floor where the tile is slightly cracked. "It feels like everything I'm learning is . . . useful. I know that sounds lame but it's true."

"What are you learning that's so . . . useful?"

I have no idea how to answer that one but Rachel comes to my rescue: "Practical things so we can take over our family businesses as soon as we graduate."

I shoot her a grateful look. She glances back as if to say, *Why are you being such a dumb-ass, Adam? Tell her I'm just a friend.*

Sarah barely acknowledges Rachel. "Don't you miss us?" Uh-oh. I feel the undercurrent of tension in that question. Actually, it's not a question.

"I do," I say. "I miss you guys a lot."

"But . . . ?"

"There's no but."

"There's always a but," she says. "Unless you're miserable, there's a but. Are you miserable?"

"No, but—"

"See," she interrupts. "I told you there was a but."

I'm losing the thread of this conversation or argument or whatever it is we're having. I look desperately for her shadow, the limpid one I love, but it's hiding behind her glazed eyes. Are we having a fight? I feel hot all over. Rachel's face is as red as mine, in sympathy. What does Sarah want me to say? I don't know. I settle for the truth.

"Sarah, I was miserable coming here. I didn't want to leave New York. I wanted to keep going to school with you and Jeremy and Carlos and . . . and *you*. But I didn't have a choice. And now it turns out that there are some really cool people at that school. Like Rachel here. You'd like them too, if you ever met them. You'd like Rachel if you'd give her a chance."

Sarah's face, which should be softening at the sheer desperate truth in my words, is slowly turning to stone. "Well, that's cool," she finally says. "But someday you're going to have to come back to the real world and what are you going to do then?"

"No, that's just it. This *is* the real world. For me."

Rachel makes a throat-cutting motion with her hand. I've said too much. Revealed too much. Because who in their right mind would ever say a boarding school was the "real world"? But I'm talking about everything. All of it. The whole soul guide way of life.

Sarah's eyes sparkle with tears. "So you like it here better than New York."

"I didn't say that," I reply, even though it's true.

"Yes, you did."

"I'm sorry, Sarah. I'm saying everything wrong."

I stare at my cup of coffee, which I haven't even touched. Rachel was right, way back on our first day at school, when she told me we can't be with so-called normal people. I imagine telling Sarah the whole truth, the real truth: *Hey, baby, I'm the Grim Reaper. You want to have a really sick time? You can party with me until you drop. Like, literally drop. As in, drop dead. But hey, we can disco while doing the Limbo because even suicide can't separate us. I guarantee, I'm dead right for you.* Yikes. Even I want to run away screaming.

"Well, just so you know, I have new friends too," she says. "After what happened when we had our fortunes told, I started searching. I belong to this new movement called The Light. We have youth groups all over New York. All over the world. We believe you don't have to die. That death is just a myth."

Sweat beads pop out on my forehead. I suddenly wish I was anywhere but here. "I've heard of something similar," I say slowly. "I wish you'd stay away from them."

"Well," she snaps, "you don't have any right to say what I can or can't do. I like the people I'm meeting there. I like what they have to say. I don't want to die. Do you? If you could learn the secret to eternal life, wouldn't you do it?"

She grabs my arm and it feels affectionate, as if, for just a moment, she's overcoming her anger about Rachel. "You should come. At Thanksgiving break."

"I don't know. I don't even know yet if I'll be home for Thanksgiving." This is the first time I've gone out of my way to tell her a lie. After all, Dad said he sent money so I could come home. And I want to see Sarah then, I do. But if she's involved with La Luz—I just can't. No matter how badly I want to.

"Okay," she says, then pauses. "So is it all right if I start going out with Jeremy?"

I sit back. I hadn't even realized I'd been sitting forward until this moment. Now I need the support of the couch on my back. "Are you . . . is he . . . I mean, do you really like him?" I'm surprised that my voice shakes.

"I'm just asking if you'd be okay if I go out with him."

"It's fine if you really like him." My voice is quiet, so quiet, I can't believe how quiet. "I can't tell you who to go out with. But if you don't really like him, then I think it's a crappy thing to ask me."

She laughs then, this I-can't-believe-it snort. "As if what you did isn't totally and completely crappy," she half-yells.

"What do you mean?"

"I come all the way from New York to Maine, traveled all night to be here to meet you, thinking maybe we could talk. About *us*. I always thought maybe there might be something between us. Like, more-than-friends something. But instead you bring your girlfriend with you. And now you tell me it's crappy that I might think about going out with Jeremy."

She gets up so fast, hot coffee spills all over the front of my jeans. As my brain catches up to my lips and I open them to say something, she slams the cup on the table, stares at me wildly, then runs out the door.

The words come too late. *It's not like that*, I say in my head. *Rachel's just a friend.*

CHAPTER 23

"Well, you sure screwed that up," Rachel says.

"Thanks a bunch." I glare at her. "You could have spoken up."

"Yeah, I'm sure that would've made everything so much better." She shakes her head. "Anyway, it seems she's hooked up with La Luz. Bad news, my friend."

I look sharply at her, words on the tip of my tongue, but whatever I was going to say is lost as my heart suddenly freezes in terror. Sarah's outside the café and she's talking to somebody who looks suspiciously familiar and pointing toward the coffee shop and then he looks up at us and I draw my whole breath in at the sight of the bookseller/fortune-teller grinning at me.

"What's wrong, Adam?" Rachel asks.

I look to the right and left. The lumberjack slouches against the wall, arms crossed, watching us. His shirt shifts, revealing a tattoo on his right forearm—the symbol from the copy of *The Book of Light*, a circle with a half-circle inside it, rays like sunbeams shooting off it.

My stomach drops. "Let's get out of here."

The lumberjack stands upright and starts to walk toward us. He waves at somebody behind me, and I glance back out the window. Sarah's gone but the bookseller is standing there, nodding. Nodding at the lumberjack.

I grab Rachel's hand. "Don't look back."

We walk outside swiftly, taking the side door instead of the front door. I turn my head just enough to see the lumberjack following us out of the café. He's balling up his apron and throwing it into a trash can and then he breaks into a run, heading straight for us. The bookseller comes wheezing from the other direction but I'm not worried about him. He's old and in bad health. It's this young guy we have to escape.

"Rachel," I say, half under my breath, "run back to the boat as fast as you can."

We dash between two buildings, then out to another street, heading downhill toward the harbor. I thought the boat was just a couple blocks away, but now, with the lumberjack on our heels, it suddenly feels like we're running from Maine to Massachusetts.

"Stop, come back!" the lumberjack hollers.

"Leave us alone!" Rachel shrieks.

"You can't escape us!" he yells. "We know what you are!"

We pass the bus station. I look over and see Zachary leaping up the stairs two at a time, ready to board the bus. Our eyes meet and he stops, his eyes shifting behind me to the lumberjack chasing us and the bookseller puffing behind.

"What's going on?" he shouts.

"Get out of here, Zachary!" I scream.

Principal Armand, Jacob, and another teacher—this enormous guy I know simply as "Rock"—are standing at the edge of the water near the boat. I turn just in time to see the lumberjack slip between two buildings and disappear. I hope Zachary boarded the bus safely.

Jacob holds out his arms to intercept us, as though we'd keep running right off the dock into the water. "Hey, hey, hey, you guys look like you saw a ghost."

We stand with our hands on our knees, panting, trying to catch our breath.

Principal Armand assesses us. "What happened?"

"The guy from the coffeehouse started chasing us when we tried to leave," Rachel starts to explain.

"Did you forget to pay for your coffee?" Principal Armand interrupts with a little cackle.

"He had this tattoo on his arm, like a half-sun or maybe an eye inside of a circle." I have this feeling I shouldn't say the words "La Luz," I should just let them figure it out for themselves.

The teachers exchange glances and without a word, Rock takes off, jogging heavily toward town.

"I'll round up the troops," Jacob says.

"You have the list of churches?" Principal Armand asks.

Jacob's already heading toward Main Street, but he waves a slip of paper behind his back and keeps running.

"What's going on?" I ask.

"La Luz." Principal Armand's fierce expression forbids further questions so Rachel and I step meekly onto the boat to wait.

Jacob soon returns with six students who climb into the boat. Immediately, he turns around and heads back toward downtown.

Gabe La Muerte sits next to us. "What's up?"

"Some lunatic chased us to the dock and Principal Armand thinks he's La Luz," Rachel says.

Sofia pales and sits down immediately.

"What would they do to us anyway?" I ask. "I mean, I would think they'd want to avoid us."

We sit in frozen silence until Jacob returns with another armful of kids, including Sean. Jacob and Principal Armand confer briefly, then Jacob heads back in the direction Rock disappeared.

Sean sits next to Rachel and yawns. "I bet it turns out to be a big crapload of nothing."

"You should have seen that guy," Rachel says. "He was serious. I mean, seriously intent on catching us—at least, until he saw our teachers at the dock."

"Nobody can beat soul guides at their own game," Sean says cheerfully. "Our real threat is civil war. You know, the whole crazy La Muerte–Angel feud." His words echo in the ocean breeze and Sofia and Gabe glare at him. "Or when the Reaper territory goes up for grabs."

I wonder if he's right. What is the worst threat—La Luz or each other?

Before long, almost everybody's returned, including Rock. But where's the group of Angels that accompanied Zachary and Aileen to the bus station?

Jacob stands at the prow of the boat and speaks to us, the camp spirit drained out of him. "Hey, listen," he says. "If what we heard from Adam and Rachel is correct, we believe there may be a La Luz agent roaming around this town. Has anybody seen Zachary, Aileen, or the other Angels?"

I raise my hand. "We saw them at the bus station when we were headed this way. Zachary and Aileen were about to board the bus."

"They're not at the bus station anymore and the bus left without them on board. Does anybody—anybody at all—know where they might have gone instead of coming straight to the boat? This is really important."

We all stare at him. Nobody speaks.

"This is serious, guys. Life-and-death serious."

The silence is something you can squeeze.

Jacob steps off the boat. He and Principal Armand and Rock huddle together for a few minutes, then break apart and look in different directions, scanning the horizon. Jacob sets out for the town again while Rock and Principal Armand pace up and down the dock.

All of us sit quietly on the boat for another hour. I think about Zachary, what an asshole he is. But then I think maybe he's not actually that big of an asshole. I hope he's off somewhere, goofing around—just being, well, assholey.

Jacob finally returns, only this time he isn't alone. Aileen and the other Angels—Lissette, Greg, Marcus, and Mandy—are with him. Mandy and Lissette are crying. Greg and Marcus peer out at the water. A muscle throbs in Marcus's jaw. Jacob, Rock, Aileen, and Principal Armand confer again.

Principal Armand steps onto the boat's prow and says, "We have a serious situation on our hands. Apparently Zachary disappeared right when he was supposed to get on the bus. Jacob and Rock are going to stay here on the mainland and search for him. We're going to send the rest of you back to the island so that you are safe. Please don't speculate about what's happened to Zachary. Rumors will only serve to create panic. As long as we don't know what's going on, let's maintain a respectful silence, shall we?"

As the boat pulls out of the harbor and into the bay, Rachel grabs my hand. I squeeze it back. We watch Jacob and Rock getting smaller and smaller. Waves slap the sides of the boat and get higher as we move into open water.

It feels like I'm going to my execution. Because I'm pretty sure La Luz took Zachary. And I'm going to have to tell them the truth about how La Luz ended up in Belfast.

CHAPTER 24

I don't really want to see anybody after I come out of Principal Armand's office later that night, but Rachel's waiting for me at the bottom of the stairs.

"How'd they take it?" she asks.

"Not good."

She waits for me to elaborate but I don't really want to say that I've been expelled. I'm afraid I'll start crying. What am I going to tell Grandpa? What am I going to tell Dad? I've failed. I've managed to do the one thing they told me not to do.

Rachel takes my hand and I can tell she already knows.

"I don't want to tell anybody. But you can tell them when I'm gone."

"When's that?"

"Tomorrow morning. First train out. Aileen's taking me."

"I'm sorry." She grabs my hand. It's a nice feeling, holding her hand. Not like Liliana or Sarah nice, more like sisterly nice. I don't tell her the other part. That the whole school is packing up and moving to a new location. Immediately. ("The school has been compromised due to your extreme . . . sheer . . . stupidity," Principal Armand told me.) I have no idea where they're going. And I guess I never will.

We sit there for a while and then we go join everybody in the barn. They're all just sitting around—the guys, the girls, and half the teachers. Aileen joins us; her eyes meet mine across the room. The disappointed look is still there. I've never seen anybody so frustrated. She didn't say anything in front of Principal Armand but I have a feeling I'm in for an earful in the morning when she has me alone.

I sit on the couch next to Tomás and his cousin Agwe. Usually they're perfectly turned out but today their clothes are a little rumpled.

Sean's next to them on the floor. His eyes are bloodshot with worry. He rubs his forehead with his palm. "I feel sick inside."

Me too. I have a horrid lingering uck in the pit of my stomach, made worse by the fact that I'm responsible and everybody's going to know it tomorrow.

"Nothing like this has ever happened before," Sean says. "Do you think it's because we're in Reaper territory? Do you think the Reaper Patriarch is going after soul guides, like in the old days?"

"Principal Armand says it's La Luz," I tell him.

"Man, the Reapers will do anything to hold onto their territory," Sean says. "Including teaming up with La Luz."

A few guys murmur and that uck feeling becomes even uckier.

Late that night, Jacob returns to the island. They've scoured the town looking for Zachary and haven't seen a sign of him. Rock's staying in town to meet Zachary's dad and several important Elders of the Synod, who are already en route. Several of Rock's friends—"goons," Sean calls them—have joined him and they've been extending the search beyond town.

"Do you think there's any possibility he ran away?" Rachel whispers.

Although I can think of lots of reasons why somebody like Rachel, or somebody like me, might want to split, I can't think of a single reason for Zachary Angel to run away. "Do you?"

"I think they got him."

I feel winded by the gigantic bat she just hit me with. But then she covers my hand with hers.

"Thanks," I mutter, and remove my hand. Then I ask the most important question, one that should be keeping all of us awake at night, one that no one seems to know the answer to. "But why would La Luz want to kidnap a soul guide? I mean, assuming this is La Luz."

"Whatever it is, it can't be good."

At some point, we all stagger up to bed. Two of the teachers agree to sleep on the sofa. If there's any news, they'll let us know.

I flop into bed, all my clothes on. Despite my fatigue, I think there's no way I'm going to fall asleep. And for a long time, I just stare at the ceiling. I must fall asleep eventually, despite the questions, because somebody jiggles me awake.

"Wh—what?" I'm still groggy. My mouth tastes sour and my head aches.

It's Liliana. Her face is so close, a strand of her hair tickles my cheek. A shaft of moonlight illuminates her face and I almost reach up to caress her cheek. But then she blinks back tears, flings herself off the bed, and stands by the window, looking down toward the shoreline.

"Who are you, Adam?" she asks.

I look at the clock—3:20 a.m. "Um . . . what?"

"Something's really wrong," she says.

"Did you hear about Zachary Angel?"

"Yes. I overheard." Her voice is low and fierce and she's almost hissing the words. Her shadow's become a cobra, spitting mad, ready to strike if she hears something she doesn't like. "What did you do this time, Adam?"

"I didn't—I—"

"Bad things happen when you're around."

"Liliana—" I shake my head. "He wasn't normal anymore. Everybody thought he was but I could tell . . . There was something wrong. In his head."

"Oh god." The cobra's gone. Her feet make a soft rustling sound as she shifts. A shy deer now, looking around for the potential predator. "What do you mean?"

"I didn't tell you that he went to Limbo with me and he got attacked by—by Her. You know who. They were sending him back to California to recover."

A sob catches in her throat.

"I'm sorry," I say.

"Do they think La Muerte is behind his kidnapping?"

"No." Of course. Of course she'd be worried about that. "No, it's La Luz."

She moans softly in the back of her throat. "Are they sure?"

I look at her and think about lying but I can't. She'll

know the truth eventually. Better if I just tell her now. "Yes. I saw the La Luz operatives. They know who I am. They followed a friend of mine up here and that's how they ended up finding me."

"Are you stupid?" There's actually no real anger in her voice, just a sort of resignation.

"I'm sorry."

She goes back to the window and stands there for a long time, peering out. The moon goes behind a cloud and the world gets darker for a few seconds. "Ignore me. Just go back to sleep."

I lie back down but there's no way I'm sleeping. I look at her figure lit up by the light of the moon. I want to get up and bury my face in her hair. I want to rest my lips on the nape of her neck. I want—

"Good night," I say.

She doesn't respond. Slowly, the silence becomes loud, a weight pushing on my chest, forcing my head deep into the pillow. Maybe I should say something else. I open my mouth to speak, and just at that moment somebody walks past the door in the hall. Pauses.

It's just my mind playing tricks. Right?

I lie perfectly still, not moving a single muscle. Silently recite a mantra from my childhood: *If you lie still, they won't know you're here.*

Another rustling sound at the door.

I break out in a sweat. Should I tell Liliana to hide? My mouth is suddenly full of cement. I breathe in and out. Maybe I should jump out of bed, yank the door open, and yell, *I'm here!* just to break the tension or to let the person know I'm onto them, whoever they are. Probably just one of the guys.

Liliana turns away from the window.

"You hear it?" I whisper.

"Yes." The band of light filtering under the door illuminates her silhouette. She pulls something out of her bag. Long. Cylindrical. She tiptoes into the bathroom.

The doorknob creaks as it turns. I pretend to be asleep, eyes tiny slits. Maybe it's a teacher checking on me. Instead, somebody creeps into the room, shutting the door behind them.

A drop of sweat rolls down my cheek and drips onto my throat. My mind screams, *Move! Yell! Run!* But I can't. I just lie there. Then I make the grand effort and, pathetically, the only thing I can manage is to flip on the light.

And freeze. *Holy sh—is that Zachary?*

"Zachary effing Angel," I yell, and leap out of bed. "What the hell are you doing here?"

"Adam." His voice is hoarse. "Adam, I need help. Please."

"We have to find some teachers. Seriously. Everybody's worried about you. What are you doing here? Why didn't you go—"

He leaps forward with a sudden, jerky movement and clamps a gloved hand over my nose and mouth. Something sharp pricks my thigh, a sweet thick feeling spreading warmly from the wound throughout my body.

Move. Move. Move! My brain's talking but my body's refusing, thighs submerged in a thousand pounds of invisible mud.

I grab the first thing my hand touches, *The Book of Light,* which I hid under my pillow last night, but my hand won't close over it. Green and yellow squiggles spiral through the air in front of me. *Pop pop pop.* Fingers like sausages. Muscles like water.

My arm flops off the nightstand. The book slides to the floor.

Zachary lets go and I follow the book, crumpling down onto the floor. The burly man from the coffee shop lumbers inside, pulling zip ties out of his pocket.

Then something flashes over Zachary's right shoulder. *Thump.* The lumberjack grunts, drops the ties, and falls to one knee. Liliana hits him again. *Thump.* "Zachary," she yells, "get away from here!"

Zachary advances toward her, syringe in his right hand. A single drop of liquid glistens on the edge of the needle.

"What the hell are you doing?" She backs away, looks like she's about to bolt. "You can't do this, Zach. Not to me. You *can't.*" Tears stream down her face

His feet slow for a second. He looks like he's pushing against a strong wind, trying to reach her. The syringe drops from his fingers and rolls across the floor toward her.

"Don't screw this up, Liliana," he growls.

"I'm your sister," she says. "You can't do this."

Liliana La Muerte is Zachary Angel's sister?

"Stay there," he warns. He nudges the lumberjack and rasps, "Get up. Come on! Let's get out of here."

The lumberjack staggers to his feet, rubbing the spot on his temple where Liliana clocked him. Grunting, he heaves me over his shoulder and stumbles out the door as Zachary holds it open.

The blood rushes to my head but I catch Liliana, quick as a flash, grabbing the syringe Zachary dropped and hiding it behind her back. Good. As long as she uses it on the right person. Not me.

"Whatever you do, stay away," Zachary says to her. "I can't be responsible for you."

My head bumps against the lumberjack's back as we hurry through the woods and down the wooden stairs. By the time we reach the dock, I'm shivering uncontrollably. It feels like a snowstorm is on the way.

The lumberjack slings me into a boat. Pain climbs up my spine as I hit a sharp corner. Zachary ties a rough cloth sack around my head.

The world goes dark and the sack quickly fills up with humid air, my hot stale breath. I huddle helplessly in the darkness.

CHAPTER 24.5

The Grim Reaper had kept one terrible secret from her lover-husband: that she suffered from a terminal, untreatable illness.

What illness? Elder #6 asked.

It really isn't pertinent to the story, he said. But what is pertinent is that it was killing her.

The disease she suffered from had been killing her all this time they were together. And finally, because her demise was near, she had to tell him. She felt he would take it as a betrayal. And so she was tentative, careful. He sensed the change in her for weeks before she approached him. And she set the stage carefully, a dinner strewn with roses, candles, and to eat: arugula salad, a mushroom risotto with wine, and tiramisu.

My love, she began, after they had finished the meal, and because they were one flesh forever, she did not need to speak another word. He understood instantly. He had, in fact, been waiting for it the entire meal.

He was distraught. He tore his hair. He

rent his frock. He fell on his knees and beat his chest. "My darling!" he cried. "My darling! I will search the world over for a cure. It can't be your time. It simply cannot be. It is not your fate to die . . . not yet!"

The Grim Reaper tried to persuade him that there was no cure for mortality. She tried hard but he was convinced there must be a way for her to evade the very thing everybody must face.

What a pack of lies, Her Excellency snapped. My son would never try to cheat death out of death's fair due.

I am only telling you the story as I understand it, from the bits and pieces told to me over the years, he said. If you wish to dispute it, take it up with your son.

The son I have not seen in sixteen years, since your daughter stole him away? The son who never let me see my grandchild? The son who is your right-hand man in everything?

Madam, you mean to say that he is, in effect, the Grim Reaper? he said.

Yes, I suppose, she conceded.

Finally he submitted himself to her inevitable death. They wept together and held each other late into the night, thinking about what was to come.

CHAPTER 25

A garish light wakes me up, along with a headache the size of Canada. I rub my temples. Everything is dull morning-breath yellow. Speaking of which, I wish I could brush my teeth. My tongue runs over the thin film covering my teeth.

Hey, Dad, where are you? Aren't you supposed to come rescue me when I'm in trouble?

"This will help."

I recognize Zachary's voice immediately. My eyes fly open. He's sitting beside me, holding out a mug of something hot. Tea, maybe. More drugs, maybe, to knock me out and turn me into Mr. Mush.

"Seriously," he says, "drink up. It'll take away the headache, give you energy."

I look around the room. Everything is stark white, like the world's been bleached. White comforter, white sheets, white bed. White floor, white walls, white chair, white filmy curtains at the windows. There's even a blank white painting in a white frame hanging on the wall. Somebody has a sense of humor.

Zachary, in his red sweatshirt and jeans, is the only color in the room.

I look down. "Gah!" They've removed my shirt and put me in a white gown, the kind they use in hospitals with the gap in the back. "Where are my clothes?"

Zachary points to my clothes, folded neatly and resting on top of a white chair in the corner.

"Where the hell am I, Zachary?"

He pushes the mug toward me again. "This is a hospital of sorts."

Now I take it. Every single joint aches. "Is there a drug in here? If I drink it, will I wake up and find out a week's passed?"

He stands and clasps his hands behind his back. "Always so suspicious. It's just herbal tea, Adam. It'll help you relax and take care of the aches and pains you are surely suffering from."

I look at him closely. Something's off. The voice is Zachary. The body is Zachary's. The posture and the words are not Zachary.

"You're not Zachary," I say.

He taps his temple with an index finger. "Ah, they said you were smart. You are correct, sir. I'm borrowing Zachary's vessel, or, as you would say, his body."

He's so pale, he matches the décor. That is, except for the dark, purply circles under his eyes.

"Who are you? Where's Zachary?"

"My name is not really important. I've had many names. You can call me Amaros. As for Zachary, he is having—how would you call it?—an extended field trip to purgatory. You so-called soul guides call it Limbo. His spirit is still animating his body; I've just replaced his soul with mine. That may seem confusing to you but I've been at this for quite some time now, so I've learned how to adapt someone's brain to fit me quite nicely."

The light behind his eyes is older, smarter, cunning. Animallike. A wolf looking at you through the eyes of a human.

I want to vomit or jump out the window. Possibly vomit while jumping out the window.

I catch a glimpse of the chain around Amaros's neck and start to feel even queasier.

Amaros notices me eyeing it. He pulls the medallion out of his shirt, a perfect circle with a half-circle nestled inside, lines radiating from it.

"Yeah, I've seen your creepy bloodshot eye," I say. "Looks like a really bad hangover."

He snickers. "And I've seen yours. A broken circle? Nobody wants broken things, Adam."

"Maybe I do," I reply, and don't even realize how true it is until I say it. Life is made up of broken things.

He nods at me, as if we have an understanding. "We have a lot to talk about, Adam. But for now, why don't you rest?"

I wonder how long I've been "resting." I hope I didn't soil my pants while I was knocked out. I intend to get them on as soon as possible.

When Amaros leaves, I swing my legs out of bed. A thin metal chain clanks against the floor. It's locked to one of my ankles; the other end is connected to an eyebolt sunk in the wall.

The room has three doors. One opens to a hall I can step into but go no farther. That's the door Amaros went through. The second leads to a small closet with nothing in it . . . thank god. The last door reveals a small bathroom. I have just enough length to get to the toilet.

After taking care of business, I hobble over to the chair with my clothes. It's impossible to get my jeans on over the chain on my leg, but I search through the pockets. My cell phone's here but a quick glance shows the battery is dead. Of course. Even if it worked, I can't imagine we'd have reception way out . . . wherever the hell we are. My fingers close around the black card my dad made me promise to take everywhere. Fat lot of good it's going to do me here. *Thanks, Dad. Thanks for the help.* Still, I manage to get my hoodie over my head and I put it in the pocket of the hoodie. You never know. Maybe I'll be able to use it to scrape the frost off my window so I can see outside this prison.

The hospital gown covers my legs, barely. Man, it's cold in here. Goose pimples break out all over my legs. I'm dying for those jeans. Hospital gown à la skirt is not exactly the kind of fashion statement I like to make.

I hobble over to the window. It looks out on a snow-covered lawn, a thick clump of pine trees in the distance. I'm guessing we're still in Maine, given the pine trees, the snow, the ocean in the far distance, and the fact that it takes so long to get from place to place in this damn state. I'm on the second floor. The window's sealed shut. Not that I could jump out, given the chain securely attached to my leg, but still.

It appears to be afternoon, possibly the day after Zachary—er, Amaros—abducted me. How long will it take someone to look for me, much less find me? It's not like Liliana was in a position to raise the alarm.

After what seems like an interminable period, someone knocks at the door. I put my ear against the wood and listen. Silence. I open it tentatively. Somebody's left a tray of food on the floor. Chicken, broccoli, scalloped potatoes.

I place the tray on the chair beside my bed, wondering if it's poisoned or drugged. It looks like perfectly ordinary food. Should I risk it?

The deep pain in my gut decides for me. I have to eat and this is my only choice. If they'd meant to kill me, they would have done it already. That is, unless this is some sick prelude. Guess I'll have to take my chances.

I eat every bite and wash it down with more tea. Not bad. Actually, I'm feeling better every minute.

Another knock on the door.

"Come in," I say automatically, and then feel stupid. I'm a prisoner, somebody knocks on the door, and I invite them in? Apparently, I'm not cut out for prison life.

Amaros saunters in. "How was dinner?"

"Why do you have me chained and locked up?"

He looks bored. "I had hoped dinner would put you in a more . . . agreeable mood."

"How can I possibly be agreeable when I'm tied up?"

He fingers the symbol around his neck. "You've encountered La Luz before. You came into contact with one of our operatives. You were with your dad, I believe? In search of a book? And then you and your girlfriend met him again a few days later?"

"Yeah, he was a real asshole."

Amaros smiles. "That 'asshole' led us to you. He recognized your father. And you. He figured out you were Reapers."

"So . . . you're interested in me because I'm a Reaper?"

"Zachary was a useful vessel. When we got to the island where your so-called school is located, he was able to get me into Limbo there. But getting into Limbo in Reaper territory is impossible without a Reaper, and we need to parlay with your father. We already knew you were a Reaper but he was also able to point us in Rachel's direction as a possible Reaper. So we are checking her out too."

I catch my breath. "You kidnapped Rachel?"

"Now, now. Be wary of using that word, Adam. You should be grateful. There's more to us than what you've experienced so far. Or heard from others."

"And kidnapping me—and one of my best friends—is going to convince me of this?"

He makes a tsk-tsk sound with his tongue. "'Kidnap' is such a strong word." Little furry ears sprout out of his head, a tail splits his pants. His teeth—long, yellowed canines—gleam.

Oh. I see. I'm not dealing with someone rational.

"I was hoping you could help me convince your Reaper relatives to 'see the light,' so to speak. Ha ha!" The creature actually laughs like he made a joke. "I need to contact your father and the safest way is in Limbo. That's where you can help me. So I don't want to harm you. In fact, I would love to compensate you for the trouble. I'm not offering you something so vulgar as money, either, though let me assure you—I could. No. I am offering you something that many men have spent considerable money trying to attain. This is why you should be grateful to our operative for putting us in touch."

I'm not speaking to this animal. Resolutely, I stare at

the wall, but then I begin to feel blinded by all the white. My eyes shift, searching for color, and I inadvertently look at him. The wolf's gone and he's back to Amaros in Zachary's body, just some old guy trying to sell me something.

"Adam, what are your feelings about death?"

"Are you threatening me?"

"No, just trying to find out exactly where you stand."

"Unlock. My. Foot."

He gets up. "Very well, have it your way. Perhaps you will be more amenable tomorrow."

He closes the door behind him and that's when I notice the book on the chair. I don't even have to look to know what it is, brown paper covering up the same symbol that dangles from Amaros's neck.

Eventually, the sun goes down and it gets dark. I'm trying to think of a way to get out of here. If I go to Limbo, my dad will find me—eventually—and I can tell him where I am so he can send out a posse to save me. Or maybe he can even travel from my Limbo to where my body is, I don't know. But will Dad make it to Limbo before She eats me alive?

Going there is the last thing I ever wanted to do. Avoided it so much that I've been sleep-deprived for a year, probably longer. But now I'm praying: *Please take me there tonight. Please.*

CHAPTER 26

And then somebody's knocking on the door and I wake up, early-morning light spilling in through the window.

Crappity crap crap crap. I didn't fall into Limbo last night.

I open the door to find breakfast on a tray—eggs, bacon, toast, and coffee. Half-and-half. Sugar. I wonder who the cook is. Amaros? The lumberjack? The bookseller? Honestly, it doesn't matter. They apparently didn't poison my last meal. I devour the eggs and bacon and suck down coffee like a drowning man.

At least eating is something to do so I don't have to think about the book, the book my eyes keep wandering back to, the book I'm not going to touch.

Then I glance at the symbol on the cover and my hand steals out to touch it.

I jerk my arm back. Nope. Not going to do it. I know Dad gave me the book, but if Amaros wants me to read it, I have this feeling I should stay away from it. At least for now.

So let's find something else to do. Wahoo! Maybe I can pick the lint out of my belly button.

I peer out the window for a while, imagining my escape route, if escape is possible.

Pace the floor.

Get a drink of water from the bathroom tap.

Sit on the floor.

Sit on the bed.

Look through the empty closet.

Look out the window.

See the book.

Sit on the bed.

Think about the book.

One hundred and fifty-seven, maybe fifty-eight, floorboards. It's hard to tell. There's a spot in the very back of the room where I can't quite reach. So there are either 157 or 158 floorboards.

A water stain on the ceiling looks exactly like a silhouette of Elvis's hair. The King is visiting me!

Glance at the book again.

Okay, it feels like hours have passed but I have a sinking feeling that I've amused myself for less than fifteen minutes.

For some reason, the death poem I read the night Sean, Tomás, and I snuck out and rowed to the nearby island comes to mind:

Coming, all is clear, no
doubt about it. Going, all is
clear, without a doubt.
What, then, is all?

If I'm going to count, I might as well count something more important than floorboards. I take a quick inventory of my "all." I suppose "all" is different for everybody. My all is mostly people.

My mind focuses on the image of a grim smile, an endless room filled with nothing but books. Dad. His shadow has always been complicated. A mountain, an ocean, a room of books. I circle around the image of him in my mind.

My mother, the fuzzy edges of her, the yellow dress, the freckles. I circle her too.

Of course, Rachel's in that "all." She's pretty much my best friend at school. I wish I'd told her more stuff. Like about Liliana and Limbo and Her.

Tomás and Sean. Glad I met those dudes.

Aileen and Jacob. Even Zachary. Yeah, okay, it sucks but my all has to include Zachary.

If I make it out of here, those are the people who will be in my life pretty much forever, I'm guessing.

Then there are my friends in the "real" world: Jeremy and Carlos and Sarah. That is, if Sarah's even still my friend. But even if she's mad, or even if she's dead, she's still part of my all.

And then there's Liliana. Yes, my all includes Liliana.

A tear pricks my eyelids. I hope I get to see those alls again sometime.

My gaze falls on the book. I turn away.

Lunch is red beans and rice with sausage. I eat as slowly as possible. Afterward, I take a short nap. When I wake up, I run in place, the chain clanking on the floor. I do push-ups. Sit-ups. Burpees. I think about all those political prisoners who kept fit while locked away, men like Nelson

Mandela. Will I be here that long? It doesn't seem possible. One night and I'm already going crazy.

There's a knock on the door and Amaros enters. "How are you doing, Adam?" He actually sounds interested in what I'll say.

"I'm fine. Unlock my chain."

"I can't do that. Have you read the book yet?"

"No."

"What a pity. So, tell me, how do you feel about your father dying?"

"Shove it. Shove it up your—"

"You know, dying isn't inevitable. There are alternatives."

Like what? is on the tip of my tongue. I bite it back.

"Let me know if you want to talk. I don't mind listening. And read that book. Trust me, you won't regret it. I'm a bit disappointed you haven't already given in to what I suspect is ravenous curiosity."

"Unlock my chain."

He laughs and walks out the door.

The next time Amaros visits—hours or maybe just a few minutes later, I don't know, time has lost all meaning here—I'm so bored that I actually ask, "Why are you so obsessed with death?"

"Oh, I'm not obsessed with death, Adam. Quite the opposite. I'm enamored with life and how to prolong it. Money, power, happiness—these things are all subservient to our need for life. I ask you how you feel about death because I've noticed it's the only way to make westerners confront their mortality. It's funny how we don't cherish life until it's coming to an end . . . Don't snicker, Adam. It doesn't become you."

"Fine," I say. "It's just—why are YOU lecturing me about death? You're a total hypocrite. You're not facing death."

"I didn't say anything about facing death. I'm saying that if you want to live forever, you must have a real loathing of death. Surely you of all people know this."

Gobsmacked, my forehead aches. Yeah, he's right. I hate death. I do. I *loathe* it.

"If you could live forever, Adam, would you?"

Whatever else, I can't tell this animal-man what I really think. "I'm too young to think about death."

He makes a beeping sound. "Wrong answer. You're never too young to be wise. Listen to your fears. They will guide you on the path to eternal life."

I wonder what Amaros thinks "all" is—if he bothers to think about it. He seems determined to hold onto his all.

"Everybody dies sometime," I say. "Maybe you've found a way to cheat death for now, but it can't last forever."

Amaros laughs in my face. It starts out as a high giggle and then reaches a low point where it shuts off completely. "Maybe you should read that book. Maybe you'll find it useful. Before it's too late."

We lock eyes as he stands. Bile rises in my throat, my soul rising up with it, through my esophagus. I clamp down hard, almost biting off my tongue. I won't let this vile man look at my soul. I won't.

"Very good, Adam. You're strong. If you cooperate, I will show you how to find eternal life. But you must give me an answer by tomorrow. Will you help me or not?"

"Is that your final offer? Eternal life?"

He smirks.

"Eternal life or what? If I say no, are you going to kill me?"

"Toodle-oo." He waves coyly as he leaves.

If Amaros is offering me eternal life, and Dad says the answer is in this book, does that mean I'll find the answer myself if I read it? Or am I saying yes to Amaros if I read it? Is this one big cosmic trick?

Aw, what the hell. I don't even know the Synod. But I know my father and he's the one who said, "Books should never be forbidden. The most dangerous ideas are those we try to suppress."

I pick the book up and flip it open.

IN THE BEGINNING, the world was made, and everything that existed was good. Every living thing was in order and death was not at the doorstep of mankind. This was how the world was made and this is how the Mysteries will restore what was good. Everything that was will be again . . .

Suddenly the light seems too bright, my eyes water at the edges, the words swim out of focus. I slam the book shut.

What does that mean? *This is how the Mysteries will restore what was good. Everything that was will be again . . .* Does it mean my mother will be returned from the place of death? Is the book talking about more than just eternal life for those of us who haven't died yet but eternal life for everybody, even those who've already passed to the other side?

I practically hit my head on the wall, I'm so startled when something or somebody thuds against the door with a grunt.

Amaros again? Already?

I open the door just as somebody pushes it open. It stops with a jarring thump, hitting my forehead and knocking me backward. "Ow!" Sparks flare at the edge of my vision.

Liliana pops through the door and grins at me. "Am I disturbing your beauty sleep?" Her hair is a wild, tangled mess, like she's been camping out in the woods for a week or maybe stuck her finger in an electric socket in order to get here or something.

I bear-hug her. "How in the world did you find me?"

"Oh, honey, it wasn't hard." She goes out the door and returns, dragging Lumberjack into the room, a needle and syringe sticking out of his throat. We haul him to the closet, folding his feet up to close the door. "I followed you guys in a boat, which I stole, and which I assume will also be held against me by the ever-wonderful Principal Armand, though after expelling me, there's not a lot more he can do to me. Then I went back for reinforcements. That's why it took me so long to come get you."

She tugs on the chain locked around my ankle. "It's a good thing I came prepared." She heaves a backpack onto the floor and pulls a bent needlelike object from the front pocket. "You wouldn't believe what people hide behind completely inadequate locks."

I turn my leg over so she can pick at the lock.

"Nice tighty-whities." She grins at my leg.

"Shut up." My leg starts to cramp. I shift.

"Don't move," she instructs. "I've got the two hard pins set and if you make me lose those, I swear I'll punch you in the crotch!"

I sit still, gritting my teeth, the cramp slowly moving up my calf into my thigh. Drops of sweat roll down her temples. My heart cramps right along with my leg.

The doorknob starts turning. "Someone's coming in," I whisper.

The lock pops open and the chain falls with a clank onto the floor. I'm expecting Amaros to step into the room, not sure what we might have to do when he sees Liliana.

But it isn't Amaros. First a riot of dreadlocks, then a face I recognize.

"Boo," Liliana whispers.

All of my muscles turn liquid in relief. Liliana's reinforcements! I unclench my fists. "Tomás!"

"Good to see you too, man." He smiles at me. "We better clear out while we can, Lili."

"Where's Dullahan?" Liliana asks.

"He's following Zachary."

"Okay, let's find Rachel first. Then we'll figure out what to do about Zachary."

I shove my legs into my jeans, making the tightywhities disappear. "Let's hurry. Please."

"What's the deal with you and Rachel, Adam? You guys seem to be joined at the hip." She winks at me. "I'd be jealous but that's not my style."

Tomás rolls his eyes. "Shut up or Sean's the one who'll be jealous."

"That little pipsqueak?" Liliana counters. "What's he got to be jealous of?"

"Never mind," Tomás says. "Let's get out of here."

We creep out of the room, then slowly down the halls, backs to the white walls, placing our feet carefully to avoid making too much noise. The enormous house we're in is perfectly silent, as though it's listening to us.

CHAPTER 27

Even though we put one foot carefully in front of the other, the stairs creak like a thousand chirping bats. We all wince but nobody comes running. Thank goodness.

The stairs open up into some sort of living room. The white furniture against the dark wood floor looks like a blizzard threw up all over the earth. Somebody's sitting on the white couch. We only know this because the shoes are visible from where we perch; we can't see the body they belong to.

But I know those shoes, the scuffed brown leather and three lace holes, laces beaten and frayed. I sat next to those shoes for two months, the best two months of my life, reading books and eating cookies and arguing about the things we read.

Why'd Rachel have to get sucked into this?

We peer around the wall. She's sitting by herself on the couch, staring straight ahead at a point on the white wall opposite her. She doesn't move. She doesn't blink. Is she dead?

"I'm going in there," I whisper.

Liliana gives me a thumbs-up.

When I step into the room, Rachel breaks out of her trance. Her eyebrows draw together in a crooked line, just a little off-center.

"Rachel, are you okay?" I whisper.

"Sorry," she replies in a voice too loud for comfort. "I thought you were my sister."

"You don't have a sister."

She glares at me. "Who the hell are you?"

"I'm Adam. And I think I may be the closest thing you have to family, as sad as that may seem."

"Well, I don't know who you are but I do know that my sister was just here talking to me. She went to get us a bedtime snack. So you can bug off."

She narrows her eyes and tries to look mean but I know Rachel too well. Deep down in those brown eyes of her, I see a pool of fear and uncertainty, clouded over by hallucination.

Liliana catapults over the couch. She pulls me with her and we hunker down behind the couch as the wood squeaks and someone clunks heavily into the room, the tread too forceful to be anybody other than Zachary. I mean, Amaros-in-Zachary's-body.

I press my cheek against the wooden floor and look under the couch to the other side. Sure enough, Zachary's sneakers line up toe to toe with Rachel's shoes.

"What'd you get us?" Rachel's voice has this excited, happy-little-girl quality to it.

"Pickles," Amaros answers in a dry voice.

"Chocolate, yum," Rachel says.

"I need your help, darling."

"Whatever you need, you know I'll do anything."

"I hope so. This is important," Amaros says.

"Just don't leave me again," she pleads. "I don't know

where Mom and Dad went and I don't think I can make it on my own." Need bleeds through every word.

"I'll try." Amaros sucks on his teeth as he speaks. "But the only way I can stay is if you help me get to Limbo. If you can't, I may have to leave forever."

Rachel bursts into tears. "But I've tried and I don't know how."

"I'll help you." He soothes with his voice, a hairbrush gently untangling a knot of hair. "Just relax and don't worry. Imagine we're doing something fun. When you get lost in the memory, you can just . . . float . . . right into Limbo."

"Okay."

"Remember how we used to make tents in the living room using blankets? Remember the dolls we made from scraps out of Mom's sewing basket?"

Silence follows.

"Good girl. Find your soul," Amaros murmurs. "Now let it go. Let it drift away . . . That's it. That's better. Much better than yesterday. Now . . . let's go!"

His shoes shift and I hear Rachel slump sideways.

"That's it! That's it!" Now he shouts with excitement, forgetting to soothe. "Come back and take me with you!"

A second later, his body thuds as it hits the floor. Through the crack under the sofa, I watch as Zachary's face slackens. Eyes open but blank.

"Tomás, get your ass in here," Liliana hisses.

I stand up to see Tomás easing his way into the room. "What's happening?" he asks. Then he looks at Rachel and Amaros-in-Zachary's-body. "Oh no. Oh no, this is not good."

Liliana's whispering in Rachel's ear now, shaking her gently, patting her cheek. No response.

I place two fingers on Zachary's neck, feeling for a pulse. "He's alive," I say.

Sean pokes his head around the corner from the other direction. "All clear?"

"All clear, as far as we know," Liliana responds.

Sean joins us. He elbows me briefly and flashes a grin in my direction. "Glad you're okay, bro."

Liliana sits next to Zachary and hugs her knees to her chest. Tomás tugs handfuls of dreadlocks as he leans back and groans.

"How the hell did they go to Limbo in Reaper territory?" Sean asks in a loud voice, too loud, especially if there's anybody else on the island besides Amaros and the lumberjack.

The reality sinks in to all three of them at the same time.

"Rachel must be a Reaper," Liliana says, milky-sweet tones stained bitter by something poisonous in the bottom of it all. "Guess they're not going to die off after all."

I wince and try to change the subject back to safer ground. "Okay, should we load them up on a boat and take them back to somebody who knows what to do with them?"

Tomás groans again, deeper this time. Liliana hugs her knees closer, one hand reaching out to gently smooth a strand of hair back from Zachary's face. Sean crosses his arms.

"Guys?" I prompt.

Finally, Liliana says, "If we remove them from this spot,

who knows what'll happen. In any case, by the time we get help, Rachel or Zachary or both of them might be dead."

"We don't even know where Zachary *is*," Sean says.

"He's right here," I say, but I know what Sean means and he knows I know it, so he doesn't bother answering.

"We need an experienced soul guide," Tomás says. "And not just any experienced soul guide. A Reaper soul guide. We're in Reaper territory, nobody else can get in there to salvage what's left of Zachary and Rachel. Which means we somehow have to reach the Patriarch." He beats a brown fist against the white couch.

"What's the worst thing that could happen to them in Limbo?" I ask.

"What do you mean? They could die!" Sean bursts out.

"Fine," I say. "Let's call my dad."

They all give me strange looks. "Anyway, none of our dads can help us now," Liliana says.

Mine can. But that's not the point. "Just . . . do you have a phone or not?" I ask. "Mine's dead."

"No phone," Liliana says. "I hate those things."

"I forgot mine," Sean says.

"Battery's dead," Tomás says.

My hands start shaking. I don't want to go to Limbo. But maybe if I do, Dad will come rescue me before She eats me up and then he can rescue Zachary and Rachel. And maybe I'll have enough time to warn him about Amaros too, so he can avoid whatever ambush that guy is surely planning.

Fear crushes my lungs. I imagine eternity as a bottomless pit. One I'm falling into. In darkness. I don't know. I don't know if I can do this. I just know I'm the only choice. If I don't do it, Rachel and Zachary are as good as dead.

"I'll go." My voice breaks the way it used to when it was changing.

"Go where?" Tomás asks.

"Where do you think?" Fear makes my voice sharp. "To Limbo."

He squeezes my shoulder. "They aren't dead yet, Adam, but they will be unless one of us finds a Reaper, and quick."

Sean stands up. "What are we waiting for? Two of us stay, two of us go find a phone so we can try to track down the Reaper Patriarch. I'll go. Who's coming with me? Adam?"

"You do what you have to do," I say. "But I'm going to Limbo. Right now."

What I'm trying to say is that I can get to Limbo. Right here. Right now. Because I'm a Reaper too. I say this in my head but my thoughts must be loud enough for them to hear because the three of them stare at me with great focus and attention.

"What!" Sean inhales sharply. "What what what?"

Liliana jumps up. "No way." Her face gets all red. She peers into my eyes, head tilted, like she's just noticing something.

"Yeah, I am, okay?" My fingers curl into fists. I don't like the awkward, apologetic way Sean and Tomás are looking at me.

"You can't be a Reaper," Liliana says. "You don't feel like a Reaper at all. You're—I *liked* you."

Liked. Past tense. This is why Dad didn't want anybody to know my clan affiliation.

"Look. I don't care what you've heard or what you think you know. My dad's the Reaper Patriarch. So I'm going in and I'm going to get Rachel and Zachary. Sean, you can say whatever prayer you want to, whatever saint you think can protect me in Limbo, cuz I'm going to need it bad."

Now I know what they mean when they say it's like someone grew a third head. "Oh man, oh man," Sean groans. "Man oh man oh man. We came here to save two *Reapers*?"

"We came here to save Zachary," Liliana snaps. "If we need two Reapers to help us, so be it."

Sean makes the sign of the cross. Then he drops his gaze and he doesn't look at me again.

"Good luck, Adam," Tomás says. "Give 'em hell. Or not. Whatever you think is best."

And there it is. *Give 'em hell.* Well, that's where I'm going. No point in delaying it. At least Tomás still looks halfway friendly, grinning awkwardly at me. But I'm the one who feels awkward now. "I really don't know how to get to Limbo . . ."

"Good LORD," Liliana says.

"Will you coach me?" I ask. Tomás is the one I turn to. He's the one who seems least likely to judge me for my family.

He claps a hand on my shoulder. "It's easy, man," he says. "You've been there before, you know how to do this. Just close your eyes. Breathe deep. Let this world—everything that worries you—just fall away. Just let it fall away, man. Then understand that the conscious state of your soul is already in Limbo and you'll find yourself there."

And so I do. I breathe in, out. In, out. Just like my meditation instructor drilled into me. Good old Dad, keeping everything secret and lying to me, making my whole growing-up years confusing, but at the same time giving me all the tools I need for this life.

Speaking of Dad . . . he's the thing I concentrate on. His lined face, his grim smile. Then I let it all go.

Coming, all is clear, no

doubt about it.

My soul tumbles toward me, a leaf sailing along a gust of wind. It trembles, tries to dance out of reach. I grab it and drag the quivering mess right into my worst nightmare.

Falling begins almost immediately.

Light has disappeared. Infinity stretches below me.

It doesn't take long for Her to find me. This time, instead of a dragon's tail and bat's wings, She looks just like the woman in the yellow dress, the woman on the endless looping train, three days dead. The fish-white flesh peels away, exposing crumbling black bones. Her blue eyes are bleached white. Her pale skin glows, illuminating the space between us.

Between flashes of light, I feel a faint . . . stirring. I think I know her. I think *I know her.*

I push Her arms away but she returns, teeth bared, hands clutching and scraping at flesh, hooking talons inside and pulling away. Blood drips down my arms and neck. I glance down at my chest, its bloody ribbons of muscle.

She claws my face. I grab Her slippery wrists to protect my eyes, my nose. Her death-softened muscles slide up Her forearms like the sleeve of a shirt.

Reeling backward, I kick Her as we fall, foot smashing through Her stomach and into her vertebrae. She kicks my kidneys in retaliation.

Going, all is

clear, without a doubt.

I sink into a memory, pillow-soft. I'm lying on a bed and my mother is sitting on the mattress beside me. Her red hair is pulled back off her forehead in a ponytail. She smiles down at me, her blue eyes loving. Her hands caress the hair off my forehead, then the nape of my neck.

She bites my skull at the back of my neck.

My mother is pulling me down the sidewalk in a wagon. The wind is blowing her hair askew. We're smiling at each other. She starts singing a song and I sing along with her:

We went to the animal fair
The birds and the beasts were there
The big baboon by the light of the moon
Was combing his auburn hair . . .

The monster stops singing and looks at me. And my mother and the monster are suddenly one and the same.

The monkey he got drunk
And fell on the elephant's trunk

teeth scrape scalp

chipped bone searing

pain

Going, all is clear.

I'm going to die.
I'm going to die.

The elephant sneezed, went down on his knees
And that was the end of the monk
The monk the monk . . .

I'm going to die. Alone.

Alone with Her. The monster who might be my mother.

no doubt about it

Was my life really ever under my control anyway?

What, then, is all?

What, then, is all?

I don't know. I don't know what "all" is. "I'm going to have to take a rain check on that one," I tell the darkness. "I'm going to have to—"

A spark of light flares for a moment.

Not the sickly glow of the leviathan but fire, growing. A soul.

It's not my dad or Jacob or Aileen. It's not Zachary. I've seen them all in this place and this blue flame is different from all of them.

Who is it?

I grab Her, this dead person, the leviathan, and I pull Her over my head so She's in front of me. I hold Her arms so She can't kick or grab or tear and I pull Her toward me. Clutch Her tight. Tighter.

And I know the truth in an instant. She's mine. This is my mother.

Whatever She is—She is *my mother.*

No wonder I'm always searching for her grave in my dreams. Because She doesn't have one. She's been stuck here in Limbo for years.

without a doubt

I'm running toward Her, a little kid, eager, crying, "Mama! Mama!" She's sitting on a moving train, looking out the window. The blanket covering Her frail body falls away and reveals a skeleton arm. She turns to look at me, dark eyes huge in Her face, skeleton arm reaching out to me. "My son," She says. "My little love."

Somebody grabs me from behind and pulls me backward.

"I love you, my boy," She calls. "I love you!"

"Goodbye, Mama, goodbye!" I call. "I love you!"

"I love you, my boy," She says. Her eyes heave huge tears.

"I love you, Mom," I say. "I love you." *Oh, how I wish I'd known You longer.*

The monster goes limp in my arms.

"Goodbye, Mama," I call. "Goodbye."

I look down. The Thing in my arms is no longer my mother. She's turned into a toddler—a little boy with dark, unruly hair, skin that is neither light nor dark but somewhere in between, deep-set eyes and bushy eyebrows.

It's me.

We fall. Me and the monster. The monster who was my mother and now is . . . me.

The blue flame of my soul goes out and suddenly I'm alone in the darkness, embracing my own corpse.

We fall.

Is this what it feels like to be dead? But . . . how can I

hold my own corpse? As soon as I ask, the corpse disappears. But I'm still falling.

What, then, is all?

If I'm dead, I'd like to pass on to the other side, get away from this endless fall. I wish I knew what it was like. If I make it there, will I recognize my mother or anybody else who might be there? Or are things so different, I won't recognize anybody because it's all brand new, like being born?

I'd like to think that my "all" will gather together on the other side someday, with me. And that I'll recognize them. I don't want to lose them. Even if half of them hate me, just because I'm a Reaper.

The scattered thoughts running ramshackle through my brain begin to coalesce around a single person.

Rachel. *I need to find her.*

I jerk upright. And suddenly, just like that, I'm sitting in the dark, the motion of perpetual falling gone.

Get up, Adam, I tell myself.

Everything's still black. With my mind's eye, I sense a soul to my right and another to my left. The one to my left exudes a sense of comfort, of being at home, of being with somebody he or she loves. The one to the right is scared and angry and alone. I'm guessing one's Rachel and one's Zachary but I have no idea which one is which.

I'll tell you what I want. I want to go left, toward the promise of happiness. So I turn to the right instead. If Amaros had stolen my soul, I'd be pretty freaking scared too.

Sand crunches under my feet. I take another step but something springy, like a trampoline, pushes me back every time I push against it. I feel up the sides and down and over the invisible wall. Whatever it is, it's impenetrable.

So I head back toward happiness, toward the smell of cut grass, and walk into a world of sepia colors—although the sunshine is so bright, it lights up a post-WWII-era housing development somewhere in Suburbia, USA.

I head toward a house in the middle of the street. It's brighter than the other ones, as if there are more pixels in this part of the street than the rest. A split-level house with a single-car garage. Freshly cut, impossibly green grass.

I press my ear up against the front door. Muffled sounds filter through the wood. Should I knock? I don't really know who—or what—is in there.

I open the door quietly and slip inside. A short flight of stairs leads up and another short flight leads down. The noises come from the lower level. I inch my way down the stairs. It's dim down here, lit only by the light filtering through a crack of the door at the end of the hall. I tiptoe toward the light, the muffled sound separating out into two distinct voices. Two teenage girls.

"We have to talk about this." The first girl sounds intense but there's something odd about her voice, like wrinkles on a baby's face. "What would you do if an intruder broke in?"

"It won't happen." It's Rachel, sounding peaceful, serene, almost . . . drugged. "The neighborhood is safe. The town is safe. That's why Mom and Dad moved us here. They wanted to get us away from all that crime in the South Side."

"I wish that were true," the other girl says. "But somebody's coming here to take me away."

"Nobody can hurt you here," Rachel insists. "I won't let them."

"What will you do?"

"Why, I'll—" Rachel pauses. "If somebody tries to hurt us or take you away, I'll protect you. With Dad's gun."

The second girl's voice quickly fills with greed, a swimming pool overflowing. "Oh, Dad has a gun? I should know where it is just in case something happens to you."

"Nothing's going to happen to me," Rachel says. "Not here. This is heaven."

"Listen to me," the first girl says. "Have you heard of the Grim Reaper? The Angel of Death?"

Rachel stays silent for a long time. When she speaks, I can barely hear her. She sounds uncertain now. "Ye-es."

The other girl's voice gets louder, insistent: "Well, you can't keep the Grim Reaper away, and that's who's coming for me. He wants to steal my soul and take it to hell. He wants your soul too. And Mom's. And Dad's. He wants it all."

A voice whispers in my head: *What, then, is all?*

"I don't believe it," Rachel says. "People like the Grim Reaper can't take souls just because they want to. There are rules about these sorts of things."

"Nice, real nice," the other girl sneers. "They've already filled your head with a pack of horrible lies."

"Who are 'they'?" Rachel asks.

"You know who they are," the girl spits. "They're the reason we're in this god-forsaken place."

"I like this place," Rachel says.

"You would." She whines, then begins to plead: "Rachel, we need to protect ourselves. The Grim Reaper is a monster. We don't have much time. Tell me where Dad keeps the gun."

The cadence of her voice is familiar. The last time, that voice sounded like Zachary, but it wasn't. And now it isn't Rachel's sister either. It's Amaros. How's he controlling her?

I peer through the crack in the door. Rachel's sitting on a lacy white bed in a pale pink room, a bedroom for a girl much younger than she actually is. The girl sitting beside her looks vaguely like Rachel but older. She strokes Rachel's hand gently.

I blink. In the fraction of a second between eyes closed and eyes fully open, I catch a glimpse of a leathery beast, sucking on a large wound on Rachel's hand. Its disgusting head is all teeth, the nose just a tiny bump with huge flaring nostrils beneath its red, beady eyes.

As soon as the light filters into my pupils, the beast disappears. Rachel's "sister" is back, gently massaging her hand.

"Okay," Rachel says, "Dad has a gun beside the bed. And the kitchen knives are sharp. Really sharp. So Mom can easily cut up all those steaks she grills."

"Thank you," Amaros breathes, and crushes her in a hug so hard, her eyes momentarily bug out. I blink and catch an image of the creature sinking two fangs deep into Rachel's chest. "Everything will be all right now, I promise."

Rachel looks down and notices her blood-soaked shirt.

She screams, but now that Amaros has what he wants, he's lost patience with her. He jerks away and snaps, "What's your problem?"

"I'm bleeding," Rachel sobs.

I crash through the door, grabbing the desk chair and smashing it against Amaros. He leaps up, snarling, and hits me with his fist, knocking me over before running out the door.

I stagger to my feet.

Rachel starts to scream, then falls back on the bed. "Adam?" she says. "Are you Adam?" She doesn't wait for me to respond before she begins panicking. "You have to get out of here, Adam. My sister thinks you guys are monsters. She's going to try to kill you."

There's no time to explain to her that she doesn't have a sister or remind her that she, Rachel, is also one of "you guys."

"Let's go." I grab her hand and pull her behind me to the stairs. How in the world am I going to get us out of this place? There has to be a way. Soul guides enter Limbo all the time and somehow get back to life. It's just that I've never done it consciously before.

We're halfway up the stairs when a gun roars behind us, a bullet shattering the railing. Huge chunks of wood rain down on us.

We bolt into the kitchen. I slide behind the counter and jerk Rachel down on the linoleum floor, hiding behind the wooden island.

Amaros calls from the stairs in the hall: "I see you figured out how to get to Limbo, Adam." He's dropped the pretense of speaking in a girl's voice. His real voice is raspy, elderly, the voice of a man 150 years old or more.

"So what?" I call back.

"Our deal still stands." His voice reaches me after what feels like forever, like he's speaking through a loudspeaker but it has to travel down a long, long hallway. "I'm not after you. If you help me now, I can show you the path to eternal life."

Maybe if Amaros keeps talking, he won't shoot. "What do I have to do?"

"Help me lure your father to Limbo. Death is his game and, as such, he's completely wrong about life. He's become so powerful and wealthy because he profits from the souls he's supposedly helping."

"What do you mean?" *Keep talking, Amaros*. "My dad isn't wealthy."

"Hahahahaha! Your dad's a multibillionaire, you idiot. And he became wealthy by one simple equation: more death equals more wealth. He's doing his job very well, don't you think? All I want is to stop the madness. We should all have the opportunity to live forever."

"You mean we get paid to usher souls to the other side?"

"Hahahahaha," he laughs again. "You don't know the first thing about the evil business you're profiting from."

What the heck does it mean to profit from death? I still can't wrap my head around this. I mean, how does it work? Who pays us? And in what kind of currency?

"We're doing this to help people," I say.

"Now now, Adam, don't fool yourself. If you were so altruistic, wouldn't you be doing it for free? Or not doing it at all? Maybe helping people live forever, be with their loved ones, instead of dying? Leaving everything they've ever known or loved?"

Maybe Amaros—or whoever this is—is right. But he isn't speaking the whole truth. "Maybe that's true," I call, "but you're also sick. What do you have to do to live forever? Take other people's bodies so your soul can just keep on going, indefinitely? That's selfish, man. You're in this for you."

He's silent for a second. Maybe he's never thought about it this way before. In the silence, Rachel moans and that seems to stir Amaros again.

"We don't have much time, Adam," he warns. "You have to choose. Life or death. Me or your father."

"Why should I believe anything you say?"

"Unlike your father, I've never lied to you."

"But she's been lying to *me*." Rachel slugs me on the shoulder. "That isn't my sister, is it?"

"No. You don't have a sister."

She scowls.

"I'm sorry."

"I knew this was too good to be true." She frowns as if she's just come out of a dream, noticing the blood pooling on the white linoleum. She panics, suddenly and completely. "Fuck! Adam! Am I going to die?"

"No!" I shout. "No, you're not. Now think. Is there a weapon in here?"

"In the kitchen closet," she whispers. She's breathing hard, trying to hold onto herself. "Mom always kept it loaded. You know, for shooting rabbits in the garden." The effort to say all that costs her; as soon as she finishes speaking, she passes out.

The kitchen closet is across the counter. A universe away.

"You have ten seconds and then it's over, Adam," Amaros calls. "I'm coming up there to prepare for your father and if you're not with me, you're against me."

I slide over the counter to the kitchen closet and open the door, expecting some sort of BB gun. At best, a .22. And there it is. A freaking twelve-gauge shotgun. Only Rachel would be so demented, she'd imagine a suburban mother who shoots garden rabbits with a twelve-gauge.

I grab the gun as Amaros charges up the stairs. He jumps into the room, revolver in his hand. I point the shotgun at his head and he halts for just a second before turning and leaping, crashing through a window, then runs down the street, disappearing from view.

I bend down to feel Rachel's pulse. It's thready but she's still breathing.

Rachel's desire for a family and a home was so huge, her imagination ran away with the details. I open a drawer and find dish towels, which I press against her wounds. After a few minutes, the bleeding slows to an ooze.

Just as I'm wondering what I should do next, I feel it. A presence I know so well, I almost pass out in relief. The front door opens and I yell, "Dad! We're upstairs in the kitchen! Get here quick!"

He takes the stairs two at a time. "What are you doing here, Adam?" He stops and stares at Rachel. He becomes very still for a second, face ashy-gray. "Who is this?"

"Rachel. My friend." I add, "Apparently, she's a Reaper."

"She *is* a Reaper," Dad says. He smoothes the hair back from her face. Like he can't help himself. "She looks exactly like your mother. If I didn't know better, I'd—" He stops. "Well, she's not your mother. But she's related to her, I have no doubt. Where'd she come from? I'll have to speak to your grandfather about this when we get back."

"Are we going to get back?" I can't help but ask.

"Why wouldn't we?" Dad's tone is mild and then I realize he doesn't know.

"Somebody named Amaros lured us here so you'd come. I don't know his real name. He's with La Luz."

For just a moment, Dad looks old, really old, like three hundred years old or something. "Fine," he says. "Let him come find me. He'll soon realize he's made a mistake. In the meantime, I have to save this young woman."

Sutures and needles appear in the air. Dad sews Rachel's wounds up with a dexterity and simplicity that suggest he's had some practice doing this kind of thing.

"I thought we just escorted souls to the other side," I say. "But you're like a doctor."

He grimaces in what I now recognize as his grim Grim Reaper smile. "Some souls get kicked into Limbo accidentally. It's not yet their time. You have to figure out the difference so that you can help some souls return to life."

"Amaros was sucking blood from that wound on her chest."

"He did that to control her body and her world," Dad says.

I think back to how pale Zachary was when Amaros was inhabiting his body.

"She didn't know he was doing it, though. He tricked her somehow—she thought he was her sister. But she doesn't have a sister. She doesn't have any family at all."

Dad looks up then and smiles at me. "I wouldn't be so sure, son. I think her family quota—and yours—has become exponentially larger."

"You really think we're related?"

"I'd stake my life on it. I just wish I knew where she came from. She's . . . a complete surprise."

So this is what my mother looked like. Straight, thick, reddish-sandy hair. Freckles all over her nose and cheeks. A long hooked nose and thin lips and a wide smile. She does look just like the woman in the train that goes around and around and around in my dream.

Dad gathers Rachel in his arms and whispers in her ear, a soft crooning, almost singing: "Rachel." Voice low and intimate, something that creeps inside your heart and warms you with its intensity of knowing who you are and caring about you. "Rachel."

She opens her eyes and I sag in relief.

"You came," she says to Dad.

"I came," he agrees.

"I should be scared but I'm not," she says.

"You have nothing to be scared of, darling," he says. "It's not your time."

"This whole place is a lie," she says. "It's everything I ever wanted and it's all a lie."

"Limbo is never a lie, dear. It simply manifests our greatest desires or worst fears."

"I thought I had a sister." She begins to cry. "I thought I

had a sister and a mom and a dad. I thought I had a *family*. And it's all a big fat lie."

"You do have a family," Dad tells her. "Adam's your family. I'm your family. My wife—Adam's mother—she was your family. For the moment, it doesn't matter how—it's just enough to know we're claiming you. You're not alone anymore. You're ours."

Rachel looks from Dad to me and back to Dad. Then she returns her attention to me. "What are you staring at?" she asks crossly.

I laugh in sheer, utter relief. Rachel's back. She's back, man!

"She's going to be all right, son," Dad says unnecessarily. "Now go! Go back to your body. Go back to life. Limbo's dangerous if La Luz has infiltrated it."

"I don't know how."

He's still working on Rachel, but he pauses long enough to push his glasses farther up his nose. "What do you really care about? Back in life?"

It feels cheesy to say it. I squirm. "You."

He smiles. "But I'm here, in Limbo. You need something else. Something that's there now at this exact moment."

"I'm not sure."

"It doesn't matter what it is, it just has to be something that draws you back to your body. Once you have somebody or something in mind, latch onto it and don't let your mind wander."

I hand him the shotgun. Then I stand there. What do I care about so much that it will bring me back to life? I remember that time when the thought of Sarah pulled me back from Limbo at Coney Island. Would that work again?

Dad gestures impatiently. *Get on with it, Adam.*

Rachel's head slumps against Dad's chest and he begins to sing. I've never heard him sing. He has a strong baritone. A nice voice. I wish I'd heard him sing before.

I leave the kitchen to concentrate. What do I care about? Something I care about enough that it will take me back to my body?

I think about the school, the music, the books, Aileen's simple instructions, Jacob's belly-laughing lectures. Tomás and Sean being smart-asses at dinnertime after a long day studying. Rachel with her crummy foster-kid shoes. Liliana, sneaking into my room and holding my hand as we fall asleep. Principal Armand. Principal Armand? His cold blue eyes suddenly seem to twinkle at me.

The walls of the living room start to fade.

What the heck. *Am I in love with school?*

That thought jerks me back to Limbo. I'm staring at a painting of a snowy woodland hanging over the fireplace mantle. Dad's singing to Rachel in the kitchen.

No. No, I'm not in love with school. Or Principal Armand. I'm in love with all my friends. With the life they brought me. School is just the backdrop.

I concentrate again and this time the walls disappear completely. Slowly, the white room materializes in front of me. I float above my body in Amaros's house. Sean sits next to Rachel on the couch, biting his nails. Rachel's skin is almost as white as the couch except for two tiny circles of pink dotting her cheeks. Liliana kneels near Zachary's body, Tomás between us, one hand on each.

My body twitches on the floor. It lacks a shadow, but if

anybody were to look up, really look, they'd see it floating toward my body.

"I think he's coming to." Liliana sounds relieved.

I'm almost linked to myself when my eyes fall on Zachary's lifeless body. He's still stuck in Limbo. The scene in front of me disappears and I crash back into darkness, the endless fall into the abyss.

CHAPTER 27.5

And so the time came. It was, as they say, inevitable. But the lover-husband had held out a thin glimmer of hope to his bride and she did not wish to go. Also, there was their son, a young boy now four years old. She did not wish to let go of life with all its joys and sorrows.

So she held on. She refused to cross over.

What do you mean, she refused? Elder #5 spoke. The Grim Reaper? Refused to die?

Yes, he said simply.

They looked at each other blankly. Finally, one of them queried, So your daughter became stuck?

He nodded. Worse, even. She became a nightmare. A demon. One who tried to take the boy.

She tried to take the boy to Limbo? Her Excellency asked. She looked around at the other Synod Elders. Their faces were bleak. She tried to take him out of life? To the other side?

Yes.

My god.

It was a dark and stormy night. The Grim Reap-

er's soul was going, going, but she was clinging with everything she had to life. The Grim Reaper had always been macabre and so her Limbo was, ironically, a cemetery. As she held on with all her might, she sensed her son's soul nearby. She reached out and snatched—and she took her son's soul straight into Limbo with her. She took him and she wouldn't let go.

The lover-husband was forced to choose between saving his son and making sure the love of his life crossed to the other side. He chose his son and abandoned his love in Limbo.

The Synod went silent for a moment. He stood in front of them, head bowed.

She is there still. She's in Limbo yet. She has never crossed the River Styx.

Her Excellency finally spoke, her voice gentle: We understand at last, John. We understand what you have been trying to tell us.

CHAPTER 28

I stop myself falling almost immediately. I don't know why, I just know I don't have to do it anymore. Also, She—the one who apparently was my mother, and I'm going to have to ask Dad about that as soon as I get a chance because he has some explaining to do—is gone, maybe for good. When I stand up, I'm back in the foggy darkness between souls. Rachel's is to my left, like before. To my right is the other soul locked into the sounds and smells of the ocean, barricaded behind an enormous, invisible wall.

Using my fingers, I seek a crack or hole—something, anything, that will let me through. But I can't reach the top and no matter how far I walk in either direction, I can't seem to reach the end of it. By leaning against it with my full body weight, I can push the barrier forward about a foot and feel sand crunching underfoot. Then it springs back and I stumble.

Why could I go right into Rachel's world but not this one? Something about it doesn't feel right. There has to be a way around or through this barrier. Walls have to conform to the rules of logic, even in Limbo.

As I think, I keep pushing. Suddenly it gives way and I lurch through what feels like a thick wall of sand.

My breath catches, a quick choking sensation, and then I'm dusting off my clothes and standing up to look around me at Zachary's Limbo.

White foam swirls over my feet. Waves crash onto a beach. Millions of stars twinkle in the night sky and artificial lights wink in the distance. They resolve into a riot of moving colors as I approach.

The heart of Zachary's Limbo turns out to be a carnival situated on a giant pier. A huge Ferris wheel revolves slowly out over the water, gondolas shining green and white, while carousel music tinkles in the wind and horses, lions, and tigers pump up and down. Tilt-A-Whirl cars spin and whoosh over the gyrating floor. Swings orbit a giant purple octopus.

The carnival is empty.

I roam the streets, swept clean of the usual food and garbage and bird poop, and head toward the center of the park, a black eye in a sea of moving light. It turns out to be a massive wooden roller coaster. My thigh muscles ache as I zigzag my way to the entrance, following the sounds of banging and clanging.

"Hellooooo!" I yell.

To my surprise, Zachary emerges from the operator's box. He's dressed in grease-stained overalls, a large wrench in his hand. A wound gapes in the back of his neck where, I'm guessing, Amaros was sucking his blood not too long ago. He's so pale, I wonder if a single drop of blood remains in his body or whatever you call your body in Limbo.

"Hi," I say.

He drops the wrench and winces as it falls through a crack and tumbles to the ground twenty feet below. "Sorry, Dad," he mumbles.

I realize almost immediately that he's talking to me. "I'm not your Dad, Zachary."

"I'm sorry I flunked out of school. But I'm still an Angel. I can still be useful."

"Look, you haven't flunked out of school. Somebody kidnapped you, stole your body, and left you here in Limbo."

It's almost as if he can't hear what I'm saying. Tears stream down his face.

"What is this place?" I ask.

"My favorite part of summer was when you'd take us to the Santa Cruz Boardwalk," he says. "So I made this place for us."

I had always pegged Zachary as the guy who would own Hollywood. I never would have guessed he really wanted to be a carny. Would he be that sketchy guy with ratty hair and a beer belly who runs the children's rides?

"This place was a dump when I got here but now I've got all of the rides running," he says.

The Zachary I know would be bragging, and if he was talking to me that's possibly how he would sound. But talking to his dad—or rather to somebody he thinks is his dad—he just sounds vulnerable. Like he's done something to be proud of but he's afraid I'm going to crap all over it.

And that leaves me in a conundrum. We're in Zachary's Limbo. What am I supposed to do in his Limbo when he thinks I'm somebody else? Am I supposed to convince him that I'm just Adam? Or am I supposed to go with the flow, pretend to be his dad?

And if I'm his dad, am I his real father—who sounds

like he might be kind of a dick, if you want to know the truth—or the father he'd want me to be? Should I give him a big bear hug? Slap him on the back and say, *Atta boy, Zachary! I'm so proud of you, son?* Or should I piss all over his accomplishments?

"That's great, Zachary," I say. "What's wrong with the roller coaster?"

The eagerness in his eyes dies. Of course, I had to comment on the one thing in the whole park that doesn't seem to be working. Guess I chose a behavior exactly like his real dad, by accident.

His shoulders slump. "You always said people come for the roller coaster. I'm trying but I don't know if I can fix it."

"It's all right, Zachary. The rest of this place is amazing."

"Thanks?" He masks his surprise, hammer clanking as he bangs on a part of the track that looks slightly bent.

"Listen," I say, hoping to get his attention—his *real* attention—for just a few seconds. "We need to go now. We need to get back to your body."

A cross look twists and distorts his face. For just a second, I think he sees me, Adam, but then the flash of reality is gone. "I'm not going anywhere until the roller coaster works," he says.

"Hey, no worries. But why don't you take a break? We can walk down to the beach and you can see how great this place looks." Maybe if I get him to the edge of his world, away from the core of his desire, I can convince him to come back to life.

He glances at the hammer in his hand and wipes hair out of his eyes, leaving a huge smear of black grease across his forehead. He stares at the roller coaster, then out at this world he's created. "Okay," he finally says.

We walk toward the entrance. I'm reining myself in, trying not to seem too eager to get out of here. Zachary walks slowly. He keeps turning his head to look back at the swirling lights.

Then, for a split second, the whole carnival goes black—as if it blinked. When the lights come back on, they warp slightly before returning to normal.

"What the—?" Shock wrinkles across his forehead.

But I already feel it. Him, I mean, if he deserves a pronoun. Amaros is here in Zachary's world. We've officially run out of time.

"We have to hide," I say, and steer Zachary into the nearest building, an old-fashioned arcade lit by rows of pinball machines.

"Why?" Zachary shouts over the loud pings and rattles.

"Somebody dangerous just showed up!" I yell. "Do you have any weapons?"

"What?"

"Weapons!" I scream. "We need weapons!"

"What kind of person do you think I am? This is a place for kids. No weapons allowed."

Just my luck. Rachel had a twelve-gauge hidden in the kitchen of *her* world. Couldn't Zachary have imagined one teeny-tiny weapon into his? I wonder if Amaros was able to bring Rachel's gun into Zachary's world.

My question is answered a second later when a burst of gunfire erupts outside the arcade. Sparks fly as bullets riddle the machine next to us. We dive under a pinball machine. Bullets whiz over our heads and explode, shattering the wall behind us.

Zachary starts to panic. "We have to put a stop to this before the rides are damaged."

"Stop worrying about the rides!" I shout.

Zachary pins his mouth against my ear. "What the hell is going on? You show up and suddenly somebody is coming after us with a gun? What did you do, Dad? Who'd you piss off this time?"

Zachary's dad sounds like a real winner.

"Let's just get out of here, Zachary."

We crawl in the opposite direction from the gunfire and huddle behind the last pinball machine. A few feet away, I spot a door.

"I'll open the door," I tell Zachary. "Then you make a run for it."

I jump out from behind the pinball machine even as bullets riddle the wall above my head. The door's locked.

I dive headfirst back to safety.

"You can't escape, Adam," Amaros calls. "If you come out nicely, maybe we can talk this over and come to some sort of arrangement."

"What do you want from me?" I yell. Maybe if I keep him talking for long enough, my dad will come and rescue me again, like he did in Rachel's world.

"I just want to talk, Adam. You should know that nobody can come and rescue you. I've put in all sorts of defensive devices to keep people from accessing Zachary's Limbo."

"You mean that awesome barrier you erected? Yeah, that defense worked real well to keep me out."

"Weeeelllll," Amaros stretches the word out, "I made some unfortunate errors which have already been fixed. The real question you should be asking, Adam, is not whether somebody can come in here and rescue you but whether you're lucky enough to get out alive a second time."

I consider our situation.

I'm not ready to die. But I can't compromise. Amaros is sick. Sicker than sick. I mean, I saw him *feeding* on Rachel. That wound on Zachary's neck tells me he was also feeding on Zachary not too long ago. There's no way Zachary and I are getting out of here alive if we give him what he wants.

So if I have to die, I have to die. But I'm going to make this as difficult as possible. "I'm not going to die!" I yell.

"Adam, you may be right. Our operative tagged you as special from the first moment he saw you. But if you don't cooperate with me, I will definitely hurt you."

His footsteps echo through the arcade.

"I'm coming to get you now," he sings.

"Zachary, where is the key to that door?" I whisper.

"I don't know."

I grab him by the shirt and pull him toward me so that our noses are practically touching. "You do know where the key is. This whole world is your freaking fantasy."

Zachary's head is down. He can't look me in the eye.

"Imagine it! Imagine where it is and pull it out of your damn pocket."

Amaros's shoes scrape against the floor. He's getting closer.

"I—I don't know," Zachary repeats.

I slam him against the pinball machine so hard, his head flops. "For god's sake, Zachary, just check!"

His hands shake as he fumbles with his pockets. "It's not there." Tears make trails through the smudges on his face.

"You have the key. I know it." I reach into the chest pocket of his overalls, willing there to be a key, my hand closing over the familiar indented surface of a metal house key. "See?"

A sob catches in his throat but I don't have time to be nice. We have just a few seconds before Amaros will be in point-blank range. "Get up and help," I hiss, jerking him up. We push the pinball machine to a center aisle for cover while I unlock the door. The machine starts banging, lights flashing, as bullets thud into it.

I slide the key into the lock and push the door open. We jump through. Bullets ping against the Tilt-A-Whirl.

"The haunted house," Zachary pants. "We can hide there."

We run past the Ferris wheel and plunge inside. Neon purples and greens light up the interior. Zachary's teeth and the label on his overalls glow bright white in the funky black ultraviolet lights.

We jump onto the tracks. As we tunnel deeper into the ride, mechanical skeleton prospectors with pickaxes lunge at us. Loud screams and howls reverberate from speakers in the walls.

"Can we get to the top?" I ask, wondering if that might give us the vantage point to see what's going on, maybe offer us an escape route.

Zachary shoves a black curtain aside, revealing steel girders and wires creeping over the ground like vines. A rung ladder trails up the wall into the dark. He begins to climb and I follow, head swimming as I mount the ladder. But there's no wraith waiting below us. My mother is gone. Maybe She's gone forever. That's something I still need to think about. Later.

Zachary opens a hatch in the ceiling and crawls through. I follow, hauling myself up onto the roof. We hide behind a flashing purple *HAUNTED HOUSE* sign and peer through the gap between the two words at the amusement park below.

Amaros appears relaxed, lounging on a bench opposite the haunted house. The bench is nestled between the legs of a large plastic clown holding up a gigantic plastic ice-cream cone. Amaros holds the gun loosely across his legs.

"I know you guys are up there!" he shouts. "I don't want to hurt either of you but I'm about out of patience! When that happens, I promise I won't miss!" He pats an assault rifle, quite a jump up in class of weapon from the revolver he'd found in Rachel's world. "Look, I helped Zachary refine this place so I know a thing or two about it, including where to get things! Stop the BS now! Next shot kills!"

He pulls a lighter out of his pocket, flicks it open, watches the flame idly. Strolls casually over to the haunted house and holds the flame underneath the heavy purple curtains that drape the ride from top to bottom.

Zachary pales. "This place will go up like kindling."

"Amaros, if you kill us both in Limbo, you won't have

a body to go back to!" I call. I sound a little desperate but that's the crux of it . . . I am desperate.

"Ha!" His laugh echoes off the buildings. "I don't need your body! Limbo is an ever-revolving door of souls. Somebody else will come along. The only reason I'm entertaining your little—game—is because I want to talk to your father. So don't be stupid! Come down and talk to me!"

The drapes ignite suddenly and fire eats away the curtains, moving slowly toward us on the roof.

Zachary slides to the ground, puts his head between his hands, groans. "We're gonna die, aren't we?"

"I don't know," I say. "But let's make sure that asshole doesn't get what he's after, okay?"

Zachary nods slowly. "Okay, Dad, I'm with you."

Flames shoot up through the haunted house sign. Sparks fly up toward the stars.

I peer over the side. Amaros saunters back to the bench and sits down, gun across his knees. Waiting.

"What's holding up the curtain?" I ask Zachary.

"An iron bar," he says. "I installed it myself."

I look him dead in the eye. "It's faulty, isn't it?"

"No, everything's good, Dad. I took a lot of time. I was careful."

"No," I say. This time I don't ask. I just state, "It's defective."

"No," he insists. "I put in the best of the best."

"No," I say. This time it's more than a statement, it's an accusation. "You put in whatever you had."

My words take instant effect. They weren't true a second ago, but suddenly, because Zachary absorbs them and accepts them, they become the truth. "You're right, Dad." He swallows. "I can't do anything right."

The instant he says these words, the bar breaks. Purple curtains whoosh as they fall. Zachary watches, shocked. "That could have hit a child!"

I don't feel good about what I'm doing, messing with his head, with the perfect world he created. But I don't know any other way out of this. He *has* to reimagine everything as crap.

I just hope he'll accept my apology. After. When we're safely out of here.

Amaros stands up, aiming his gun at us.

"Look, there are no children here, the only people who can get hurt are us," I say. And I make the leap. Maybe I'll burn in hell for this. Maybe it'll save us. "That clown over there isn't supported by anything, is it." I state this as if it's an established fact.

"I—I—I thought I did that," Zachary stammers.

"It's not bolted down, is it!"

"No," Zachary admits.

The metal clown creaks. We look over the edge. Amaros glances back in horror and starts to run as the clown pitches face-first into the pavement. Its outstretched arm holding the ice-cream cone crashes into the haunted house's façade and lands with a rending shriek, ripping a gigantic hole in the front.

"Now!" I yell at Zachary. "Let's go!"

We half climb, half slide down the ladder, crouching low to keep out of the line of fire. I have no idea where Amaros went, only that he headed back toward the Ferris wheel.

"I'm sorry, Zachary," I say.

"For what?"

I don't answer. I just do what I decided to do, diving right into his mind. And then I run helter-skelter through this world he so carefully created. I remove memories of tightening huge bolts, of putting the lid on the generator gas tank, of wiring the rides correctly.

Zachary quickly lets his mind shrink to a small knot somewhere nearby as I take more and more control of his world. "This is just like you, Dad," he mutters at some point. "Wrecking everything I ever created. Thanks. Thanks a lot."

The changes wreak havoc immediately. The cars on the Ferris wheel drop off and crash through the pier into the water below. The Tilt-A-Whirl cars come off their moorings and skid across the wood boards, crashing into other rides.

I glance at Zachary. He sits back and folds his arms across his chest.

"Do it," he says. "But don't expect me to help you."

As I burrow deeper into his head, I feel myself split off from him. Like a bird, I circle in the air above us, watching as the world collapses below. I see myself, body erect and arms raised to the heavens. Amaros runs through the wreckage as I demolish one ride after another. The roller coaster erupts into flame as he jumps into the sea, swims to the sandy beach, and scrambles over the dunes.

Then he's gone.

Something sweet spreads from my mind down my esophagus and settles warmly in my belly. Much like the shandies we drank the first night of school. All I want to do is rip and shred and tear, more and more and more. The noise is incredible, a roar in my ears that I feel from my teeth to my toes.

But I look at my feet and notice Zachary. Perfectly silent. Huddled beside me. He isn't crying. He isn't anything. He's just sitting there, hunched into his overalls, staring at the wooden pier.

"Are you okay?"

He tries to lift his head but he can't.

The sweet feeling crashes into bitterness and I snap back into myself, sinking to the ground beside Zachary. It feels like I've been swimming through mud. Like I'm lost in a world of muck and algae. I wipe the sweat from my forehead.

"I'm really sorry, Zachary."

It sounds as though I'm speaking through a tunnel. A long tunnel. And I'm not even sure if there's anybody there at the other end.

"It's okay, Adam." He can barely get the words out.

"You finally realized I'm not your dad, huh?"

He nods. We sit. I put my arm under his back and prop him up so he can look around. "Wow, what a wreck."

"I'm sorry I ruined it," I say. "I know you worked hard."

His eyes are clear. "You did what you had to do." He sniffles. "I should hate you, Adam. But I don't. Remember that, okay? Because it's going to kick in, later, what you did to me. I don't hate you. I know you aren't asking, at least right now, but I forgive you. I do."

"Okay," I say.

"And I have to apologize too. I'm sorry for spying on you."

"Spying on me? You mean for La Luz? I already know about that, dude. You were out of your head or something. I think what happened when we went to Limbo together affected your brain somehow. Made you more vulnerable."

"You're right. But I'm talking about before. Back at school, before going to Limbo. I was spying on you for my family. For the Angels. They wanted to know who you were. What powers you have."

"What?" I stare at him. And then I realize it doesn't matter. I don't have time to think about this. And neither does Zachary. I crouch, arm under his shoulder to help him stand up. "Actually, forget about it. We can talk about it later. Right now, we have to get out of here."

Zachary shakes his head. "I know where I am. I thought I would be scared, but I'm not."

"Zachary? I hate to burst your drama here but we can get back."

He smiles at me. Gentle. Ironic. "Don't ask me how I know, but my body's dead. I'm not going back to life. So please . . . say goodbye to my mom and Liliana. Tell them I love them."

"Is Liliana really your sister?"

"Half. We only found out when she sneaked into Principal Armand's office last year and found her birth certificate in his files. We share the same asshole dad. That was just before she got expelled."

"Did she get expelled because of that?"

He shrugs. "It's too late for me to worry about it." He slugs my shoulder, halfhearted. "Hey. Will you say goodbye to Rachel too? I liked her. She was different."

"Then why were you such a dick to her?"

"You know, just because *you* interpreted everything I did in a negative light doesn't mean—" He stops and sighs. "Never mind. It isn't important." He licks his index finger and makes an imaginary mark in the air. "Never thought you'd be the one to take me to the other side. I'm your first soul, the first one you helped cross Limbo. That means you'll never forget me. You know what? I'm glad it's you. Maybe you'll forgive me now for taking you to Limbo that time?"

"Stop talking, Zachary! Maybe I can revive your body. Can you hang on long enough for me to go back to life?"

"Just throw me into the sea."

"No." Somehow I have the feeling I shouldn't do anything for Zachary now. He has to do this himself.

"What the hell, man! After all that you did to me, you won't even help me? Just like my old man."

I sit back on my heels. "Whatever you are going to do, you've got to do it. This is your world and I'm not going to hold you back. And I'll be here with you. I just can't do it *for* you."

Zachary raises his fist, starts to grab mine. Then he blinks. "Sorry, I'm not mad at you. I'm mad at my dad." He mumbles something under his breath, eyebrows scrunched together as he scowls. He stands, hunched over like an old man. He looks at me one last time, his face a mask of frustration and hatred. "I'm done with you, Dad." Then he shakes his head, vision clearing. "See you on the other side, Adam."

He jumps over the rubble, sprinting toward the ocean,

dodging the large debris, hurtling the smaller bits of wood and metal and broken lights.

I run with him. Side by side. We get closer and closer to the farthest end of the pier and then he hurls himself off the end. Just when he reaches the apex of his jump, a gigantic wave shoots up from the sea and swallows him.

For a moment, I feel the wave's cold, salty embrace as it crashes against the pier, and then it all disappears.

CHAPTER 29

Darkness embraces me again, a soft touch this time instead of the icy fingers of death. My body feels like it's congealed in a vat of lukewarm Jell-O.

Is Zachary really dead? I wonder.

Yes, he really is, I answer, almost immediately.

In fact, my memory of him has already changed. It's missing shape and heft, like the time I left my backpack at a coffee shop and returned and knew, without even looking inside, that somebody had emptied it. Zachary is just an empty backpack in my mind.

What about me? Am I dead too? I don't think so but how would I know? Do you remember anything from life or Limbo when you reach the other side or have you lost all consciousness of who you were before?

I can't see anything or hear anything. Am I breathing?

And then I feel it again. The fear. What the hell? I thought I'd gotten rid of it. But it's there, at a distance, weaker but waiting. Definitely waiting.

A small shot of gladness wiggles its way through all that warm Jell-O. Because if the fear is still there, it must mean I'm still alive. And that means I have to think of something that will recall me back to life.

I think about my friends again. Rachel and her freckles. Tomás's pipe. Sarah's smile. Liliana's grin.

And Dad. His serious face looks at me from across a greasy table, his chopsticks neatly placed on their holder, only a few grains of rice missing from the round mound in his bowl. In his eyes, I see the reflection of someone, and for a moment I think it's me. Until I see the long red-brown hair and freckled face and beautiful smile . . .

If I get out of this, I'm going to sit down and have a long talk with Dad about my mother.

A bright light pushes painfully against my closed eyelids and tiny hairs from the plush white carpet tickle my nose, making me sneeze.

"He's coming to!" Rachel says.

I roll over and look up at her. She's sitting beside me, dark circles under her eyes. I struggle to sit up and get to my feet.

"He's alive!" she cheers. "He walks! Does he talk?"

I lean over and puke all over the white carpet. Rachel jumps sideways to avoid getting sprayed. "Ewww, Adam!"

Liliana huddles on the floor, Zachary's head in her lap, caressing his blond hair with her brown fingers. Her shoulders shake as she gazes down at his white face.

"Lili," I say, my voice squeaky and thin, "Zachary told me to tell you goodbye."

She grips his body tighter. "He's not coming back?"

"No," I say. "He's free now."

"Free?" She bites back the word. "Shut up already. I don't want to hear it."

Sean and Tomás help Rachel to her feet. When she looks at me with her hazel eyes and frank gaze, I can't hold it in anymore. I start weeping. She grabs me in a hug. "Thanks," she whispers. "I couldn't have survived that alone."

"I don't like this." Sean frowns. "Three of you go to Limbo. The Angel is dead and only the two Reapers made it back alive."

He looks at me and then Liliana looks at me and Tomás too, and I meet their silent accusation head-on. "You guys know I would never hurt anybody."

"Look, Adam, or whatever your name really is," Sean says, "I *don't* know you. I just found out you're a Reaper, a secret you've apparently been keeping from us."

Rachel shivers. "Why does it matter so much? Let's just get out of here. It's creepy. I don't want to wait for other members of La Luz to show up. Because you do know that's who was behind all this, right? You do know they're the ones who took Zachary's body and my body and lured Adam to Limbo? It wasn't the two of us. It wasn't the two horrible, awful Reapers. It was La Luz. The bad guys. Remember?"

When nobody responds, she shakes her head. "Forget it. I don't mean to be rude, but you'll never understand. Your stupid prejudice blinds you to the truth."

Sean shuffles his feet. Liliana peers off into the distance.

"Rachel's right." Tomás speaks casually, as if he's just commenting on the weather to a neighbor. "La Luz might show up any second. So let's get out of here."

"What are we going to do with Zachary's body?" Liliana asks.

"I'll carry him," I say.

"No, I will," Sean says.

We have a stare-down. Never in the last three months did I imagine I would have a stare-down with a Dullahan. Between a Dullahan and a Reaper, though, there is no contest. He looks away.

"Just give him a hand, Sean," Liliana says.

Sean takes Zachary's feet and I grab him under the arms. We heft him up and walk backward, carting him outside the house and down a ramp toward a dock. Rachel leans on Tomás and Liliana and they trail after us.

We slide into the boat, heaving Zachary's body onto a chair and propping it up. Sean glares at me until I sit next to the corpse.

Guess now that I'm a Reaper, I get all the crap jobs.

"What about the lumberjack?" I ask. "He's locked in the closet. He'll die if we leave him here."

"So let him die," Liliana responds. "He would have done the same to you."

"Adam's right," Tomás says.

"Fine, one of you go open the door. Hope he's not awake," Liliana says.

Zachary starts to fall over when I move but Sean holds him upright. As I jog toward the house, I have this horrible feeling they might leave without me but I'm just going to have to risk it. I can't leave somebody to die, even if he was one of the people responsible for getting all of us into this mess to begin with.

The house is oddly still and silent. I take a deep breath and try not to think about it as I run up the stairs and to the room where I was a prisoner only a few hours earlier.

The lumberjack is still out cold, drooling on the bathroom tiles. I unlock the door so he's not trapped.

Then I see it. *The Book of Light.*

Dad said it shouldn't get in the wrong hands. I better take it. But where can I hide it? I look around the empty room and finally at the lumberjack. I need his jacket more than he does.

A few seconds later, I'm wearing his plaid jacket, the bootleg copy of *The Book of Light* hidden safely in its deep pockets, as I make my way back to the boat.

Zachary slumps heavily against my shoulder as I take my seat next to him. When I shift, his head topples forward. I ease it back and smooth his hair out of his eyes.

"Move over." Liliana grabs the wheel out of Sean's hands. "*I'm* the speed demon."

Sean slouches into a seat facing the water and glares steadily away from the rest of us, or maybe just me. Rachel and Tomás huddle together, his arm gently supporting her. Liliana glances at Zachary every few seconds, eyes rimmed a pinky red. Every once in a while, her eyes shift to meet mine then flit away, guilty butterflies.

We race over the ocean to the distant coast. It takes about an hour before we reach a harbor I don't recognize. We tie up the boat and everybody gets out.

"Since nobody has a working phone, I'm going to go find one and call my dad," I mumble.

"You do that," Liliana snaps.

"Good idea," Tomás says. "We're in his territory. He'll know what to do."

Though the harbor and docks are empty, I'm lucky to

find a pay phone outside a gray, weather-beaten shack. An ancient phone book dangles from a rusty metal cord. I call Dad collect.

He greets me with a question: "Where are you?"

"Some harbor in Maine that I don't recognize."

"I'll look the phone number up." He's silent a moment, then says, "You're in Winter Harbor, Maine."

"I don't know where that is."

"It doesn't matter. Just get to an airport—nearest airport, that'd be Bangor—and fly to New York. Do you have Zachary's body?"

Of course Dad would know if there was a loose soul rattling around Limbo in his territory. "Yes. We couldn't leave it on the island."

"Good. It would be very messy if police get involved. So you must bring Zachary's body to New York. I'll make sure he gets home for burial."

"How are we going to get him on a plane?"

Dad's quiet for a second. "You still have that card I gave you last August?"

I feel its sharp edges inside my hoodie pocket. "Yeah." I'm also still wearing that stupid hospital gown underneath the lumberjack's jacket. The ends flap in the wind. I'm going to be surprised if they don't arrest us at the airport. I imagine telling the police that I didn't just escape from the loony bin with the body of a dead boy.

I put the phone between my ear and shoulder while I strip myself of the hospital gown. I put the lumberjack's coat back on and zip it up. It smells faintly of tobacco and coffee.

"With that card, you won't have any problems," Dad says.

"Okay." I'll believe that when I see it.

"Good job, son. You helped Zachary across. That took skill and care."

The quiet pride in his voice brings a tear to the corner of my eye. I wipe it roughly away.

After we hang up, I page through the phone book until I find a taxi company. I can't imagine they'll be too pleased if I call them collect so I shout back at my friends on the boat, "Does anybody have a quarter?"

They search their pockets, then Liliana runs up the dock to hand me a quarter. As I reach for it, her hand closes back around it, into a tight fist. "Don't screw this up, okay?"

The cab company has a shuttle to Bangor International Airport. I make arrangements and Liliana and I walk back down to the boat. I glance at her sideways, wondering what she's thinking, but she doesn't say anything. One time she cuts a sideways look at me, a hard look, and I quickly turn away.

We put sunglasses on Zachary and prop him up on a bench between me and Sean. When the cab arrives, we lift him carefully, as though we're assisting him, not carrying him.

Rachel gets into the front seat of the cab. "You don't mind if I sit here, do you?" she asks, distracting the driver long enough for us to manhandle Zachary into one of the backseats.

"What's wrong with him?" the guy asks. "He's not doing drugs, is he? If he's been using, he has to get out."

I look deep into his eyes and do my best impression of Dad. "He's a little under the weather, sir. He'll be okay in a few hours."

"He just had some Dramamine so he wouldn't get sick on the boat and it's knocked him out," Liliana chimes in. "He's my half-brother and he's *always* been like this." She rolls her eyes, exasperated.

"Okay, just so long as he doesn't yak in the backseat."

"No sir, I promise he won't."

We sit silently on the ride to the airport. It seems to take an eternity as we wend our way over rough roads through small farm towns. How are we going to get Zachary's corpse on a plane? And what if he starts smelling bad?

At the airport, I hand the driver the black plastic card Dad gave me.

"What's this?" He stares at its smooth, blank surface.

"Just run it through the credit card machine." Praying it'll work.

Tomás is already pretending to dig in his pockets for nonexistent money.

"Well, by golly." The driver's eyebrows shoot up like happy arrows. "That worked." He hands me the receipt and I notice that the card automatically gave him a 100 percent tip.

Thank god. My hand trembles as I shove the receipt in my coat pocket.

The driver is so thrilled with his tip that he doesn't notice Sean and Tomás having trouble getting Zachary out of the side door. Rigor mortis has finally set in. They prop him up on the sidewalk so he's leaning against the luggage.

Tomás sits next to him, one hand behind him, gripping his shirt to keep him from tipping over.

"Now what?" Sean's shrill voice pierces my thoughts.

"My dad said we should fly to New York right away."

Sean's long hair flops over his eyes as he shakes his head emphatically. "Count me out. I'm not about to head into the Grim Reaper's lair with the body of the Angel Patriarch's son on board. I'm going to be safe in Chicago when the bloodbath erupts. Tomás and Liliana, you guys should come with me."

Tomás nudges my foot and tears spring to my eyes. The gesture makes me realize that Tomás, at least, is still my friend. "Sean's right, Adam. If we go with you, things will be more complicated in the future. Hopefully the clans can sort this out so nobody else dies."

Liliana's fighting back tears. "Guys, I'm sorry. I'm going with Zachary. He's my brother. I can't—I can't leave him."

Tomás scrambles to his feet, opening his arms wide. She rushes into his embrace and sobs even as Zachary keels over sideways. I heave Zachary back to a sitting position. Dead bodies are a real pain.

"Do you guys have your IDs on you?" I ask.

Everybody looks sheepish. What prepared rescuers I have here! I'm guessing Zachary doesn't have his hidden in his jeans either. Great, one dead body, five teenagers, and not a single ID among us. Hope Dad's magic credit card really is magic.

"All right, guys," I say, "how are we going to get Zachary inside and on the plane? Let's figure out the IDs as we go."

Rachel prods me with her elbow and points at an empty courtesy wheelchair sitting beside the drop-off curb. "First things first. We can use that to get him on the plane, assuming they let us on."

I wheel it over and we haul Zachary up and onto it. His sunglasses dangle off his face and Sean readjusts them.

"Is Zachary really your brother?" he asks Liliana.

She nods.

"That means . . ." He trails off.

"That means what?" Liliana glares at him.

"So the La Muerte Matriarch is your mother . . . and the Angel Patriarch is your father?"

She regards him impatiently.

"How is that even possible?" He gawks at her.

"Has your education been deficient in sex education, Dullahan?" she says. "Do I need to remedy that right now? Insert Tab A into Slot B?"

Sean mumbles something that might be a half-apology. "That wasn't what I meant."

Although I understand why Liliana's angry, Sean's confusion is understandable. From everything I've read, this is an aberration. Not just because the Angels and La Muertes hate each other with a blood feud dating back five hundred years, but because neither parent relinquished their rights to Liliana or to their clan. They had a child and kept her paternity secret . . . That is 250 percent against the rules. Not sure if my dad's crime is worse.

"Anyway, the proof runs in my blood," Liliana says. "I don't know where that leaves us."

"What are you planning to do about it?" Tomás asks.

"I really don't know. Well. If you guys are flying to Chicago then I guess this is goodbye." She hugs Tomás and grimaces at Sean.

Sean looks dejected as he and Tomás split off and head inside.

Rachel, Liliana, and I shamble into the airport. I wheel Zachary up to a counter and ask the friendly flight attendant manning the counter whether there are four seats available on the next flight to New York.

She types something and checks the computer screen. "We have a mixture of first class and coach seats available, sir."

I pull out the black card. It worked in the taxi but still, I hold my breath. Paying for the tickets is only the first hurdle; the next is getting on board without IDs, and the one after that is not letting on that we're lugging around a dead body.

The ticket agent swipes the card, stares at her screen, then turns it over, gazing at it with some confusion. Then she turns it over again. "If this is what I think it is," she says, "you'll have to talk to my superior."

"Oh brother," Liliana whispers. "Your dad had this all planned out, did he?" She rolls her eyes.

"You don't accept this card?" I ask in a low voice.

The ticket agent breaks out of a trance. "Oh! Oh, yes. Sorry. We *definitely* accept this card. I just . . . I've just never seen one. I've only ever . . . heard about them." Her fingers start to shake and she giggles. "Sorry, it makes me nervous. I'll be careful . . . One moment, please." She walks through a side door.

"Now what?" Liliana asks. "Are we about to be stormed by FBI agents?"

Instead, a fat man in a uniform comes puffing up to us. "Sir, I'm so very honored you chose to fly with us." He hands me the card and I pocket it quickly, just in case. "I don't believe the accommodation on this flight will be up to your standards. I do have a small private jet ready for takeoff. I've already alerted the pilot on call. He will arrive in fifteen minutes. You and your travel partners can be in the air in less than thirty minutes."

"Uh . . . thanks?" I say.

"No sir. Thank *you*. Please follow me."

I grab Zachary's wheelchair but Liliana steps forward and yanks it from me.

"Sorry," I say to her retreating back.

"Give her some time," Rachel says.

Our guide uses his badge to usher us through several doors, the last one leading right out onto the tarmac and up to a small jet. A service truck screeches to a halt in front of us and the whole back drops level with the ground. The driver jumps out and motions for us to get into the back. Liliana wheels Zachary in while Rachel and I follow. It lifts us up to the airplane's door.

We step inside its large interior, furnished with comfortable leather chairs, a love seat, and a sectional that wraps around a table. A crew member straps Zachary's chair to the plane floor. Rachel and I sit on the sectional, while Liliana flops down on the love seat next to Zachary and glares at us.

A flight attendant asks us what we want to drink. Rachel asks for orange juice, Liliana for a spritzer with a twist of lime. I ask for water and drink one glass after another, ravenously thirsty for some reason.

A phone next to me rings. When I pick it up, Dad says, "You made it."

"How'd you know?"

"The card activates a few automatic functions. They called and told me you were at the airport. I arranged for a spare airplane to be made ready for you. They'll fly a new one to Bangor for the businessmen it was intended for. Everyone will be comped the flight, which should keep the protests to a dull roar. You still have Zachary?"

"He's here." So stiff, it looks like you could break his arm right off without even trying. "What are you going to do with him?"

"Don't worry, I'll take care of everything and arrange for him to be sent back to his father. I'm just glad you're safe. Who else is with you?"

"Tomás Eshu and Sean Dullahan said they were going to Chicago. Rachel's here and also Liliana La Muerte."

"I see." He clears his throat. "And what does Liliana intend to do?"

I look over and my heart breaks a little for her. She's staring out the window, one hand resting gently on Zachary's forearm. "Dad. She's planning to go with Zachary. He's her half-brother. Did you know that?"

The silence from the other end goes on so long, I think we've lost our connection.

"Hello? Dad?"

"All right, son. I'm here. I'll make all of the necessary arrangements for Liliana as well."

"Okay," I say.

We hang up. I get the feeling Dad isn't thrilled with Liliana's plan to escort Zachary's body to California. From everything I know about the La Muertes and Angels, it does seem a little foolish. They could do anything to her. Her expulsion from school and her lack of "official" place in the soul guide world make her totally vulnerable.

The pilots arrive a few minutes later. They introduce themselves, then quickly head into the cabin. Less than thirty minutes after handing my card to the ticket agent, we're in the air, headed for New York.

Bet Sean and Tomás have barely bought their tickets. Bet they're stuck in Bangor for a few hours more, at least until somebody can FedEx them some IDs. I'm not gonna lie, Sean was such a jerk about me being a Reaper, the thought fills me with immense satisfaction.

Rachel conks off shortly after takeoff. She puts her head on a pillow and before long she's drooling all over it. I'd wipe the drool off but I don't want to wake her up.

Liliana looks out the window and pretends I don't exist.

I wonder what secrets she's hiding and what she's trying to prove. What does it mean for her to be half La Muerte, half Angel? What does her existence mean for all the clans?

I have so many questions and I don't have the first clue how to answer them. If Rachel is a Reaper, who are her parents and why did nobody know about her until recently? Why didn't the Reapers, my family, know about her? How did my mother die and why did she become a ghost? If

Rachel and I are both Reapers, what happens now? And now that I've been kicked out of school, what's going to happen to me?

And what about Sarah? Is she lost forever or can we rescue her from the clutches of La Luz? Are we still friends? Is there still a possibility for us? Or is she so mad, we are irrevocably over?

Even though I'm watching Rachel drool and Liliana ignore me, my mind is everywhere else but here. Just as it feels like my life was beginning, it now feels like it might have come to an end. Or maybe it's just another beginning.

My eyes start to droop. I jerk myself awake, afraid. What if I end up back in the graveyard?

Then I remember that I took care of that. My mother's ended her infinite journey around and around the train loop. We broke the circle. She's passed to the other side.

I push my part of the sectional into a reclining position and rest my cheek against a pillow. It can't take longer than a few seconds before I fall into a deep and completely dreamless sleep.

The first one in . . . I don't even know how long.

I wake up as the airplane begins its initial descent. The flight attendant stands up and takes away our drink glasses and we buckle up for landing. We bump down on the runway and start to taxi. We taxi some more and then some more. And then some more.

"Maybe the pilot's driving us to my apartment in Brooklyn," I joke.

Liliana grunts. Rachel gives me a wan smile.

A million years later, it feels like, we turn into a large hangar and through a window I see the giant doors close behind us. The plane is a tiny Skittle lost in a warehouse. We pull up beside an ambulance and a black SUV. As soon as the door opens, four paramedics climb in and set to work on Zachary.

Dad's waiting at the bottom of the plane steps, tall and gaunt in his black overcoat, looking like he hasn't slept in weeks. He nods at me and smiles at Rachel. He holds a hand out to Liliana. She takes it and he bends down to kiss it. "Liliana, sweetheart," he says, "with everything that's going on, you shouldn't go to the Angels. There's an ongoing investigation into your expulsion and that decision may soon be reversed. Things are really getting dangerous. Plus, you're next in line for the succession. This is going to cause problems. Huge problems. Maybe war."

Though her face looks strained, her voice is clear and determined. "I *have* to do this."

Dad sighs. "I knew you'd say that. La Muerte women are always determined." His rueful smile takes the sting out of his words. He hands her a black bag. "This has everything you need if you change your mind. If you need to run. And if you do need to run, please find your way back here. We'll protect you. The whole Reaper clan." He sweeps his hands out to include me and Rachel.

They look at each other for a long time, and then her eyes meet mine and then Rachel's, and finally she nods. "Thank you." Simple but elegant. I practically burst with pride.

She walks toward the ambulance where they're loading Zachary's body.

I hesitate for a second. But I can't let Liliana just walk away. Too many things happen in this world that we can't control. At least I can say a proper goodbye.

"Hey, wait!" I hadn't realized I was running until I skid to a stop beside her.

She's standing behind the ambulance door, searching through the bag's contents. She holds the bag open toward me and I catch a glimpse of women's clothing and toiletries. Two passports zipped into a clear interior pocket. She unzips it and shows me both of them—one American, one Canadian. I flip one open. The passport is for one Christina Lopez, with a birth date eighteen years ago. I don't know how in the world he did it but the picture in the passport is Liliana. A recent photo, right down to the highlights in her hair. She looks serious. Four small fat manila envelopes contain stacks of one hundred–dollar bills. There must be at least twenty thousand dollars in just one envelope alone.

She mutters something I can't understand. When she's done, she covers her face in her hands. "Tell your father thank you again. He thought of everything."

"He usually does," I say.

She smiles, faint lines wrinkling across her forehead, and leans forward, as if she's going to hug me. Instead, she places her hands on each side of my face, her fingers gentle, and presses her lips against mine. She tastes of lime and spritzer and her lips are warm and soft as they linger.

She drops her hands and lets them swing loosely at her side as she steps away. I grab them.

"What . . . ?" I start to say.

She looks apologetic but extricates herself, turning away, following the paramedics to the ambulance.

"Bye, Lili," I call.

She turns back for just a second. *"Adios, amigo."*

I can't move. Everything in me wants me to follow her, to stick with her, to keep her in my sights. But I don't. I just lift my hand and wave goodbye, though she doesn't look back. She climbs into the back of the ambulance with Zachary's body and one of the paramedics closes the door. They drive slowly outside.

And just like that, Liliana is gone.

"Didn't you guys just meet today?" Rachel asks.

"No." I don't say anything else and Rachel, because she's Rachel, doesn't pry.

Dad's standing by the black SUV, his back to us, talking to a man in a dark suit.

"Is Zachary gone?"

"Yes," I say.

"Good!" He turns and faces us. "I'm so glad you are both safe."

Rachel bursts into tears. Dad takes a step toward her, his outstretched hand unsure. She throws herself into his arms and he pats her back gently.

A suspicious lump in my throat is making it hard to swallow.

"There, there," Dad says. "You're ours now. You're family." He brings me in close for a hug. My forehead touches Rachel's and tears smart my eyes. I hold both of them, throat hurting. I have no idea what the future holds. I don't know how to interpret Liliana's kiss—was it, *Goodbye, it was nice knowin' ya,* or was it a promise? But these two! I know where I stand with them. They mean . . . everything.

Arms around us, Dad leads us to the SUV and we climb in the back. The man in the suit slides into the passenger seat. The driver straps his seat belt on and turns the key in the ignition.

"Reaper compound," Dad tells him.

"Is that what you're calling our tiny-ass apartment?" I ask.

He laughs. "That rattrap? I rather liked the place. It was small, but it served us well. It kept you hidden. Safe. Now that everybody knows you and Rachel are Reapers—or they will shortly—we might as well live in the actual Reaper compound. It's in Manhattan. The Upper East Side."

I feel in my coat pocket to make sure *The Book of Light* is still there. First chance I get, I'm giving it to Dad.

Okay. Not really. Maybe I'll read it first.

Dad pats my knee. "We have a lot to talk about, Adam."

We put on our seat belts. The driver rolls up the windows and puts the car in gear. Rachel sits beside me, her hand touching mine loosely, in a friendly way. I smile at her as we drive out of the hangar into a cold, cloudy New York day.

LIST OF CLANS MENTIONED IN THIS BOOK AND THE TERRITORIES THEY CONTROL

Italy

Mors (Letum)

Japan

Shinigami

North America

Angel (California)
Ankou (Louisiana)
Crowley (Tennessee, Kentucky)
Cu Sith (territory unlisted)
Dullahan (Midwest)
Eshu (Caribbean & Belize)
La Muerte (Central America, Mexico, US-Mexico border regions)
Pesta (Minnesota, Ontario)
Reaper (Eastern Seaboard)
Samael (territory unlisted)
Yamaraja (territory unlisted)

Allison Sattinger

J.L. Powers is the award-winning author of three young adult novels, *The Confessional, This Thing Called the Future,* and *Amina*. She is also the editor of two collections of essays and author of a picture book, *Colors of the Wind.* She works as an editor/publicist for Cinco Puntos Press, and is founder and editor of the online blog, *The Pirate Tree: Social Justice and Children's Literature.* She teaches creative writing, literature, and composition at Skyline College in California's Bay Area, served as a jurist for the 2014 NSK Neustadt Prize for Children's Literature, and is launching Catalyst Press in 2017 to publish African writers.

Mark McCall

M.A. Powers is J.L.'s "little" (but much taller) brother. He has a PhD in the oncological sciences from the Huntsman Cancer Institute at the University of Utah in Salt Lake City. He is currently a stay-at-home dad and lives in Maine.